BANDIT COUNTRY

BANDIT COUNTRY

Martin Evans

ATHENA PRESS
LONDON

BANDIT COUNTRY
Copyright © Martin Evans 2007

All Rights Reserved

No part of this book may be reproduced in any form
by photocopying or by any electronic or mechanical means,
including information storage or retrieval systems,
without permission in writing from both the copyright
owner and the publisher of this book.

ISBN 10-digit: 1 84401 951 9
ISBN 13-digit: 978 1 84401 951 9

First Published 2007 by
ATHENA PRESS
Queen's House, 2 Holly Road
Twickenham TW1 4EG
United Kingdom

Printed for Athena Press

All characters and events in this book are fictional and any resemblance to actual places, events or persons, living or dead, is purely coincidental.

Street Plan of Belfast

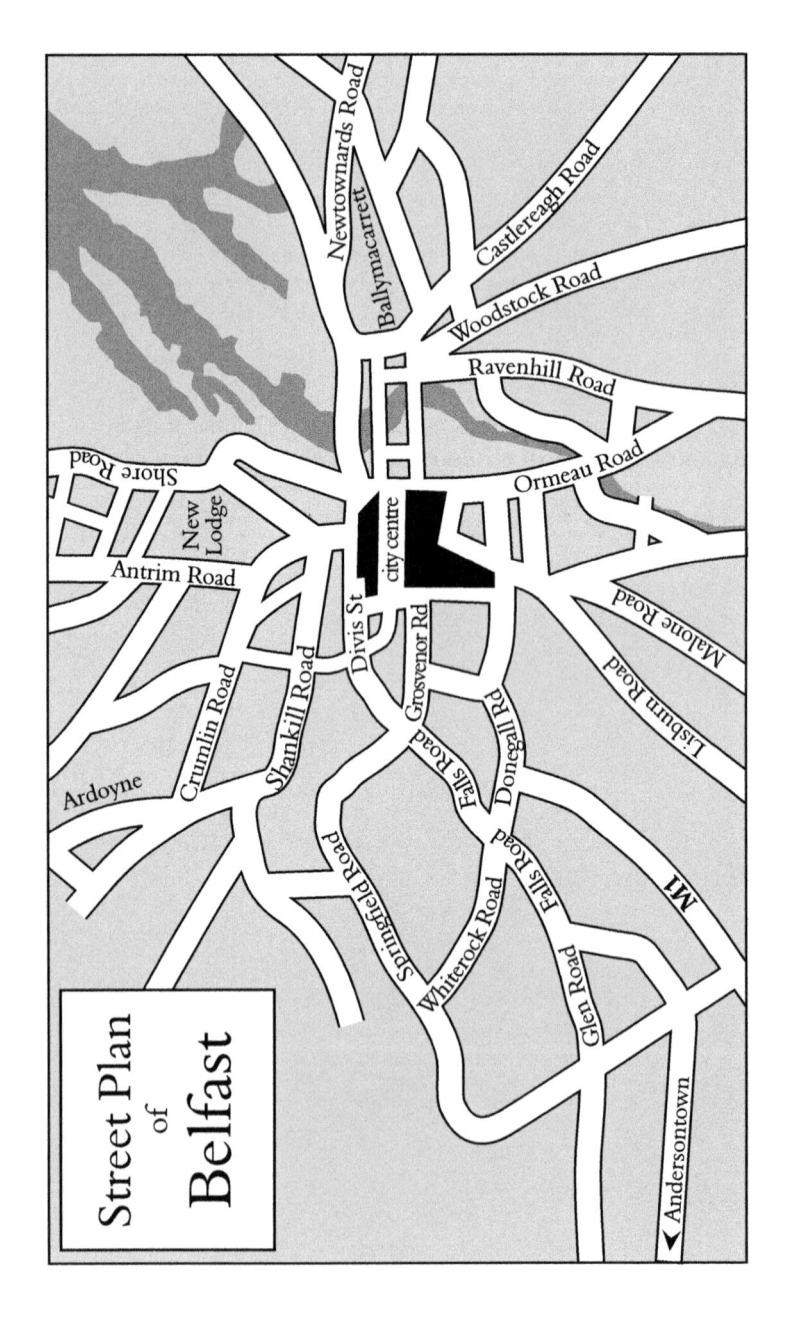

Part One
The Players

When Volunteers are trained in the use of arms they must fully understand that guns are dangerous, and their main purpose is to take human life, in other words to kill people, and Volunteers are trained to kill people.

> An extract from Appendix One,
> The Green Book IRA Training Manual

Chapter One

16 November 1978

Inside the mobile patrol vehicle it was cramped and dusty and claustrophobic, and smelled of stale sweat and cigarette smoke. Trooper One sighed and moved his limbs for the umpteenth time to get comfortable. As he did so he kept his eyes peeled at the rear window for any sign of trouble, his posture crouched and his weapon, a self-loading rifle in his arms, primed and ready for action. Opposite him, Trooper Two did the same, looking out of a slit in the side of the vehicle. Two Royal Ulster Constabulary men rode in the front, right up against the dashboard of the armoured van, practically.

All were in working uniform, with the soldiers of the Royal Anglian Regiment in full combat gear of dappled camouflage jacket, trousers and helmet. The RUC men sat in front in their distinctive dark green uniform and shirt and black tie, with peaked cap and the crest of crown and harp proudly displayed since the inception of their predecessors, the Royal Irish Constabulary, in 1822. They wore their latter-day customary flak jackets under thick waterproofs, with holstered Walther PPK pistols on their hips.

They had just come back from the area around the B135, where it converged with the A29 road to Newtownhamilton. Their patrol had lasted a whole eight-hour shift in and around the backroads of the open country consisting of thick hedgerows, wild grass and rocks, which rose up and down the dale. But now, thankfully, their shift was nearing the end, much to the relief of the four men in the vehicle. They were tired of peering into the night and were hungry and in need of a hot drink and something to eat. It was a chilly November night with howling wind and falling temperature and the appearance of frost was visible on the road and the grass verge alongside.

Trooper Two looked at his watch as Trooper One looked out of the rear and said, 'Won't be long now, mate.'

'Thank God for that,' Trooper Two replied. 'Being in here is like living your life inside a tin can.'

Trooper One smiled and said, 'Now you know how a sardine feels.'

'Yeah, I reckon I do,' Trooper Two replied. He put his weapon down and said to the other trooper, 'Fag?' as he produced a roll-up from a tin out of one of his pockets.

'Don't mind if I do,' Trooper One said and reached to take it.

This little banter set off a similar dialogue between the two RUC men in the front. The RUC reservist in the passenger seat next to the driver commented, 'I'll be glad to get home tonight. I've felt ravenously hungry all this shift and besides, my missus is cookin' bangers and mash with her own special gravy that you have to taste to believe.'

'You lucky bastard, I daresay my wife will be out with her sister till gone eleven at the bingo at the local hall. So I'll probably have to cook me own supper again,' the driver replied.

'Yes,' sighed the reservist, 'she's a good'un, that wife of mine.'

The four men fell silent for a while, as they drove the mile or so at the end of the B78 from Newtownhamilton that took them right into Markethill in County Armagh. The lights were on in the station and everything looked normal from a distance as they approached; the roads and area were deserted. The men in the vehicle started to relax and become less alert. They'd had a boring shift that had jogged tediously along, with nothing eventful or memorable happening.

Like beckoning beacons, the lights in the police station shone gloriously in the night. The station was a square, two storey building with a sloping roof, three white chimneys and a small wood observation post attached to the outside wall, with a crash-barrier in front.

It was now as they got nearer to the station that things were to happen which would catch them off guard. Suddenly there was a flash of movement in the dark and the RUC reservist in the passenger seat who, catching a glimpse of it out of the corner of his eye, said, 'There, look over there.'

The driver peered out and said, 'I don't see it. Where exactly is it?'

'Over there,' the reservist pointed, as the armoured patrol vehicle came out of the turn and straightened.

'OK, OK,' the driver said, 'I see it! I see it!'

The reservist pointed at the body lifeless and not moving in the middle of the road, parallel to the station and illuminated by the beam of the headlights as they came to a halt.

This was an unexpected situation and as such was met with a little heady expectation and some trepidation, as the RUC men gathered their wits about them and got ready to respond. Turning around, the reservist told the soldiers in a firm voice, 'You boys stay here and we'll investigate to see if it's booby-trapped or anything. After all, we don't want you nice English lads on our conscience should anything go wrong now, do we?' he added, tongue-in-cheek. He and the driver got out of the vehicle and approached the body.

On closer inspection, the body was a young man lying face down, splashed in blood and groaning. His dark jacket and brown trousers were ripped and torn from the impact of the fall, so supposed the two RUC men. He was shaking and twitching and looked a ghastly sight.

The driver looked at the reservist and commented, 'My God, he looks in a bad way. He'll have to go to hospital right away.'

'Hold your horses,' the reservist told him, and cautiously approached the body until eventually he stood over it. Up to this point, the lad's groans and twitches had been the only sign of life. But as the reservist bent over the body and rolled it right way up, things changed in an instant. Within a split second he was staring down the barrel of a 7.62 semi-automatic Tokarev pistol, pointed in his face. The youth was wearing a black balaclava with cut-outs for eyes and mouth.

Shocked at the appearance of the gun in the hands of the supposedly injured youth, the reservist looked horror-struck and froze for what seemed like an eternity. Then he uttered the words 'No, no, you really don't want to do this' as he fumbled for his own gun.

'Too late copper,' replied the youth, in a gritty, tight-lipped tone. He pressed the trigger and fired straight away at point blank range, shooting the policeman between the eyes with a single bullet. His expression fell blank and he died instantly, dropping his gun, as he hit the ground.

Jumping up, the youth lost no time and shot the driver twice in the leg and arm as he failed to respond quickly enough. The driver went down and writhed on the ground as the youth stood over him and calmly executed him with a shot to the side of the head.

Inside the mobile patrol vehicle, the two soldiers who had been momentarily stunned by these events leapt into action. They threw themselves out of the vehicle and began firing volleys of 7.62 rounds, in quick, continuous bursts.

The youth was crouching and firing back defiantly as the troopers' attention was diverted by a car that screeched on to the scene.

'Take that, you bloody Irish bastards!' shouted Trooper Two, as he fired from the rear of the armoured vehicle.

Meanwhile Trooper One ducked behind the bonnet of the vehicle and shot at the car as it made a spectacular turn in the middle of the road. Two figures in the rear of the Ford Escort opened the door and yanked the youth in bodily. 'Get in Liam,' a masked man shouted. He held a 9mm Thompson sub-machine gun, the favourite weapon of the Mafia in the '20s and '30s in the USA: a weapon dated but effective. 'Keep low an' keep your head down,' he added.

Though the troopers shot at the Ford, they only managed to hole the bodywork a little and smash the back window. The getaway driver put his foot down as the Ford came out of the spin and shot off at high speed. The masked man with the Thompson was managing to fire so rapidly and effectively that the soldiers had to keep their heads down as the car sped past, down the road and out of sight. The ambush party had fled the scene of the crime before any hot pursuit could be arranged. However, Trooper Two did think that he saw the faintest glimpse of a woman with red hair in the car, though in all the noise and excitement and confusion he could not really be sure.

As the car fled out of sight, RUC men poured out of the station and into the road to see what all the shooting and confusion had been all about.

A chief inspector, his rank apparent from the insignia and pips on his uniform, collared Trooper One and asked in an arrogant voice, 'What happened here?'

'A terrorist action,' Trooper One said correctly.

'What, did you think that I thought it was a bloody Sunday afternoon picnic, then?'

'No sir,' Trooper Two stated as he put down his smoking weapon and spoke up for his mate.

Looking at both troopers sternly, the chief inspector said, 'You two, my office – now,' and the troopers entered the RUC station to be debriefed by the Inspector, so that he could get a handle on things.

Yet far across the sea in England no one had heard of these events, for they had not been officially reported, including in the London suburbs of Barnet and Borehamwood. Hardly anyone knew of Borehamwood and yet, most seemed to have heard of Elstree Studios; no wonder really, as it had been described as the 'British Hollywood' with just about every major star in the world coming to make films there.

The reason the place was known as Elstree and Borehamwood was really quite simple. Before there were council houses built after the Second World War, there was no Borehamwood, only Elstree, which had been a rural village for as long as any of the inhabitants cared to remember. It was once described rather disparagingly by Michael Winner as, 'Nothing but a turn-off from the A1,' despite the number of blockbusting movies that had special effects done at the MGM studios there; movies like George Lucas' Star Wars, and Steven Spielberg's Indiana Jones movies.

However, none of that meant a jot to the eighteen-year-old Martin Strong, who lived at the top of Bullwalk Road in a nice, neat little brick terrace house, with a small front garden and high privet hedge, and a little black iron gate. The council house backed onto the playing fields of Hillwood Secondary Modern School, where Martin and his friend, Alan Thompson, were playing football. The goalposts were still up, but the nets had been taken down leaving just the white, mud-splashed posts, to play between. Maybe the class had been in too much of a hurry to put them away or the caretaker too lazy, either way they were still there, for the use of the two eighteen year olds. Bored on a grey and windy Autumn Saturday, they had decided to have a good kickabout till dinner, for something to do.

Martin Strong was five feet nine inches tall, square-faced, honest looking and slim as a pencil with a mop of mousy coloured brown hair. His mate, Alan Thompson was taller with shaggy, shoulder-length blond hair that waved about when he moved and made him look somewhat like a sheep dog. Even so, he was good-looking and had those attractive blue eyes that made him hugely popular with the females of his acquaintance. He also had endless chat, something that the quieter Martin Strong did not always have.

Alan lifted the ball up and kicked it out to Strong, who chased after it and quickly trapped it with his feet to stop it. He rolled the ball back on his foot and flicked it into the air. Juggling on his instep, he turned and ran at the goal towards the facing Thompson, who rushed out at him. Just as Thompson approached, Strong deftly chipped the ball over his head. Despite Thompson being taller than Strong and having a much greater reach, Thompson was unable to stop the ball as he sprang into the air with his hand outstretched. The ball sailed between the posts while Thompson fell to the ground and landed in the only puddle in the goalmouth with an exclamation of disgust. He retrieved the ball and wiped his dirty jeans where they were wet and muddy.

Strong was ecstatic and jumping about very pleased with himself. In a loud voice he stated, in imitation of a commentator's tones: 'And the crowd goes wild, as Jimmy Greaves does it again and puts Spurs ahead in the dying minutes of the final.'

'Bah, get away with that,' Thompson remarked. 'When was the last time that Greaves played for Spurs? He's a football personality on TV now, not a player.'

'Maybe so, but he's still the greatest footballer to me.'

'Take some penalties Mart, I'm a bit rusty. Let's see how good the great Greavsie is at that, eh?'

'Yeah OK,' Strong replied, as Thompson bowled the ball out under-arm and it rolled fast across the firm ground towards

Strong. Placing the ball on the bald penalty spot in the scrubby looking penalty area, Martin steadied himself as Thompson moved from side to side and clapped his gloved hands together, looking alert. 'Ready?' Strong asked, foot on the white plastic ball.

'Ready,' Thompson shouted back, as he swayed and tried to anticipate what Strong was going to do. Moving back, Strong took a great long run-up and at the last moment over-stepped the ball: as Thompson dived left, Strong side-footed the ball low in the right-hand corner of the goal.

'You tricky bastard!' Thompson exclaimed, annoyed at himself for falling for the oldest trick in the book. He picked himself up and retrieved the ball again.

'Yep that's right,' Strong agreed. 'That's me.' They played out for another hour, and then picked up the ball and went home again.

Later that evening, Strong returned home from a good night out with his mates drinking lager down at the Red Lion pub. On the way home he had popped in the local fish and chip shop and bought himself some greasy chips, which he polished off sitting on his sofa in his front room as he watched the Late Night News.

There on the TV screen he saw the familiar hangdog expression of the Northern Ireland Correspondent for the BBC recount the events of the shoot-out at Markethill RUC Station the night before.

The reporter was saying, 'Last night at about 10 p.m. two RUC officers were returning from a routine patrol; they left their vehicle to examine a body lying in the road, when a youth ambushed them and shot them both dead at point-blank range.'

'Do we know anything else?' the smooth, good-looking presenter Andrew Simmons asked in the London studio.

'Only that there was a shoot-out as the youth escaped in a getaway car and soldiers on the scene gave returning fire.'

'Do we know who is responsible for the attack?'

'Not as yet, Andrew, but the general feeling from those I've spoken to on the scene since seem to think that it was probably a killing aimed at the increasing pressure by the security forces and police on the IRA.'

'I see,' Andrew Simmons remarked. 'And will the forensic people and firearm experts be able to deduce much more?'

'It is hoped so,' the BBC correspondent replied. 'As you can see behind me, the area is cordoned off and there are great skid marks but the RUC assure me they will be able to tell us a lot more later on. This is Dennis MacMourne for the BBC, County Armagh, Northern Ireland.'

'Thanks Dennis,' Andrew Simmons said, as the Northern Ireland scene on the screen behind him, with soldiers and police milling about, switched back to London. 'And now, here is the rest of the news.'

Switching off the TV, Strong's tired mother, Jean, yawned and commented, 'That's enough of that, the world's a bad enough place without watching and hearing about all that violence.'

'But Mum,' Strong remarked, giving his thin mum with her tight brown curls and fag in her mouth a squeeze. 'That's where I'm going shortly with the Regiment. Northern Ireland – there will be a lot of it about.'

'Then you be careful and don't get yourself shot, for me and your father couldn't stand it.'

Strong's stocky and dark-haired father had as usual fallen asleep in the armchair in front of the open fire, and was snoring loud, while the mongrel dog lying in front of the fire whimpered as it too slept.

'I won't, I promise,' Strong said, kissing his mother on the cheek. 'Goodnight Mum,' he said, then stroked the dog.

'Goodnight love,' she said and he closed the door and made his way upstairs to bed.

Armagh, Northern Ireland

The Catholic cathedral dedicated to St. Patrick was begun in 1840. Building stopped during the Great Famine and for years afterwards. The walls were no more than fifteen feet high when JJ McCarthy resumed construction, changing the style of Duff's modest perpendicular gothic design to loftier decorated gothic. The outside was finished in 1873 and the finest view of the spires could only be seen from the city's west and north-west approaches. The Pope and many of Europe's royal families kindly helped with the builders' bills, but by far the largest share of the cash was raised through collections, bazaars and raffles. Speaking of which, a grandfather clock, a prize in the 1865 bazaar, to this day waits in the sacristy for a lucky winner to come forward.

Statues of two archbishops flanked a long flight of steps up to the grand entrance. Those were of Primate Crolly who began the building and Primate Mac Gettigan who ended it, with the addition of Cardinal Logue who later improved the interior and made it beauteous with a brilliant display of mosaic, paintings, stained glass, Italian marbles and the local red 'Armagh marble'.

Going about his duties the altar boy in cassock and surplice put out the candles and arranged the green and gold cloth on the altar. He collected the silver chalice and put the lid on it, bowed to the cross and quite smartly disappeared into the vestry, the service over.

The interior of the cathedral was cool and the mood sombre and serious as the woman faced the altar and knelt and crossed herself, then stood up again. She wore a full-length black coat with wide lapels and belted in the middle, and shoulder-length red lustrous hair. She waited impatiently on the cold seat of the darkly polished pew at the back. For the umpteenth time she checked her wrist watch and saw that only ten minutes had elapsed since she last checked it.

Looking at effigies of the Virgin Mary and the grandeur of her surroundings, she was startled out of her reverie as a hand touched her on the shoulder. She quickly looked around to see a small boy in navy jumper, grey short trousers, knee-length socks and scuffed tan shoes.

He was a round-faced little boy of about ten with mussed-up hair and a cheeky face and manner. Without any preamble he said, 'I only have two things to say to you.'

'And they are?'

'Commitment to an organisation is what?'

'Belief in that organisation,' she replied, pat.

'Commitment to the Army is what?'

'Total belief in the Army.'

These were a couple of lines from Appendix One and extracts from the Green Book –the IRA Training Manual.

The recognition code over, the boy said, 'Correct and follow me.' He turned quickly turning on his heel; she only caught him up at the open door.

'You're tall,' he commented, enquiringly.

'Five twelve,' she said, with a hint of sarcasm.

'But pretty,' he added, as he made his exit and went down the steps of the cathedral and out the gate.

'So glad you approve,' she replied in her thick country brogue.

Pulling him back by the scruff of the neck as he marched off, she said, 'In here with me.' She pulled him on to her lap as she ducked in to a back seat of the parked, lumbering Austin Princess and shut the door.

'But it's a hearse,' he said, in real surprise.

'What better a car to be parked outside of a church, now I ask you?' Liam O'Connell piped up, sat next to the driver. 'Now are you goin' to give us directions, or are we goin' to stay here all bleedin' day, not knowin' how to find your da's place?'

The Shamrock pub was a shabby, two storey down-beat affair in the middle of a short block of huddled-together shops in the mean backstreets located a couple of miles from the Catholic cathedral. It had a big, oblong concrete courtyard at the back with a six foot high wood fence surrounding it and heavy padlocked gates. Those were soon opened on the shrill blast of several honks of the Austin's horn. When the car drove in to the yard and the occupants got out of the sleek, black hearse.

'Fat Billy' shut the gates and padlocked them again, then turned to greet his visitors effusively.

'Mairead O'Connell,' he said and hugged the brown-eyed twenty-four year old redhead, noting her high cheek-boned face, its typically Irish beauty and perfect complexion.

'Fat Billy,' she said and returned the compliment with a kiss on the cheek.

'My God, colleen, but you've shot up,' he wondered. 'It doesn't seem five minutes since me an' your da used to take turns of bouncin' you on our knees, when out at the pub at Castle Blaney on a Saturday night.'

Down at the mouth she replied, 'Yes well, that won't ever happen again will it?'

Giving her a squeeze of reassurance, he replied apologetically, 'Me an' my big mouth.'

'No it's all right, really,' she said, not wanting any further embarrassment.

'And who may I ask is this good lookin' fella?' Fat Billy asked with restored gusto.

'That's my brother, Liam.'

'Never!' Fat Billy exclaimed. 'You've shot up too, what are you, six feet?'

The big-boned man with the small head perched on wide shoulders, handsome features and jet-black, swept back hair replied, 'Six four. And if it's any consolation, I don't remember you, either,' shaking hands with the pudgy-fingered Fat Billy.

'You're never that skinny lad that was always gettin' sick with something or t'other? You're a sight to behold me lad, a real, livin' breathin' Errol Flynn, so you are.'

'Oh, come on now,' Mairead said. 'Now you're stretching the blarney, Billy.'

'Why not?' Fat Billy chuckled. 'We Irish are famous for kissin' the Blarney Stone.'

'Kissin' it, yes,' Mairead smiled, 'but not killin' it t'death.' Everyone laughed at that.

'So who are these, then?' Fat Billy enquired, shaking the hands of the two lads next to Liam so vigorously that they really thought their hands would drop off.

'These are Padraic Duffy and Sean Maguire,' Liam said, introducing them.

'Now are they, then?' said Fat Billy, standing back and taking a good look. 'Glad to be makin' your acquaintance.'

The two boys nursed their hands. Sixty-year-old 'Fat Billy' was so called because of his fat face, girth and body. However, he had a firm grip in his hand, and his fat build did not prevent him from moving surprisingly quickly, if and when he chose to.

Small Padraic Duffy was scruffy, nineteen and built like a sparrow with thin arms and legs. He had painfully boyish features and a mass of tight brown curls on his head, overlapping his brow and Sean Maguire was twenty, slim and well-muscled. His short blond hair, parted in the middle, gave him the appearance of a clean-cut, respectable lad.

Everyone wore faded blue jeans and the boys had zip-up parka jackets on. Compared to the rest, Mairead, with her slender body, long legs and good looks, was positively elegant in her full-length coat, like a well-groomed clothes horse.

'I could murder a pint,' Duffy said, as he looked longingly through the open door at the bar and the taps waiting invitingly inside.

'Guinness do?' Fat Billy asked, as he wiped his mouth at the thought. He patted his wide girth and the others noticed the coloured plastic apron with the large green shamrock on the front.

'Is there any other?' Duffy enquired.

'Course not,' Fat Billy replied.

'A shamrock?' Maguire pointed out, in a critical tone that implied he thought it a bit sissy for a grown man.

Picking up on the tone, Fat Billy said indignantly: 'It most certainly is, an' right proud of it I am too. So get yourselves inside now, an' the first dozen or so drinks are on the house.'

Stepping behind the bar as they filed into the room, Fat Billy went on, 'Just let me know your pleasure lady an' gents.'

'That'll be four pints of Guinness then, landlord,' Liam said, as they pulled out the chairs and sat around a stained table in the darkened corner of the dingy pub.

'No need to be so formal me lad,' he shot back, grabbing a glass and putting it under the tap, pulling the lever and pouring out a strong, full pint of dark Guinness with a good frothy head on it. 'I'll not be offended if you call me Fat Billy.'

'So be it, Fat Billy,' Liam said. 'How much do I owe you?' reaching into his trouser pocket.

'Keep your hand in your pocket,' Fat Billy said, 'I wouldn't dream of it. These are on the house, an' so are the rest you'll be drinkin' here today.'

Liam had not really believed the flannel he had been fed by the jovial landlord, and therefore said with a grin, 'Well Fat Billy, you're a man after me own heart.'

'Then right glad I am,' Fat Billy replied, as he finished pulling two of the pints and set them on the bar and got on with the rest of the order.

'Can I have a Guinness?' the boy, who was Fat Billy's grandson, whined.

'No you can't, you'll have sweet lemonade an' like it,' Fat Billy remonstrated, as the boy pulled a face and sat with the others.

Fat Billy brought the drinks over to the table on a tray, and joining them with a pint of Guinness of his own, he raised a glass and said, 'Now good people gathered here, I only ask one thing of yous people an' that is that yous join me in a toast an' a recitation: "Commitment to the Republican Movement is the firm belief that its struggle both military and politically is morally justified. And that the Army are the direct representatives of the 1918 Dáil Éireann Parliament. That as such they are the legal and lawful government of the Irish Republic, which has the moral right to pass laws for, and to claim jurisdiction over the whole geographical fragment of Ireland: its maritime territory, airspace, mineral resources and means of production, distribution and exchange of all of its people, regardless of creed or loyalty".'

After the few words all the visitors joined in with the well-known passage from Appendix One of the Green Book. When they finished, Fat Billy shouted, 'Here's to a Republican Ireland, the Irish Tricolour and Michael Collins, hero of the 1916 Easter Rising. Long may he reign in our hearts!'

The boy sipping his lemonade and the others their beer around the small table all concurred with the sentiments and fine words expressed by Fat Billy.

It was at this juncture that Liam tapped Fat Billy on the arm and reminded him, 'What about the business now?'

'Ah, bejesus, surely there's plenty of time for that.'

'No I don't think so,' Liam insisted.

What Fat Billy did not know, as the others laughed cheerfully and supped their pints, was that they had less time than he thought.

Getting up from the table, Duffy said, 'I think Liam's right. So come on Fat Billy, show us what you've got.'

'Yeah,' Maguire joined in, 'it's about time.'

'Very well,' Fat Billy said. 'Drink up an' follow me.' They all downed their drinks in two seconds flat, including the boy.

Walking across the room, Billy reached for a set of keys hanging behind the bar and opened the door beside it. Switching on the light inside, so as they could see their way, he started down the few worn stone steps to the dimly lit, musty and damp cellar below.

Seeing them walk off, Mairead supped up too and called out, 'I'm just goin' to the fishmonger's to get us a little something for tea.'

'Got enough money?' Liam asked of her.

'I have indeed,' Mairead said, affecting a haughty air. 'Am I not a woman of independent means?'

'So you are,' Liam agreed.

Down in the cellar, they removed a false wall and Fat Billy used a crowbar to prise the lid off one of the two beer barrels in the cobwebby corner. 'What do you think of these beauties?' he asked, as he tenderly brought out a heavy package wrapped in oil cloth, smelling of grease and sealed with black masking tape. Liam gave him a hand as they laid the package on the cold, stone floor. Fat Billy unwrapped it to reveal half a dozen spanking new AKM Kalashnikov rifles, made in Romania.

Picking one up, the delighted Duffy said, 'Yes, they should be just the job.'

'How about ammunition?' Maguire asked.

'Thousands of rounds in the other barrel,' Fat Billy said. 'Here, open it with this.'

He handed the crowbar to Maguire, while Duffy handled, sighted and played with the trigger and moving parts of the Kalashnikov. Fitting a clip into the rifle, Duffy enquired, 'Is there anywhere we can practice and get a better feel of this baby?'

'Next door,' Fat Billy said. 'It's for that purpose, that's why I had it padded and sound-proofed.'

While Liam and Fat Billy talked shop, Duffy and Maguire went next door and played with their new toys, shooting at the metal targets to their hearts' content. The boy looked on eagerly.

'What say we enjoy another excellent pint of your Guinness?' said Liam.

'That's an excellent idea,' Fat Billy replied and clapped Liam on the shoulder. 'Why didn't I think of that?'

'Because I got there first?'

'Probably.'

Before he left the cellar however, Liam turned and poked his head through the inset door, and when the loud cacophony of gunfire died down he looked at Duffy and said, 'Remember, I expect those guns loaded soon, so don't take all day about it.'

'We hear you,' Duffy reassured Liam, and right away they packed up the shooting and followed Liam out of the cellar. While Liam went to the bar with Fat Billy, Duffy and Maguire exited through the door to the courtyard. They lifted the tailgate of the hearse and began to unload the empty coffins from the back.

Inside the pub, Liam and Fat Billy sat down at the table to talk, full pints in hand. 'So what have yous been up to recently,' Fat Billy began. 'You weren't a part of that shootin' of them poor unsuspectin' RUC constables at Markethill the other day, were you?'

'We were,' Liam announced proudly, 'and in the future we're goin' to be up to a whole lot more,' he boasted.

'Such as?' Fat Billy asked, and Liam rather foolishly blurted out the forthcoming plans of the Active Service Unit.

Duffy and Maguire meanwhile, were doing the donkey work, filling the coffins with arms and ammunition from the treasure trove in the cellar.

'Looky here!' Maguire exclaimed. 'How I'd like to blow a can off the road with this,' he said, in an excited voice, hefting the weapon and posing with it.

'What's that, then?'

'This here is a Russian-made RPG-7 rocket launcher complete with payload,' Maguire said proudly, 'and some landmines and grenades.'

Soon after, Duffy and Maguire were carrying a full coffin out to the hearse when Duffy suddenly said, 'It's no good, I can't hold it. My arms are breakin', they feel like they're being pulled out of their sockets.' With that, he let go of his end and the thing twisted out of Maguire's grip and crashed on to its side on the concrete. The lid flew off and the contents spilled out on to the ground.

A passing postman walking home happened to notice the accident through a split in the wooden fence. Putting his eye to a knothole he looked into the yard and saw two youths acting very suspiciously as they gathered up the rifles, ammunition and grenades. Seeing enough in that short space of time, the postman hurried to the end of the street and turned a corner and entered a telephone box. He lost no time in dialling 999 and asking for the police. The message was relayed to the station at Markethill, and control soon dispatched a patrol in the vicinity to look into the matter.

'Do you think anyone saw us?' Duffy asked in a worried tone, as he collected up the items and he and Maguire finally put the lid on the coffin.

'Shouldn't think so,' Maguire said, in his typical cavalier fashion.

'But what if they did?'

'You'll "what-if" till the day you die,' Maguire remarked. 'You know your trouble?'

'No,' Duffy said, sounding thick.

'You worry too much,' Maguire explained. 'Now come on, let's get this over with, then we can have another pint or two.'

Ten minutes later the Shamrock fell silent as a stranger entered the bar. Liam and Fat Billy had been so enjoying themselves that they failed to hear the Divisional Support Unit's armoured mobile van draw up. They looked up from their pints to see standing in the doorway an RUC constable of many years' standing, large as life and twice as ugly, with a junior colleague by his side. Protecting their rear was a British trooper guarding the outside entrance. He was armed with an SLR at the ready, while another soldier in the van was in communication with RUC headquarters Knock and the local army base, Gough Barracks.

The RUC constable was a bitter and twisted veteran of the conflict over the years, and was a Protestant, a policeman and a man vehemently opposed to Republicanism in general and the IRA in particular. He was big and broad and tough with pugnacious features and an obnoxious manner. To ensure that those in the room got the message, he and his colleague opened their thick waterproof coats to display their weapons, both to frighten and to intimidate.

In three large strides the constable crossed the room to the table and Fat Billy. 'Are you open or what, then?' the constable demanded to know. 'It's that dark in here, that from the outside it looks closed.'

Kowtowing to the constable, Fat Billy smiled and said, 'I'm always open and always ready to serve the famous an' well-renowned RUC, you know that, Constable.'

'Are you indeed; then you'll also know that we never drink on duty.'

'Of course, of course,' Fat Billy said in a wheedling tone. 'What about yous make an exception on account of me havin' a drop of quite exceptional malt whisky, made in these fair isles, so it is.'

'Don't try and humour me, you Catholic piece of shite,' the constable uttered, kicking away the chair that Fat Billy sat on so that he fell on the floor.

Scrambling awkwardly to his feet, Fat Billy said breathlessly, 'What is it yous want to know then, there Constable?'

'You sarcastic fat bastard!' the constable angrily exploded, and drawing his long baton hit Fat Billy several blows about the head, one of which caused a deep gash in his forehead. Blood ran from the gash into Billy's eye as the constable screamed, 'The last time you told me anything it cost me two of my best men, you Republican fucker!'

'I don't know what you're on about,' Fat Billy protested as he fell back.

Not finished with him, the constable said to his RUC colleague, 'Help me get him up.' They forced Fat Billy up against the bar, the RUC man holding him upright as the constable laid into him with baton blows to the chest and arms and midriff. Fat Billy folded retching on the floor. Not satisfied with that, the constable then put in the boot and gave him a good kicking too. Fat Billy screamed shrilly as he rolled across the floor and over to one of the coffins by the door that led to the outside courtyard. As he came to a stop he bumped into the last of them, knocking the lid off it so that the constable noticed the weapons inside.

'Well, well, what have we here?' the constable asked of no one in particular. He bent down and peered at the weapons inside, and picked up a Kalashnikov high-velocity assault rifle.

Liam looked up and said, 'See if you can guess.'

'And whose funeral is it, then?'

'Yours if you're not careful,' Liam said, his Tokarev pistol in hand. 'Now put the rifle down and move away.'

Chapter Two

'So you're in charge, are you?' the constable stated, and glancing at his colleague instructed him curtly: 'Draw your weapon and shoot any of these Republican fuckers if you get a chance.'

'Yes sir,' the policeman replied.

Meanwhile, down in the cellar, Maguire and the boy had been working while Duffy was in the courtyard loading the coffins onto the hearse. On hearing a loud voice above, Maguire had smelt trouble and turned out the light so that he and the boy were hid in the dark, before climbing the steps noiselessly to look out through a chink in the door. Putting his eye to the hole, he had a limited view of an RUC man and the exit door leading to the street outside. He tiptoed back down the steps to the cellar.

Hearing that his grandfather was in trouble the boy anxiously whispered, 'What shall we do?'

'Nothing, just watch and listen till the time is right,' Maguire told him. He had seen Duffy doing the same thing at the outside door to the courtyard. Except, out of sight, he had his trusty 9mm Thompson to hand, should it be needed.

While all this was going on, Mairead was two doors down at the fishmonger's and blissfully unaware of everything. She was in a queue of one, behind a poor, harassed woman, drably dressed in hat and coat who had a noisy brood of kids with her. That, quite frankly, Mairead could have done without and she thought to herself, I would have drowned them at birth, if they'd belonged to me. But then the poor simple, stout woman with the scarf round her head had probably never heard of a birth control pill. Anyway, she seemed blissfully unaware of her youngsters' shortcomings, as they whined and moaned and argued among themselves.

Eventually, the woman and her brood did leave the premises, but it took a long time and a lot of argument about what each in turn was going to have as Mairead cooled her heels.

'And what can I do for you?' asked the pleasant man that was the fishmonger, in a slightly soiled white apron.

'Three large mackerel, if you please,' Mairead said, just as pleasantly.

Looking along the glass counter and at the display on the front slabs the fishmonger said, 'It seems they've all been sold out here. So I'll just pop out the back and see if there are any there, if that's all right?'

'It's all right with me,' Mairead said, as the fishmonger disappeared out the back. It was only now, standing there, that Mairead smelt the whiff of shellfish and freshly caught herring assault her nostrils as she waited at the counter. She idly moved over to the glass window and display, watching the harassed woman and her brood of kids walk along the narrow, steep street.

It was then that she spotted something she did not bargain on seeing, and that was the armoured van parked outside the pub. For a moment there was alarm and despondency; she was panic-stricken and her heart began pounding nervously. But she soon caught a hold of herself, and had calmed down by the time the fishmonger reappeared.

He carried three generous-sized, floppy, strong-smelling mackerel in his hands. 'Will I remove the heads and tails for you?' he enquired.

'No, I like them that way,' Mairead said, as the fishmonger weighed them on the scales. He wrapped the fish in large white sheets of paper and popped them into a brown paper bag.

'That'll be one pound and fifty-nine pence,' the fishmonger said. He took her money and rang up the till, then shut it with a clang and gave Mairead her change.

'Thank you,' the fishmonger said, 'call in again now.'

'Thank you, I will,' Mairead replied, with no such intention in mind, as she put her change away in her purse, and shut her handbag.

She left the fishmonger's and walked along the street. To all intents and purposes she looked calm and steady as a rock, but inside she was like a quaking volcano full of emotions and her thoughts were racing. She tried to focus on what she had to do for survival and for the cause of Republicanism, for the long war to continue. That last thought summoned up in her the will and determination to follow it through. Bitterness and anger welled up in her at the occupation of her land by the British: her home, her Ireland, and she felt good about what she was about to do.

Approaching the pub at a jaunty walk, she was alert and ready as her eyes took in the quiet street and any watched for sudden movement. As she walked up to the pub doorway she was greeted by the trooper standing guard with his SLR in his arms, positioned side on blocking the entrance.

Smiling sweetly, Mairead looked him in the eye and said, 'Be a gent will you and hold these, as I've got to adjust me tights before they fall down.'

'Certainly,' the soldier said politely and put his weapon down for the pretty colleen as she thrust the fish in his hands. While she had his attention she put her foot on the low wall surrounding the outside of the pub. Proudly showing off her gorgeous long legs encased in black tights, she displayed her knee-length leather boots and above those the concealed holster, strapped to her shapely thigh. By the time the trooper registered what he was seeing it was too late and, Walther PPK in hand, she pointed it at him and shot him three times in the face. The soldier crumpled to the ground mortally wounded and clutching his bloody face. Cool as a cucumber she then turned and sorted out the other soldier sat behind the wheel in the van gawping and open-mouthed. He scrabbled for the radio as Mairead leant in the nearside window and shot him in the chest and arms. Fumbling for the grenade in her handbag and pulling the pin, she tossed it in the van. The explosion was contained, but still managed to blow out the doors, windows and sides of the vehicle as Mairead walked away. Stepping over the soldier in the doorway, she entered the pub with the fish in her hands.

The explosion outside threw everyone momentarily, and they had forgotten about Fat Billy rolling about the floor in agonised pain, hurt and bloody. But he still had the presence of mind to take out a knife, and stab the blade up to the hilt in the back of the constable's thigh. Now it was his turn to scream, and his RUC colleague, his gun drawn on Liam, turned instinctively and shot Fat Billy several times in the shoulder.

Then all hell broke loose, as Duffy ran into the room and, hurling abuse, riddled the RUC junior with his 9mm Thompson with the effect of spinning the RUC man around before he fell dead. Just then the constable dropped his baton and raised his Walther PPK to shoot Mairead, who was still standing by the doorway.

Spotting the action, Liam called out, 'Mairead, hit the ground!' and she threw herself headlong under the nearest table as shots from the constable rang out. When the firing stopped, Liam got up from where he had ducked and broke a chair over the constable's head, knocking him out cold. Then he stepped forward and shot him in the head.

'Thank God that is over, t'be sure,' Fat Billy remarked, as they all put their weapons away.

'You're glad,' Liam said angrily, 'no more than we are, nearly being compromised like that. For Christ's sake, this is supposed to be a safe house.'

'It's all right for yous to go moanin' on but he wasn't goin' to kill you,' Fat Billy remarked uncharitably. 'That mad bastard had it in for me!'

'Your probably right,' Liam said, 'so what did you tell him that got him so riled about losing two RUC?'

'Only false information about yous and your unit.'

'Oh, I see,' Liam said, it dawning on him that the RUC were the two he killed several days ago playing possum in the middle of the road. A good and successful operation that his OC would be pleased with later.

'I'm leakin' something bad,' Fat Billy remarked, as Liam handed him his hanky to stem the blood.

'Never mind all this chit-chat,' Mairead reminded them, on her feet again. 'We've got work to do before they send out another patrol to find out what happened to this one.'

'Yeah, you're right,' Liam said, dragging the body of the deadweight constable across the floor and towards the cellar door. 'Duffy, get the body outside and bring it in, and his weapon too. And you and Maguire and the boy clean up too and put the bodies below.'

'No, yous can't do that,' Fat Billy pointed out. 'Jesus, Mary and Joseph, are you tryin' to get me hung.'

'And why not?' Liam asked.

'When they finally sort out this mess the first place the army will search will be here.'

'He's right,' Duffy said, fraught with worry like the rest and running his hands through his hair. 'God knows, I don't like it any more than you do,' as Mairead glared at him, 'but he's right.

'Call the Brigade,' Fat Billy remarked, 'they'll know what to do.

'Are you sure?' Mairead queried, feeling somewhat inadequate having to ask for their help.

'Just do it, for Christ's sake!' Liam commanded. 'Time's wastin' away.'

Reluctantly, Mairead picked up the old-fashioned black telephone behind the bar and called the number. She was unable to resist looking at her reflection in the large mirror on the back wall as she dialled and listened for the tone that she was through. She used the number she had been told to commit to memory. It was changed every week or so.

She was soon through and a smooth female voice answered, 'Yes, who is calling?'

'This is Tricolour-7 an' we're in trouble and need assistance,' Mairead said, rather dramatically and feeling foolish. There was a short pause, then the voice asked, 'Where's the best club for a night out?'

'Connolly's is the best one,' Mairead replied, giving the recognised code for that week. It was a real Republican club in Belfast, set up and run by ex-prisoners.

'Where are you?' the smooth voice asked.

'Shamrock pub in Armagh.'

'Right caller, sit tight and someone will be with you presently.'

As Mairead put down the phone, Liam asked, 'Well, what did they say?'

'Someone will be here presently.'

'Then let's clear this place up and tidy as much as possible,' Liam commanded, and everyone jumped to it.

Taking Liam aside, Mairead said, 'Can I see you outside a moment,' and they exited into the courtyard outside.

'All right, make it quick and tell me just what's eatin' you, will you?'

'It's Fat Billy. I don't trust him, that's all.'

'But he was a friend of our father's.'

'A long time ago,' Mairead reminded him. 'And what about that statement by the RUC constable that he'd given them information?'

'False information only.'

'But can you be sure?'

'No, not exactly. No one can be really sure, not without being there and witnessing it for themselves.'

'My point exactly, Liam,' she said, 'and until we can be sure, I for one, am not happy with his glib talk and free speech. So if you don't mind, let's do something about him.'

'That's a bit extreme,' Liam remarked.

Mairead interjected, 'May I just say that he's compromised us once already. Does he have to do it again before your suspicions are roused?'

'I guess not.'

'Good, now you've got the wool out of your head, maybe you'll see a little reason and some common sense.'

'I still think it's a little extreme, for a harmless old man that has given more years than either of us care to remember to the Cause.'

'Anyway, I'll not argue with you,' Mairead said, 'I just want something done about him before he runs off at the mouth to the wrong people and gets us all in trouble.'

'All right, you've said enough,' Liam said tersely. Making a gesture of finality with his hands, he walked away.

Mairead followed tugging him on the shoulder and, turning him round, she looked at her brother and spelled it out for him. 'You've got a simple choice. It's either him or us. You can't have it both ways.'

'That's not an easy decision.'

Pulling him forward and kissing his forehead, she said, 'You're my brother and I love you, but no one ever said commanding this unit would be easy.'

'I'll not kill him,' he said resolutely.

'No one said you had to.'

'Just as long as you realise that.'

'I do.' And they went inside.

The thing to do was to take Fat Billy and the boy, his grandson, out of circulation. That was easily done by binding and gagging their hands and feet and leaving him in the dark, musty cellar, then locking the door and walking away.

'What do yous think you're doin'?' Fat Billy asked aghast, before Mairead gagged him.

'Never mind,' she smiled at him. 'It's all for your own good.'

Some time later; 'What shall I do with these?' Maguire asked, holding the mackerel in the brown paper bag. 'Keep them for our tea,' Mairead said.

'Do as she says,' Liam commented to Maguire. 'Put them behind the bar for now.'

'No, I've got a better idea,' came a voice from the doorway.

'And who might you be?' Liam asked, stepping forward to confront the stranger standing there.

'I'm the Undertaker,' replied the man in a flat, sombre voice that went with his attire of black suit and hat, his hatchet features and pipe-rod thin body. He looked sixty if he was a day.

Looking him up and down, Liam asked, 'Are you the someone they've sent?'

'I am if you're Tricolour-7,' the Undertaker replied.

Pleased and shaking his hand, Liam said, 'Good, we've been expectin' you.'

'So I hear,' the Undertaker said, as he and Liam moved further into the room. 'Now then, we've not long,' he continued succinctly. 'For time is of the essence.'

Spotting the coffin, the Undertaker enquired, 'How many more of these have you and how many bodies and what transport?' For 'trouble' on the phone meant 'army', and 'assistance' dead bodies. The message being relayed to him soon after the Brigade received the call, the Undertaker had been on his way immediately.

'A hearse and two more coffins, and three bodies all together.'

'Then get the bodies into the coffins ASAP.'

'What about discovery?' Mairead pointed out.

'Just do it and quickly,' the Undertaker said, taking charge.

'And the guns?' Liam queried.

'Doesn't the hearse have a false bottom?'

'I believe it does,' Liam said brightening, seeing a way out of the mess. He had forgotten this detail in the commotion.

'Then I believe that is solved,' the Undertaker said. He poured himself a small whisky from behind the bar, the same Irish whisky that Fat Billy had tried to tempt the constable with, as everyone else did as he said. 'Hurry good people,' the Undertaker commented, 'for I warrant a mobile patrol will be here sooner rather than later.'

Everyone rushed around in a panic except the Undertaker, who quietly poured himself several more glasses of the finest malt whisky he had sampled in many a year.

'Just as a matter of interest, how did you manage to get here so quickly?' Mairead asked outright.

'Don't bother yourself worryin' about that little lady,' the Undertaker said, allaying her suspicions. 'I have a place of business not far from here.'

The A25 runs between two waters at the north end of Camlough, a ribbony lake which supplies the taps of Newry and is known as a first class angling spot. The South Armagh hills peter out at the border in small rock strewn, stone-ditched fields fringed with yellow whin. The road continues beyond the Dorsey (a pre-Christian defensive earthworks contemporary with Navan fort) down towards Crossmaglen, population some 1,200. This remote village had an exceptionally large market square, an army base and a reputation for, among other things, horse-breeding and handmade lace.

Crossmaglen was a cattle market town and was known to the British Forces as XMG. Its location, right on the border, made it a favourite of 'players' preparing in Dundalk on the other side and shooting over the border to have a pop at the British Forces.

The big square in the town centre comprised a number of small buildings, with metal railings in front for livestock and all overlooked by Banki Sangar, an observation post located some one hundred metres away from the security forces base that the troops lived in. The post was named after an unfortunate paratrooper who got blown up, a sangar being a corrugated iron and steel structure. Used to defend the place were three general purpose machine guns, an M79 grenade launcher and smoke dischargers. Also at hand were radios, and much needed flasks of tea and sandwiches were always on the go.

There was something very dispiriting about the cold winter and dull, grey November afternoons in particular. It didn't help when as a soldier you had to do your watch detail on such days, looking out at a desolate and isolated countryside more suited to cattle and farmers than the modern soldier and warfare. Such were the unspoken thoughts of the young men kitted up and in the Royal Anglian Regiment, newly arrived and helicoptered in only days before.

They were fresh recruits in a new and hostile land, fighting a guerrilla war that most of them had only glanced at in pictures on the news bulletins back home; a war that most of them never really knew or understood or cared about till now. But by the end of their four month tour their ideas about the war were formed and their understanding would be crystal clear. A war of hate, extended over the centuries in a curious mix of history, politics and religion, ground up into a volatile and explosive mixture that threatened to blow up at any moment in their faces. There on the stony ground was where those new recruits would do their real training and where the complexities of the situation would be brought home to them in no uncertain terms.

Stamping their feet and rubbing their hands, they tried to get warm, exposed to the elements out in the open as they were. They looked out over the area, wishing they were home, or back in the relatively safe and comfy confines of the army base close by watching Top Of The Pops on the small TV. Anything, but the boring chore of watch duty in an observation post perched up in the clouds like some glorified bird table.

Standing there feeling glum, Martin Strong felt something hit him on the arm and looked down at the horrible white mess on the sleeve of his camouflage jacket.

The pale-faced and spotty private known as Man United looked at him and laughed. 'Bird shit!' he laughed again. 'Do you think that bird is trying to tell you something about Spurs' chances in the Cup this year?'

'Maybe, the sodding thing,' Strong said, looking like he sounded – disgruntled.

'Never mind mate. Have another sandwich and a mug of tea and you'll soon forget about it,' the curly-haired, brash East Acton said, so called because of the area in London he came from.

Taking the lid off the plastic flask and filling three tin mugs, Man United helped himself to the pile set below the concrete parapet and asked Strong, 'What sandwich do you want?'

'Got any ham left?'

'No, only cheese and pickle.'

'That'll do,' Strong said, taking the sandwich and sinking his teeth into the white bread. East Acton slopped some of the weak tea as he set a mug down near him.

'Man United,' Strong enquired of him, 'that's a strange name.' He swallowed what he was eating, washed down with a slurp of tea.

'Nah, it's his nickname,' East Acton interrupted. 'Ain't that right.'

'That's right, ever since I was about twelve and started Barnet Comprehensive. Just down the road from where we live. I guess it stuck over the years, as I was always bending someone's ear and rabbiting on about the likes of George Best and Dennis Law and Bobby Charlton. The three best players in the whole world!' Slurping his tea, he helped himself to another sandwich.

Not having that, Strong stuck his oar in: 'Don't forget about the likes of the great Greavsie, probably the most consistent goal scorer in the League. Plus the flying Scot, Alan Gilzean – and the best keeper ever, Pat Jennings. You know I've seen him pluck the ball out of the air one-handed, and there aren't many that can do that.'

'Too right!' East Acton agreed. 'But you know mates, better than footy, my favourite pastime is girls. Especially ones with big tits.'

'You horny bastard,' Man United said, finishing his sandwich.

'So how many birds have you had?' Strong wanted to know, particularly interested and all ears, as was Man United.

'I've had a few,' East Acton boasted, 'and I aim to get me a few more after this tour is over.'

'Good for you,' Man United said. 'And who was the best?'

'Don't know about the best,' East Acton replied, 'but the biggest. Well, I can tell you about her.'

'Go on then,' Strong urged as he and Man United slouched inside and sat glued to his every word.

'Cor you want to see this sister of one of my mates in the flats back home. Shit, she'd put Raquel Welch and Brigitte Bardot to shame.'

'Get away with you,' Man United said, slurping more tea.

'I don't believe it,' Strong said, 'well I mean, I've seen a lot of pics of that Raquel Welch and especially in that fur bikini out of *One Million Years BC* and wow.'

'Yeah well,' East Acton remarked, 'you ain't seen nothin'' till you've seen this bird.'

'So how big is she?' Man United asked, as impatient as Strong for the end of the story.

'She's simply enormous,' East Acton said, his enthusiasm getting to them. 'Bloody great footballs she's got on her chest.' Drawing them into his narrative he said, in a confidential tone, 'I got her alone on the settee one day when her brother was out of the room and asked her outright. She looked at me a little funny and said, "I don't rightly know offhand, but I'd guess somewhere in the region of 40DD plus" and pulled up her jumper.'

'Bleedin' hell!' Man United exclaimed and spluttered into his tea as he took a mouthful, nearly showering the others.

'Christ, you sure?' Strong asked, fascinated like his mate but still a little doubtful.

'As God is my witness,' East Acton said in a reverential tone.

'What were they like to feel?' Man United asked, bug-eyed at the thought of such big tits.

'God knows!' East Acton said, 'before I could find out her bloody stupid brother came back and wanted to play Monopoly as it was raining outside, and she pulled her jumper back down.'

They all laughed, Strong pointing his finger, 'You bloody liar!'

'I am not,' East Acton said, as he and they choked with laughter.

It was half past four in the afternoon and already the light was growing dim and the dark creeping over them as they chatted oblivious, but all that was to change as the chore of doing watch duty in the observation post suddenly became positively dangerous.

Their chatter was interrupted by the crack, crack-crack of rifle fire as someone took pot-shots at them. Dropping his mug, Strong remarked, 'Shit! They might have waited till we'd finished tea.'

'Where did that come from?' Man United asked, as he and the other two ducked down, with bullets pinging and whining over the cramped and low sangar.

'Can you see the bastard?' East Acton asked.

'No, where the bloody hell is he?' Strong asked, the question nagging at all of them as they crouched behind the sandbag and inner metal walls.

Just as they were getting a fix on where the rifle man was, there were more shots from the other direction. Very quickly they assumed their positions as trained, and soon returned fire with GPMGs set on continuous fire. Tilting the machine guns on the tripods down into the market square, they aimed their fire in the direction of the gun flashes they saw and the rifle men shooting at them. Strong, Man United and East Acton all had a different target to shoot at. The 'players' shooting at the soldiers were each firing from the concealment of the small buildings located around the market square. Temporarily they had the upper hand; they had surprised the troopers in the sangar with their bolt action sniper rifles and could fire them. But they were no trained snipers, and no match for the soldiers by any stretch of the imagination.

The rat-a-tat of the GPMGs chewed into the small buildings and took great chunks out of the masonry, riddling the brickwork. The bolt action rifles hardly got a look-in as the troops' overriding fire got on top of the situation. Not for long, however, as a Nissan Hiace van appeared on the scene, its tyres screeching as it shot in a tight curve around the deserted market square. Travelling at high speed, it drove past the sangar, and then flashed out of their view.

'Look out for the frontal assault,' Strong called out.

'How can you tell?' Man United wanted to know.

'He's got a feeling in his bones,' East Acton said. 'Ain't that right, mate?' Strong just nodded, his eyes taking in the van fast approaching them once again.

'Here it comes!' Man United cried out.

The van barrelled straight for them and then, turning at the last moment, drew alongside the sangar. Two balaclava-ed youths were hanging from the back of the van sticking their 7.62 Kalashnikov rifles in the air. The fearsome and efficient weapons were on automatic as they fired straight up at the sangar, forcing the troopers to duck, as the gunmen shouted, 'Up the Ra. Up the Ra-Ra-Ra!' – the local name for the IRA. The fire rattled the sangar with a commotion like a lot of stirred-up bees.

Strong and the others then returned fire on the moving van. Strong shot out the glass in the driver's side window, Man United riddled the side of the vehicle and East Acton shot one of the snipers hitching a ride in the back in the arm, and the other in the leg, as he clutched on to the passenger's door handle. As quickly as it had begun, so it was all over, in less than two minutes everything was quiet and returning to normal.

Expecting a little more, the three troopers stayed tense and full of expectancy at their positions for another five minutes before standing down and realising it was all over.

'Christ, that was exciting!' Man United remarked.

'Exciting but deadly,' said East Acton, adding his two-pennyworth.

'Now we know why they call it Bandit Country,' Strong said and laughed, relieving the tension.

'Course we do,' East Acton and Man United chorused.

'That's right, they're the bandits and we're the good guys,' Strong added.

Suddenly the radio burst into life, 'Base to sangar, you all right up there, over?'

Picking up the radio East Acton replied, 'Sangar to base, we're all right. Seen a bit of action but otherwise OK, over.'

'Well, let us know if you need any help, sangar – over.'

'Will do base. Roger and over and out,' East Acton replied and put the radio down with a silly grin on his face. He looked at his mates, Strong and Man United, who could no longer control it and burst out laughing too. Then all went silent. All of them were thoroughly relieved they had survived their first, real action.

In the city of Armagh, the Mall used to be the city's racecourse and many of the Georgian townhouses along its length still have large balconied first floor reception rooms enabling a good view of the starting and finishing posts. At the northeast corner, the Sovereign's House contains the museum of the Royal Irish Fusiliers. It was built in 1810 of stone left over from the courthouse. On the west side was a rather extravagant little church with a campanile. Approaching this and within a short walk was a one-storey detached building with a pointed roof – a funeral directors. Its woodwork was black and its sign was in letters of tarnished gold. It was an old family establishment that went back decades, and it was here that the bodies and the IRA unit led by Liam O'Connell came at the urgent request of the Undertaker.

Though a not very big premises, it had a small back room, a kitchenette and a front room large enough for a very presentable showroom, complete with the very best and most expensive caskets on view to the purchaser of a bereaved family. They were fine elm wood caskets, satin-lined with lovely brass-work and fittings. Artfully arranged were a variety of price lists in leaflets detailing the arrangements and services available, to pick up and browse through. During working hours a boy and a girl, family of the Undertaker, helped out by taking messages over the phone and speaking to the many prospective clients in the showroom who needed assistance or advice.

Otherwise, the blind came down on the door and it was firmly shut, with the Undertaker using the back rooms for lodging and sleeping when not actually working or out and about. It was a somewhat spooky arrangement to the layman, but the Undertaker, now in middle-age, had known no different since as a small boy he would assist his father before him when he was not at school.

Sharing the place with the dead, and all the pungent smells and unusualness of the situation was quite commonplace to him; he thought nothing of it. For his new and temporary visitors however, the experience was somewhat creepy and unnerving. They sat around a dull and dusty varnished table, eating their beans on toast within spitting distance of the three dead bodies from the shoot-out at the Shamrock pub. It was a uncomfortable situation, no less so, for the fact that dead bodies have terrible personal habits like breaking wind and releasing the trapped gases inside, and even making odd noises and sitting up when least expected. One of the soldiers sat bolt upright almost, and seemed to stare accusingly at Mairead who felt physically sick at the sight of it.

The Undertaker gently pushed the torso back down with the remark, 'There's a gent, now. You don't want to be scarin' the little lady. 'Tis right scared she is, so you go to sleep now like a good soldier boy.'

'It's enough to give you the willies,' Mairead said, pale-faced. 'Us eatin' our beans and them lookin' on disapprovingly.'

'Granted, it's not ideal, but then would you rather be sharin' an RUC cell,' Liam piped up.

'At this moment,' Duffy said, his mouth full of beans, 'there's no contest, I can tell you.'

'Me too,' Maguire said. 'But how long do we have to stay here, I ask myself?'

'Not long, just a day or two, till the coast is clear,' Liam reassured.

'A day or two,' Mairead said, 'cooped up in here with the cast from The Mummy's Curse. Jesus Liam, I know sacrifices have to be made for the cause, but right now, you're really pushin' it.'

'Maybe so,' Liam said, 'but that's how it's got to be.'

'So what's the plan?' Maguire enquired.

'To smuggle you through the checkpoints and the British lines and out of Armagh,' the Undertaker said.

'You'll never do it!' Duffy commented.

'Course we will,' Liam said, 'for God's sake all of you, have a little faith, will you?'

'Duffy's right, it'll never work,' Maguire remarked disbelievingly.

'Have you got a better plan?' Liam asked in a challenging tone to Maguire. 'And you, and you,' Liam continued to Duffy and Mairead.

'No,' they chorused.

'Then, shut up,' Liam snapped, and to Mairead in particular added: 'Earlier on, you told me to command, so let me get on with it and be as good as to give me some backin' when I ask for it.'

Shooting a look at him she said, 'Sorry I spoke, I'm sure,' in that aggrieved tone that only a woman can assume so well.

Maguire then spoke up as everyone else went quiet, 'If we are smuggled through the lines, what about the bodies?'

'Them too,' Liam said succinctly, 'the same way.'

While they ate, the Undertaker quietly and unassumingly went about his business, firstly draining the blood out of the bodies and replacing it with formaldehyde through a series of tubes and bottles. The gas, formaldehyde, being a short-term preserving agent used in the trade to bring back the colour and texture of the skin, in a well known process to arrest the natural decomposition of the body. It was used for purely cosmetic reasons, as were the lipstick, blusher, false eyelashes, foundation cream and wigs and dresses, which the Undertaker now applied to the three corpses. The women's clothes and padded bras helped to complete the illusion; it was one of life's ironies that these brave and courageous soldiers who served their country faithfully should be dressed as a woman in some sick and comic farce at the end. That was the plan, but would it work? Everyone had serious doubts, including Liam himself.

The rifle company lived in what were termed as 'submarines' in the security forces base. There were long corridors, three beds high but sadly without lockers. Everything was painted regulation green and your kit was on your bed or under the bottom bed. The whole base was as a spider, with submarines coming off the central area like legs. The rifle company and troops that did not fit into the submarines had the bad luck to be billetted in the garden sheds in the compound. These were linked by duckboards and usually submerged in ankle deep mud. Covered in anti-mortar mesh, the whole place was no better than a building site, with a thick layer of frost on the roofs.

Smoke pervaded the area any time day or night, with the unforgettable smell of fried egg sandwiches and chips wafting from the nearby cookhouse. Wet floors and the horrible smell of damp clothing had to be contended with. Better still, there were no windows and the heating system was very poor to say the least, so as a consequence it was either very cold or very hot, with no in between.

It was 6 a.m. and roll call was after a quick bit of breakfast. That was if you shifted yourself to get there in time. The sergeant, in a bullfrog voice, shouted, 'Up and at 'em on this fine morning me lads. Let's be havin' you,' as he walked through, shaking the 'I'll only have five minutes more' types awake, banging their mess tins and mugs and generally making a right royal row so that no one could sleep through the din.

The way things were going Strong, Man United and East Acton were not going to make it to breakfast on time. Mainly for the reason they'd only had four hours' kip after coming in from a twelve hour patrol. This made them rather reluctant to do as the sergeant bid them. Their bodies were telling them they were still tired and exhausted and crying out for more sleep.

The others in the room were bustling about in and out of it hairy-arsed and bollock naked, shaving and showering and getting dressed for breakfast. Strong, Man United and East Acton pretended to be fast asleep and not hearing the bull-voiced sergeant, shouting at the top of his voice, 'Get up you lazy bastards and get up now!'

Coming to Strong's bed at the end, he paused and looked down. 'Are we awake enough for a cup of tea?' he asked. 'Well, you soon will be!'

With that the sergeant, who had thick forearms, a barrel chest and large hands, took hold of the mattress Strong was sleeping on and gave it a great heave, tipping the whole lot up. Strong fell in a tangled heap on the floor among his bedclothes, hitting the floorboards hard enough to wake him up. Looking a bit dazed and not quite with it, the sergeant said to him, 'Good morning Mr Strong I trust you had a good night's sleep,' in his sarcastic voice. Then he looked at his watch and said, 'You now have two minutes to get dressed and to get to breakfast. Do I make myself clear!'

'Yes, Sergeant,' Strong said meekly, scrambling to his feet.

Turning on the others, the sergeant said, 'Would any of you like a personal call too?'

'Er, no,' Man United said, panicking. 'See, I'm getting up,' as he rolled out of the middle bunk in his red and white football socks.

'Me too,' East Acton said, jumping out of bed in his white ankle socks, vest and underpants.

'Good,' the sergeant said, turning around. 'I am glad to hear it.'

Chapter Three

20 November 1978

At 5.05 a.m. all the men were assembled in the Nissen hut used as a briefing room. After a lot of banter and scraping of chairs and general hubbub, the men of the Royal Anglian Regiment settled down as the sergeant at the desk took his seat. He was at the top of the room and facing the men as he took the register for the roll call. When he had finished two men in uniform entered the room and all attention turned to them, as the sergeant got to his feet and, springing to attention, saluted the two officers. 'All present and accounted for, sah,' the sergeant barked. To those in the room he added: 'Now shut up and be quiet you squaddies. The colonel has something he'd like to say.'

'Good morning men,' the colonel began. He was a rather handsome looking man with Sandhurst stamped all over him. A fine moustache and grey hair gave the forty-eight year old man a rather distinguished appearance. 'I'm pleased to take this opportunity to talk to you men, as up to now, I've really not had a chance. You might have realised by now, even with your limited experience, that things can get pretty hairy around here. Which is why we are having this talk now and not when you first arrived.'

There was a pause and the men got restless and broke out with a few comments. The colonel raised a refined eyebrow and smiled appeasingly, as the sergeant reminded them, 'Settle down, you squaddies, now. Officer talking. So mind your p's and q's.'

'Er quite,' the colonel said. 'Now, to tell you more about the situation around here that you will be dealing with, I hand you over to Captain Dixon.'

Captain Dixon was of the Special Investigation Branch, but did not announce that. Indeed, the colonel did not refer to it, either. Dixon was short, of slight build, had close-cropped brown straight hair and a plain appearance with no distinguishing features. Aged thirty-six he was then on his fifth tour of Northern Ireland, the work getting no easier as he looked out at the sea of optimistic faces and wondered briefly how many would be maimed by the end, or killed. Putting away such bleak thoughts he went into his 'meet the men' mode.

'Welcome to Northern Ireland,' Dixon said in a bright, cheery voice. 'I hope you will enjoy your stay with us and that everything will be satisfactory. That room service is up to the usual high standard and that you're able to find the time to relax on our golden sandy beaches and get yourself an all-over tan to show the folks back home.'

'Is he for real?' Strong asked.

'Where?' Man United shouted out. 'That's what I want to know, where is this golden beach?', while East Acton commented, 'An all-over tan, that'll do me, son.'

There was much laughter as he'd known there would be and Dixon waited patiently for the men to settle down again.

'Sadly,' Dixon said, 'I was joking, and here is where it all gets serious so pin back your ears and listen carefully. Who knows, you might even learn something.'

Pointing to a large, colour map of Northern Ireland fixed to the wall he continued. 'Ever since the withdrawal of the SAS in 1974, one area of Northern Ireland has remained totally impenetrable amid the successes of security forces elsewhere. That has been the wild border country of South Armagh, centred on Crossmaglen.'

'Bandit Country,' Strong said out aloud, and Dixon acknowledged it as he picked up a swagger stick to point it out on the map. 'That is right, Bandit Country, as labelled by Merlyn Rees, the Northern Ireland Secretary and the Brits that have served over here. Never a natural part of the Protestant North, its inclusion in Northern Ireland's geography was one of the more foolhardy political errors of partition. For as you might know, the Irish Tricolour flies here as readily as the Union Jack in London. Has anybody anything to say on that?'

'What about the IRA?' Man United asked, out of interest.

'It is no secret that throughout the Troubles the IRA has

consistently sustained a classic, rural guerrilla war in this area, hopping back and forth across the multitude of border roads to friendly territory in the Irish Republic. This is not to say that the Irish Government, as Mr Ian Paisley and the Protestant ultras maintain, condones terrorism. For it does not. However, the advantage to the IRA is a clear-cut one, in that the IRA does not recognise the border, but the British and Irish security forces do. Which tends to make hot pursuit in either direction, both covert and in uniform, utterly and diplomatically impossible.'

'Are you finished?' the colonel asked.

'Finished sir,' Dixon replied, and looking at the men asked: 'Are there any questions?'

'Yes, sir,' East Acton said. 'Instead of all this pussy footin' around, why don't we just round up all the IRA and shoot them?'

'A nice idea,' the colonel interrupted, 'and don't think we haven't thought of it, but the politicians, you know. They are a touch sensitive on the subject and I'm sorry, but there it is. The politicians are our masters, whether we like it or not.' Smiling, he looked at East Acton in the front row. 'But a good question, nevertheless.'

'Anyone else?' Dixon asked of the men, like the colonel, still amused at the question by East Acton.

A trooper in the middle of those seated held up his hand. 'Yes sir, I have a question. When can we shoot at them?'

'Another good question,' the colonel pointed out, turning to Dixon. 'Well Captain, when can a soldier shoot?'

Very carefully, so that it would sink in with all the others, Dixon explained. 'A soldier can only give returning fire on making contact with the "players". On no account are we allowed to shoot first and ask questions later. For this is to be avoided if you don't want to be charged and criminally prosecuted.' A brief pause, then, 'Neither is a soldier to be allowed to open hostilities either, only shoot when you're shot at. That is the policy and that is what we on the ground have to adhere to. These should help clarify it for you,' he said, touching a stack of yellow cards.

'Sounds a bit bloody ridiculous to me,' piped up a trooper at the back, and there were murmurings of agreement among the men.

The sergeant spoke out, 'Watch your language trooper, when replying to an officer.'

'Even so, Sergeant,' Dixon added, 'he has got a point as all of us here would acknowledge. But as I said before, that is the policy here and we have to abide by it, despite the feelings we may have about it.'

'Now, are there any more questions?' the sergeant asked. 'Speak up you squaddies or forever hold your peace. This is your chance if there is anything you want to get off your chest.'

Dixon looked at them. No one put his hand up and everyone seemed to realise for the first time the predicament of their work in keeping the peace, there in 'Bandit Country'.

'All right then, I'll hand you back to the colonel.'

'Yes thank you, Captain, for explaining the rules of engagement,' the colonel said. 'I'd just like to take this opportunity to say that if you have any problem my door is always open, and to wish you well in your posting here.'

Before the colonel could go on, the sergeant took a step near him and pointed out Strong, Man United and East Acton. 'And before you go,' the colonel said, 'I just want to congratulate these three troopers at the front for their splendid work in beating off a surprise attack the other day. Well done, and keep up the good work.' He shook hands with the three troopers briskly.

With that, the colonel and Dixon left the room and it was left to the sergeant to dismiss the men and dish out the cards. 'Fall out and take one on your way out.'

They were riding along through the green and rough country on what was a bright frosty morning: Liam O'Connell in the passenger seat, the Undertaker behind the steering wheel of the hearse, along the A29 road that bent right out of Armagh and up towards Charlemont.

At the B28/A29 junction outside Moy, two miles south of the Argory, was the ruined Charlemont Fort built in 1602 by Lord Deputy Mountjoy. Though not signposted they would continue right on to the Armagh/Tyrone border, where the star-shaped fort faced across the Blackwater into the territory of Hugh O'Neill. It was in 1598 that he resoundingly beat the English at Yellow Ford, a few miles from Charlemont, his power increasing. The campaign by Essex was a miserable failure and Elizabeth I now sent Charles Blount and Lord Mountjoy to crush O'Neill once and for all, the fort being an important part of the English strategy.

'So the hearse parked outside the cathedral was yours all along,' Liam commented.

'That's right,' the Undertaker said. 'As for the Ford Escort, that was spirited away and probably is in some garage being broken up for spare parts.'

'And what do we do now?'

'If we get stopped let me do all the talking, and act polite if they talk to you at all.'

They were just leaving the huddled housing estates on the outskirts of the built-up part of Armagh city behind, when sure enough, up ahead was a vehicle checkpoint. It was manned by soldiers of the Royal Anglian Regiment, armed and ready and tense.

'Oh God, here we go,' Liam said nervously, patting the Tokarev pistol under his black suit jacket for reassurance.

'No need for that at all, at all,' the Undertaker explained in a whimsical voice that did not go with the sombreness of his looks – or his profession. 'If you just keep your nerve, we'll soon pull this off. Believe me, I used to smuggle whisky, guns and explosives long before you were born. So I know what I'm talkin' about.'

'Did you now,' Liam said smiling. 'I never knew you were such an old rogue.'

'Did you not? Well, the sum knowledge of what you do know is nothin' to write home about is it?'

'I guess I'm just a beginner compared to you.'

Seeing the hurt look on the face of the movement's most dedicated young man, the Undertaker reached across and patted his knee.

'Ah dear Lord, forgive me. For I have a dreadful arthritis in me bones this cold mornin' and I shouldn't be takin' it out on you.'

At that, Liam brightened and said, 'It's all right really.'

'No, it's not,' the Undertaker said, as they approached. 'Now remember, let me do all the talking.'

Martin Strong stepped in front of them and holding his hand up, indicated for them to stop. The VCP was a hastily set up one, as were most of the vehicle checkpoints. It was nothing more than a dark green Hotspur Land Rover in army markings parked on a grass verge with a plank of wood across two large oil drums as a barrier to stop any oncoming traffic. Man United was in the Land Rover, which had a mesh grille covering it to ensure against rocket attack and to protect the windscreen, while East Acton, alert eyes seeing everything, was behind the barrier with an SLR in his arms. As the friendly Strong approached the hearse on the driver's side, the Undertaker pulled smoothly to a halt.

Winding down the window, the Undertaker winked at Liam and put on his politest voice. 'Top of the mornin' officer, and what is the trouble, may I ask?'

'No real trouble, just a routine check,' Strong corrected him. 'Not unless you've seen a blue Ford Escort with bullet holes and a white flash on its side on your travels?'

'No, I can't say I have.'

'No, I didn't think you would have,' the friendly Strong said, leaning in the window. 'Can I see your driving licence or any other credentials you might have of ownership of this vehicle, please sir?'

'You can,' the Undertaker said and duly handed over his driving licence to the trooper. Strong deftly handed it to Man United in the Land Rover, who radioed the details through to army headquarters. Here the details were thoroughly checked out in minutes, and the all clear was returned.

'He's clean and the vehicle checks out too,' Man United in the Land Rover called out and handed the licence back to Strong, who in turn gave it to the Undertaker.

'Where have you been and where are you going?' Strong asked.

Liam was tempted to chip in and remark, 'To Scarborough Fair, where else?' after the pop song by Simon and Garfunkel, but wisely stayed quiet and instead watched and learned from the charade.

'We've come from Armagh and we're on our way to Moy and a funeral there with the Ryan family that we might not make if you hold us up much longer.'

'Bear with me sir,' Strong said politely. 'Would you and the passenger get out of the vehicle and stand by the road side?'

While the Undertaker and Liam did that, Strong searched the interior and under the seats. He then informed the pair that he would need to frisk them. After his body search the Undertaker got back in the hearse and resumed his seat. The trooper came around to his side and patted down Liam from his shoulders to his feet as he held his arms aloft on request.

'Who are you?' Strong enquired.

'I'm this man's nephew,' Liam replied.

Liam was just feeling pretty smug with himself and the stupid Brits when Strong exclaimed, 'Aha, what's that?'

Shooting a look over, the Undertaker saw a quick flash of panic on the narrow features of Liam, who nearly had a heart attack on the spot. For the trooper had felt something metallic about his chest area and demanded of Liam, 'Let's be having it now.'

'What?' Liam queried, being deliberately obstructive.

'You know what,' Strong replied firmly.

'Oh this old thing,' Liam said, reaching in his jacket and pulling out his Old Holborn tobacco tin – much to the relief of him and the Undertaker.

'Open it!' Strong demanded, sensing there might be something untoward about it.

'What for?'

'I want to know what is in it.'

Opening the lid of the tin, Liam fingered the tobacco mixture and remarked, 'Why, me 'baccy of course. What else would be in it?' as he played dumb.

'Put it away,' Strong ordered, 'and get back in the vehicle.'

'Yes sir,' Liam said, and did as bid.

Trying a different tack, Strong walked around the back of the hearse and lifted the tailgate to look at the coffins he could see arranged in the back, through the window. Curiosity getting the better of him, he was about to reach out and touch the brass plate on the lid of the one in the centre, when quick as a flash the Undertaker was at his side. He was anxious to have no more close calls and to put the trooper's inquisitive mind at ease that they were just in fact a hearse with three coffins on the way to a funeral. The Undertaker was prepared to say or do anything that would reinforce that false impression.

'Open this one!' Strong demanded, 'I want to look inside for myself.'

Picking up a crowbar the Undertaker said, 'This is highly irregular and shall be reported to the Bishop of Armagh, and he will be none too happy about it, I can tell you.'

'I don't think we need trouble him with such a trifling matter, do you?' Strong remarked in a firm tone, as he defused the proposed threat.

'Now you come to mention it, no,' the Undertaker said gulping, as he hastily forced the lid off the centre coffin.

Peering in at the satin-lined coffin, Strong asked, 'What's that God-awful smell,' as he got the full assault on his nose and senses. He looked at the shut eyes of the grey-haired old woman in a slightly musty condition in a cheap, flowery cotton dress.

'Oh that, sir, it'll be the formaldehyde,' the Undertaker explained. 'We use it for the preservation of the body.'

'Preserve the body and kill off the mourners I shouldn't wonder,' Strong remarked cheerfully.

'Can I go now?' the Undertaker asked, as he spotted another vehicle coming towards the checkpoint. It was a broken down campervan painted in psychedelic colours, with a family of tinkers aboard and luggage and kids hanging off at every angle.

'Yes, be on your way,' Strong directed, 'and be quick about it.'

The Undertaker took him at his word and quickly set the lid back on the coffin and pulled the tailgate down. Jumping behind the wheel, he moved off, before the trooper changed his mind and took a closer look at the coffins and their occupants.

'Phew that was close, so it was!' the Undertaker remarked, changing gear.

'I thought we'd had our chips when he pulled me up like that.'

'We nearly did,' the Undertaker said.

Taking the tobacco tin out and the lid off, Liam offered, 'Have a smoke?'

'Don't mind if I do,' the Undertaker replied, reaching over one-handed.

'Sorry, they are only roll-ups, but I've no proper fags on me,' said Liam.

'Don't be a-worryin' about that, me and roll-ups are no stranger to one another. When I was smugglin' that's all we had to sustain us in our hour of need. That and a wee flask of the good stuff, the elixir of life, Irish whisky. Fresh as the mountains of Mourne.

'Ah the whisky,' Liam remarked. 'But more to the point, what about that stink: what caused it?'

'Not formaldehyde, though I'll grant you it does whiff somewhat, but rotten fish, now there's a different story,' the Undertaker explained.

'So that's what happened to the mackerel? I did wonder, as you cooked us beans on toast, the other night.'

'It was the mackerel all right. I slipped it under the cardigan of the body, so that anyone getting near would get a good whiff of it. It never fails,' the Undertaker said, sounding gleeful. 'It gets them every time.'

Liam ginned. 'And on to where, now?'

'On to Moy, like I told the good trooper, and more especially, that wonderful Blackwater River that runs through it. There we'll just undress these good people, set fire to their clothes an' let them float away down stream and unload all our problems at the same time.'

'You wily old rogue,' Liam said.

'Not so much of the old,' the Undertaker pointed out, as they left the checkpoint behind in the distance.

The vicarage next door to the elegant little Saint Mary's church was just a small affair; a low, concrete pebble-dashed building with large picture windows and a garage alongside, enabling anyone to park a car inside, then pull down the up-and-over door. Inside the garage, an inset door in the wall opened into the hallway of the house, allowing easy access.

As they entered, Mairead, Duffy and Maguire were greeted hospitably by the housekeeper, who bid them enter the kitchen and sit round the formica-covered table. She chatted away to them in small talk, and poured each of them a good strong cup of tea. She offered them all a good thick slice of home-made fruit cake, which she took from out of a large Quality Street tin.

Some fifteen minutes later the man of the house appeared, and bid them to enter the cosy and comfortable sitting room, where a warm coal fire was burning in the grate. There were two easy chairs covered in floral dust covers with large cushions, and a long settee set beneath the five foot picture window, showing the garden and the home-grown vegetable patch. Mairead and Duffy chose the settee and Maguire the chair against the back wall. The man of the house sat in the chair nearest the door, which he shut before sitting down with them.

The room was peaceful and calm. Not even the traffic outside could be heard, and the only sound inside was the big grandfather clock, on top of the marble mantlepiece, ticking.

The man of the house was fifty-nine and dressed in black – a small, plump man with white tufts of hair either side of his pink shiny head, and cherubic features. It was a kind face and the three of them soon warmed to the man as they sat there in his company. He was sat so high, on the plumped up cushions in the chair, that his little fat legs did not touch the ground. He broke the silence by asking, 'Has the Undertaker been taking good care of you?'

'Yes he has,' Duffy said.

'We had beans on toast last night,' Maguire informed him. 'That was nice,' he added.

'We slept at his place last night with the dead looking on,' Mairead commented. 'It leaves you just a little spooky and frightened.'

'I'm sure it does,' the man of the house said, 'but I don't suppose they mean any harm by it.'

'How do you know? Do you have an understanding with the dead?'

'You might say that,' the man of the house said, 'for it has been known for me to have to commune with them from time to time.'

'We'll be doing a bit of that to Fat Billy,' Mairead threatened, 'if that loose-tongued, stupid Irishman doesn't watch out.'

'How did you find Fat Billy?'

'With the help of his grandson,' Duffy said thickly.

'Warm and friendly,' Maguire remarked. 'He had the guns we wanted.'

'And the ammunition and a place to try them out; and some RPG-7s,' Duffy pointed out.

'Did he now?' the man of the house replied, and to Mairead: 'And how did you find him?'

'Warm and friendly as he brought us into a trap in his own "safe-house".'

'How do you know it was a trap?'

'Soon after, the RUC and some soldiers showed up, that's how,' Duffy replied.

'And you?' the man of the house asked of Maguire.

'Well it did seem a little fishy, I must admit to that. For as soon as he put us at our ease, they showed up out of the blue, like that.'

'So is Fat Billy a traitor?' the man of the house asked outright, inviting opinions from all of his guests.

'Could be,' Duffy said, a little undecided.

'If he isn't, then he's got to be suspect, that's all I'm sayin',' Maguire remarked.

And Mairead said cuttingly, 'If he isn't, then he should be.'

'I see, as bad as that.'

'Worse, I suspect,' Maguire said, 'even though he flogs to death the fact that he and my da were friends some twenty years ago.'

'In other words you don't trust him,' the man of the house said.

'Damn right, I don't. Anyone that loose-mouthed and friendly with the RUC has got to be suspect in my book,' Mairead said.

'What did your brother Liam think about it?'

'When he got the cotton wool out of his ears and put down the ol' violin and I helped him see through the mush, he had to agree.'

'But not beforehand?'

'No.'

'And why was that?'

'Simple. He couldn't believe that a man steeped in the Cause an' its traditions could jus' go bad.'

'And you did?'

'Cynical as it may seem, yes I did.'

Duffy quickly added, 'Me too.'

Maguire went further, 'Don't see why not. After all, he wouldn't be the first.'

'No he wouldn't,' the man of the house agreed. 'Tell me, why did you go to the Shamrock pub?'

'Liam had his orders to go.'

'Did he say where he got them?'

'No,' Duffy said surprised. 'We don't question our orders, just do as we're told like good volunteers.'

'That's right,' Maguire agreed. 'Like the good volunteers we are.'

'Good,' the man of the house said, sounding pleased with them. 'Then, you are a credit to the Army, as I myself issued those orders. For I am your OC, the Operations Commander of the Armagh Brigade. And why did you think you went there?' he asked of Mairead.

'To get more guns as ours had run out in Crossmaglen.'

'Partly, that was the reason,' the OC said, 'but more importantly to test out Fat Billy and allay our suspicions.'

'Which were?' Duffy demanded to know, still somewhat dumbfounded by the admission that this cherubic man who looked so gentle and like he would not harm a fly, was their OC.

'That he was a traitor,' Maguire quickly interrupted.

'Quite so,' the OC said.

'No matter what we think or say, it has to go to the Army Council for they have to sit in judgement on it, not us,' Mairead pointed out.

'You're right and they have,' the OC said. 'Like you though, I suspect they would like to have an open and shut case with more concrete proof instead of rumour and conjecture and innuendo to go on. Which is why the Army Council has instructed Intelligence to get the evidence to that effect.'

'I just wish Liam was here to hear that,' Mairead said, sounding pleased and vindicated at the same time.

'It doesn't matter what Liam thought. You were right, that's all that matters.'

'So when is the court martial?' Duffy asked.

'A duly constituted court martial has tried this case already.'

'What was the verdict?' Maguire enquired, as interested as all the others.

'Fat Billy was tried and deemed guilty of treachery.'

'And the sentence?' Mairead asked, looking at her OC.

'The penalty for a breach of this order is, as always, death.'

'I almost feel sorry for Fat Billy,' Mairead said, knowing that the Army Council would issue the order as soon as was convenient. Fat Billy would be a dead duck, and nothing and no one could prevent it.

'Don't be,' the OC said. 'If he's guilty of treachery, and everyone on the Army Council is convinced he is, then he deserves what he gets.'

'I agree,' Duffy remarked.

'Me too,' Maguire added.

Then, just when the three of them thought there were no more surprises in store, the OC got out of his chair and went over to the mantelpiece. Looking in the oval mirror hanging there, he picked up his dog collar and put it on as he turned round and faced them.

Duffy spluttered, 'But you're a...'

With Maguire adding, 'He is too.'

Mairead sat bolt upright and remarked, 'You're a priest, no less.'

'Father Behan. And what would you have me be instead, a plumber maybe?' The OC chuckled to himself, and with his fingers made the sign of the cross and said, 'And may the peace of love and understanding, live with you now and forever, amen.'

'When I come back from my flock,' the OC said, 'then, we will speak of Christmas and the presents the Army wish you to distribute among the soldiers in our "Brits Out" campaign.'

Before the OC left the room, Duffy spoke up, 'Shouldn't we be leavin'? After all, you don't want the RUC or the Brits to catch us here, do you?'

'No more worrying on that score,' the OC said, 'for God moves in mysterious ways and the Brits will never think of looking here. They think we are all stupid micks without a grain of sense or imagination.'

'Do they now?' Maguire enquired in a put out tone.

'Yes they do and if you haven't learnt that yet, then you haven't learnt an awful lot, have you?'

With the question hanging in the air, the priest who was the OC made his way into the kitchen, bid his housekeeper goodbye, and shut the door on his way to Evening Mass in the elegant church next door.

23 November 1978

Markethill is a Protestant village where livestock markets are held three days a week in the bustling and thriving community of some 1,300. The main street of the village contains butcher shops, hardware stores and a chemist's. Churches are on both sides and there are some old grey cemented terraced houses too. It is a place, like so many, that has suffered much during the 'Troubles' in Northern Ireland.

It is a place with a strong representation of Orangemen and Orange Lodges; about 500 male members, plus two women's lodges and even a Junior Orange Lodge. At the entrance to the village are the security gates, usually open and pulled back, but, if necessary closed over, thereby sealing off all entry to the village.

Two local policemen were at this moment guarding the entrance to the town. All traffic was being stopped at the barriers as an armoured van drew up. It was waved through by the guards and proceeded into the back of the police station. An RUC escort got out of the van and opened the rear door for a boy and an older man, both in handcuffs. Soldiers brought up the rear as the RUC men ushered their prisoners inside to the custody sergeant, who sat at his desk in the corridor beyond reception.

The prisoner and the boy halted before him, as he looked up from behind the large lined open custody register. A biro in hand, he got ready to record the details of the prisoners to be booked in.

'Name?' the custody sergeant asked in a snappy voice. He was feeling a bit tetchy, as the last few nights he had found it impossible to sleep for all the noisy music, and a baby next door crying to all hours, belonging to the newly moved in young family. He was not looking forward to going home in half an hour at the end of his shift and having another blazing row with his neighbours about the racket they made.

'Fat Billy,' the prisoner in cuffs announced to the amusement of the RUC escort.

Wearily, the custody sergeant said with emphasis. 'Now, let's try again, shall we? Name?'

'William Shanaghan.'

'Better. Date of birth?'

'Fourth of July 1918.'

'Current residence?'

'Shamrock pub. Armagh city.'

'Personal effects?' the custody sergeant asked, and on the presentation of keys, money and driving licence, dropped them in a plastic bag and wrote out a label, then put the sealed bag in the drawer of the desk.

'Both involved in shootings at the same pub and address,' the leading constable of the escort said to the custody sergeant, who wrote down the details.

'Take him along to cell number one, then uncuff him and lock him in,' the custody sergeant told the escort who did as bid.

'Now, you are?' he said to the boy.

'That man's grandson,' replied the boy, pointing after the retreating Fat Billy.

'And your name?' the custody sergeant said, fed up of repeating himself.

'William O'Grady.'

'Good. Better. Date of birth?'

'The fifth of September 1968.'

'Currently residing?'

'The same place as my grandfather,' the boy said proudly.

'Take him along to cell number two and uncuff him and lock him in as well,' the custody sergeant directed the second man in the RUC escort.

There was the dull sound of a heavy metal door clanging shut as the custody sergeant made his way over to the cells and, picking up a piece of chalk, wrote their names on a board outside. As the door shut loudly on Fat Billy he remonstrated, 'You'll be hearin' from me brief over this, so you will. You're makin' a terrible mistake an' I should not be here!'

Sneeringly the custody sergeant looked at him through the open slit in door and said, 'Don't make me laugh you thick Catholic fucker.' He shut the cover and walked away.

It was gone midnight when Fat Billy was dragged out of his cell and down to the interview room further down the corridor. Realising he was not going to be set free straight away, he had decided to shut his eyes and go to sleep for a while. He chose a corner on the cold concrete floor instead of the uncomfortable concrete plinth and useless mattress, wrapping his jacket around himself as a substitute blanket.

So it was a particularly rude awakening when the two interrogators came for him. They were two detectives from the Criminal Investigation Department, one tall and thin and spotty and the other fat-faced and smelling of cheap curries and lager. Both in their thirties they would play the age-old game of Mr Nasty and Mr Nice. They entered the interview room and put a blank tape in the machine. Then they dumped Fat Billy in a low plastic chair, where he looked up with sleepy eyes at the fluorescent lighting glaring down at him from the ceiling of the stark room.

The chair was so low that Fat Billy could hardly sit up at the grainy table before him, as his interrogators towered above him – particularly Mr Nasty, the fat-faced one. Irritable and unhappy with this treatment, Fat Billy remonstrated loudly, 'You lousy Protestant bastards! I've done nuthin' an' I'm not bein' treated right an' you can't hold me like this!'

'Oh yes, we can,' the thirty-two year old 'Nice' detective said, smelling of some sweet aftershave like Brut for Men. 'We have a piece of paper in our possession that says we can do just that.'

Then the other detective bent down and into the face of Fat Billy and remarked in oily tones, 'It's a three day detention order under the Emergency Provisional Act, or seven days under the Prevention of Terrorism Act. Which means we can have you all to ourselves for seventy-two hours or more. Won't that be lovely, just you and us talking all friendly like and learning what you've got to tell us.'

'Get yourself out of my face,' Fat Billy said, none too pleased.
'Is that a threat, is it?' the 'Nasty' detective demanded to know, balling his fist.

'It is,' Fat Billy said, clenching his own, and standing up.

'Break it up, you two,' the other one said, pulling them apart. 'Now, let's have some decorum and some cooperation out of you and sit down,' he commented, as he jabbed Fat Billy in the ribs.

'What do you want to know?'

The 'Nasty' policeman grabbed hold of Billy's throat and briefly squeezed it hard with his right hand round his windpipe. 'Or, if you piss us about, then there's always the alternative,' the tone of his voice grew colder, 'where we can take you to a nice empty cell and have a whale of a time beating the shite out of you. What do you say?'

Choking, Fat Billy spat. 'To hell with that!' and lashed out at the hostile detective, kicking him on the shin and making him hop about in pain.

Restoring order again, the amiable detective looked at Fat Billy and said, 'Look, if you help us, we'll help you.'

'How?'

'Depends on how good you are to us,' the nasty one added.

'But initially as good as a brand new pack of ciggies and a cup of coffee.'

'You're on,' Fat Billy said enthusiastically, as he had been in custody for several hours and had nothing to eat or drink or smoke. Consequently, he was dying for all three, but the drag of a fag more than anything.

'I don't know why you're bothering,' said the one Billy was mentally naming Nasty. 'Let's dispense with the niceties and take the fat cunt to a cell and have the pleasure of beating the crap out of him, anyway,' as he rubbed his shin which was still painful.

'No, that's not the way and I won't be a party to it,' said his partner. 'At least, not unless it's absolutely necessary, that is.'

At that, Fat Billy was flabbergasted and went white with fear, he believing foolishly that he had a friend in the 'Nice' one. But like his partner, Nice was enjoying putting the squeeze on Fat Billy, enjoying the age old game of the 'carrot and stick' procedure.

Fitting on a knuckleduster, Nasty said coldly, 'Forget the cell, I can do it here just as easily,' as he grabbed hold of Fat Billy by the hair and set him up for a straight right to the face.

Closing his eyes and shaking his head and quivering in fright Fat Billy burst out in a shrill voice: 'All right,' he pleaded, 'I'll tell you what you want to know. I'm an IRA volunteer t'be sure, but I'm also an army spy.'

'Yeah, we know: in the Irish Republican Army,' said Nice.

'No,' Fat Billy corrected, 'the British Army.'

'Who says?' demanded Nasty. 'He's playing for time, the fat weasel, let me have him alone for five minutes. Just five minutes,' he urged his partner. 'Just let me finish this weasel.'

Ignoring him, the second detective said, 'Do you really expect us to believe that?' as he laughed out aloud.

'Yeah, really, you stupid fat Catholic mick,' Nasty said, laughing too.

'It's true,' Fat Billy said. 'Ask Captain Dixon and he'll tell you.'

'Who the hell is that?' dismissed Nasty. 'I've never heard of him. You're making it up!'

'I'm not, I'm not,' Fat Billy pleaded. 'Get on to the Special Investigation Branch.'

'Army intelligence,' scoffed Nice. 'You probably couldn't even spell it!'

'Yeah, Captain Dixon,' echoed Nasty, equally scoffing.

Just then the door was thrown open to the green-walled interview room and a man in uniform walked in.

'You rang?' the man in uniform said curtly.

'We did?' Nice asked dumbfounded, as he and his partner stood there open-mouthed and gawping at the man from the Royal Military Police's Special Investigation Branch.

Smiling and putting down his briefcase on the table the man in uniform said, 'Captain Dixon of Army Intelligence at your service gentlemen. Be so kind as to leave the room and bring back two coffees, sweet, and a packet of cigarettes. And then, leave us alone altogether, thank you.'

The two policemen left the room, scowling. Dixon immediately pressed the button to erase the tape, then turned to Fat Billy. 'So how are you?'

Brightening, Fat Billy said, 'Jesus, it's nice to see a friendly face at last.'

Chapter Four

Fat Billy relaxed now that the detectives had left the room. Now it was just Captain Dixon and him, old allies and firm friends amidst the sectarian wars and the troubles of Northern Ireland over the years.

Sitting across from Fat Billy, Dixon began his softly-softly approach.'

'You know Fat Billy, I was a young lieutenant in this service when I was first introduced to you and handed your case file to continue as an ongoing informer.'

'To be sure, you were,' Fat Billy said, 'and I thank fate and destiny, two ladies who brought you into me life. For no other wiser or astuter young man could've done a better job at handling me than you've done up to now, so you have.'

'And I share the same sentiments, believe me,' Captain Dixon said.

'No other Englishman has ever done for me what you have, so help me God, and so me an' my family thank you from the bottom of our hearts, so we do.'

'All right,' Dixon interrupted, 'turn the blarney off and listen good to me, or you'll end up in Gough Barracks as an internee.'

'Now your scarin' me so you are, with such a threat. I've heard the stories, no thanks. So what is it?'

'In all the time you've known me you've always known I had your interests at heart as well as the job, haven't you?'

'Go on,' Fat Billy said, 'tell me the worst,' as he did not like what Captain Dixon was leading up to.

'I've always tried to help you, despite you being my "squealer" and my agent.'

'Yes, now you really are scarin' me, an' my ancestors that died in the bogs fightin' you damn arrogant British,' said Fat Billy, sipping his coffee and taking deep drags of the cigarette in his mouth. 'Certainly you've always done me right an' I've tried to play ball.'

'Well now, old friend,' said Dixon, patting him on the arm, 'I'm not so sure there is a lot I can do to help you. Or if I want to,' he said hesitantly, taking out some papers from his tan briefcase with the brass locks on.

'Tell me, just tell me,' Fat Billy said in a quavery voice. 'You must be able to do somethin'.'

'You see,' Dixon said, papers in hand, 'before I came in here I took the liberty of demanding your charge sheets. And pretty dreadful reading they make, too.'

'No, it can't be, I ne'er did nothin' to them. It wasn't me, but them.'

'I've been going over it in my mind, and you see, old friend,' Dixon said, deliberately coy, 'I'm not really sure if there's anything I can do to get you out of this tight spot you're in.'

Grabbing hold of Dixon's arm for reassurance that his old friend had not gone hostile on him, Fat Billy pleaded, 'Dear God in heaven, holy mother of Christ! But you must be able to, t'be sure, I'll shop the whole lot of 'em. Only don't send me to prison an' don't let me be separated from my loved ones and my dear, dear family.'

'Let me see, it was the year of the "sixty-niners" when things all began to go wrong for you, and you began to question the motives of the Army, isn't that right?'

'To be sure, that's about right, so it is. The year of them mad bastards Martin McGuinness in Derry and Gerry Adams in Belfast. Full of hate and bitter about the situation, an' wild an' fiercely ambitious, they took over the runnin' of their areas as commanders.'

'They were young and too ambitious and just a little too violent and too trigger-happy for your taste, is that right?' Dixon prodded.

'They were, to be sure. They had their reasons, and no one is saying they didn't, with the fire in their belly from the outrage of the way they saw their community set upon by mad Protestant dogs, as whole families got burned out and shot. Who didn't? I did too, an' wanted to kill 'em with me bare hands when I found out.'

'So what was it that made you turn away from all you had previous held as dear. Was it the Provisionals?'

'Ah, the bloodthirsty Provos. They just took the gun and pointed it at anyone or anythin' they did not like or agree with. An' I'm ashamed to say, that it made me sick to me stomach an' that's when I began t'think there must be a better way. That these young pups of commanders were hell-bent on leadin' us into the great conflagration an' fires of hell an' torment an' there was no goin' back.'

'Especially, when they did no more than turned on the Officials – the left-wing and politically oriented, is that right?'

'Especially when they burst into our own Catholic bars an' shot down our friends an' colleagues of the Officials. Me friends an' me Army mates, who we'd fought shoulder to shoulder with, when they had been but a twinkle in their mother's eye.'

'How did you feel about that?'

'When that happened, well it was time to throw in the towel, for somethin' just snapped inside of me, so it did.'

'By the Officials, you mean of course those who opposed the 1921 Treaty which established the Free State and the border. The Republican Movement priding itself on being the only political organisation representing the thirty-two counties and certainly the only one fighting for the "true republic".

'To be sure, you're right. An' when that went and these puppies took over, I said to me wife that I'd had enough of it. She agreed an' said I should follow me conscience an' do what the Holy Father says in the Good Book.'

'The new breed of hard-line Provisionals which sprang up after the Protestants turned on the Catholic community with such vehement rage, and largely destroyed them; this breed did not please you, then?'

'They did not. To be sure, I agreed with the retaliation and our anger an' hate of them at the time, but later, I just had to question what it was all for and where it was leadin'?'

Dixon gave his opinion, 'It's a great pity more men of your ilk don't do the same and stand up and tell these hard men and "sixty-niners" that violence begets violence, as the Good Book tells us, and that no good can come of it anyway. That sooner or later, the only way the whole sorry and terrible mess can ever be resolved is at the ballot box and around the talks table.'

'To be sure, Captain Dixon. Where Catholic and Protestant can talk to one another friendly like and work hard for everlasting peace.'

'But will there ever be one? What with all the hurt and the suffering and the mistrust and fear between the two communities, I wonder if it will ever come about?'

'Only with trust an' patience an' good sense, things that are sadly lacking, and a great deal of compromise on both sides,' Fat Billy said, and then ended on a morbid note: 'But Englishman, will there ever be an end to the killin' an' slaughter?'

'I'd like to think so, as would the best-intentioned people and politicians, but somehow in the hard graft of political talks and compromises that hope does seem to be a little misplaced, as the sectarian killing goes on and murder follows murder. For that to happen everyone involved in peace talks around the table and on the ground will have to really want peace and will have to be willing to give up something and to compromise fully to fulfil that everlasting peace.'

'Well to be sure,' Fat Billy said, 'I never heard a better speech by an Englishman. You were so eloquent there that I quite forgot meself an' thought it must be an Irishman speaking.'

Looking at his watch, Dixon said, 'It's nearly half past one in the morning. Now, I suggest we call it a night and call a halt for a while and I'll see you in the morning after a good night's sleep. Then, you can tell me more about what happened and I can try to work out a deal to get you off these charges of GBH and murder, to name but two.'

'That sounds like a real good offer to me, an' I'll gladly sleep on it.'

'Good. Guard!' called out Dixon, and an RUC man came in and escorted Fat Billy back to his cell.

Along the main street of Richhill was a glassed-fronted shop with a recessed doorway and a sign over the top, in raised white letters on a pale blue background that proudly announced, 'Richhill Electrics'. Crammed in the small front window were toasters and three-bar fires and hairdryers and foreign fridges and all sorts in a higgledy-piggledy fashion; not so much displayed as piled into the front window, with cardboard notices written in marker pen informing any would-be customer of the hire-purchase terms and monthly payment offers.

The shop was also the sole Crankey Vending Machine agent for miles around, Crankey Vending being the company that made the ever popular Manhattan model in cream with the brown stripe. I'm sure you know the type of slot machine I mean: the one that, on receiving the right amount in coins, at the press of a button dropped a plastic cup that filled with coffee, or whatever the customer selected.

The Manhattan was the pride and joy of Crankey, and just happened to be the model of vending machine that the local RUC stations had plumped for, Richhill Electrics installing them some time ago. On the whole it was a reliable and most efficient machine; but, like all machines, it had its faults and its idiosyncrasies and it was not unknown for it to go on the blink, or even break down sometimes. When this happened, the RUC station concerned would simply place a call to Richhill Electrics and Michael O'Flaherty, the owner. Every day he would visit the stations in his small Thames van and bring a refill of drinks and cups for the machine. But some days he had to do more than just a simple quick refill and it turned into a major service job.

Michael O'Flaherty was of medium height and build with bony features, uneven but white teeth and a shock of red hair, thick and back-combed from a long forehead. He was thirty and he had run the thriving business of Richhill Electrics ever since getting out of the UDR, the Ulster Defence Regiment. When he came out having completed five years in the service, his eyes opened to a great deal of things he had previously been naive and narrow-minded about.

A good, church-going Protestant, he had agreed with his friends and neighbours that all the 'Troubles' were of a Catholic nature and agreed with them that the only good Catholic was a dead one. But serving in the UDR had changed all that, as over the years he saw terrible things that left a lasting impression; not least of all, the misery of the terrorism inflicted by the Protestant terrorists such as the UVF, the Ulster Volunteer Force.

Sometimes he had been sick to his stomach, and after five

years he'd had enough of seeing the harm and suffering at close quarters. His viewpoint changed, and he gradually began to sympathise with the Catholics, and then with the IRA. It was around this time that he returned to civvy street and started up his business, Richhill Electrics. It took a number of years and did not happen overnight, but gradually he did more and more for the IRA and the Armagh Brigade in particular. Even so, it was always with the proviso that he was never directly involved in the violent side of things. Instead, he kept his eyes and ears open as he went about his work and dealt with information, giving the IRA what they wanted in the form of good, sound intelligence.

So it was no surprise to him when he got the call one morning at 8 a.m. Picking up the receiver, O'Flaherty heard the smooth voice announce, 'We need a job done quickly.'

'Wait a moment while I get a pencil,' O'Flaherty said, as he picked one up and got ready to jot down the message. Leaning on his counter he said, 'Go ahead with the job.'

'We need a rewiring and unitary circuit job done with a good safe estimate and not too much damage to the free boards ASAP. Can you help?'

'Certainly, I'll do that,' O'Flaherty said helpfully. 'Cash on nail or usual terms?'

'Cash on the nail and will you drop the estimate off at the usual address when passing Markethill?'

'I'll do that, see you then.'

'Good and goodbye,' said the smooth voice and put the phone down.

This came from the usual smooth voice and the opening phrase was a coded message, as O'Flaherty knew. 'Rewiring and unitary circuit' meant RUC, while anything after 'much damage' indicated the person involved. The initials FB of 'free boards' referred to Fat Billy, and Markethill was the location of the RUC station. So now he knew what the latest was that they expected from him.

By 8.20 a.m. he had packed the van with all the tools and equipment and refills and drinks he would need and, turning round the sign on the shop door to 'closed', he locked the door and got in the van. Frost lay thick on the ground but now as the warm sunshine came out it glistened wet on the grass. The appearance of the sun did much to buoy the spirits of Michael O'Flaherty, as the grey clouds disappeared on this late November day. He drove along the B131 with the window down and cool outside air soon waking him up. Feeling most cheerful and whistling as he drove he soon reached the B3 intersection taking him past Forest Park, heading in a north-westerly direction towards Markethill and his destination.

Many visitors were attracted to Gosford Forest Park by the castle in the middle. The first Norman revival castle in the British Isles, Gosford Castle was designed in 1819 for the Achesons and Earls of Gosford by Thomas Hopper, who later built Penrhyn castle in Wales. It was a huge sprawling structure with a square keep, a round tower with a circular drawing room and extremely thick walls. The fourth earl sold the furniture in 1921 to pay his debts; in World War II Anthony Powell, the writer, was billeted there, when the castle was in military use. At another time it had housed a circus, complete with lions. Driving by, O'Flaherty never ceased to wonder at the grandeur and magnificence of it, and wished it was his.

'One day,' he said, changing gear as he looked wistfully at it. 'One day you'll be mine and I'll live a life of Reilly, so help me,' and he smiled to himself at that pleasant thought as he drove on and the castle disappeared behind thick trees.

Arriving at Markethill by 8.45 a.m. and hitting the queue of vehicles entering the town, O'Flaherty sat there and patiently waited until he moved up to the open gates. He was in the 'rush hour', as someone whimsically noted one day. A queue of some dozen lorries, vans and cars headed into Markethill, past the RUC station and on down the main street.

Approaching the gates, it was not long before a policeman who knew O'Flaherty well stopped him, and looking in the window said, 'Oh, it's you, Michael.'

'So it is, and how are you on this grand mornin'?' O'Flaherty asked of the sour-faced man in green uniform.

'Not as good as you obviously,' the policeman said. 'How the hell do you manage to keep so bloody cheerful, that's what I want to know?'

'I remember what me old grandma used to say and she was right. As long as you've money in your pocket and you owe no one, well life can't be all that bad, can it?'

'When it's pissing down and I'm on duty and me feet are achin' an' I can't wait to get home, I must remember that,' said the policeman, perfectly serious, even if he did sound like he was taking the mick.

'You do that,' urged O'Flaherty, 'and you'll be a better man for it, I guarantee you.'

'I will. Now tell me,' the policeman said, 'what have you in the back?'

'The usual,' O'Flaherty joked, 'timing devices and a 1,000 pound bomb.'

'Don't even joke about it,' the policeman said. 'Not unless you're going to blow up that damn vending machine?'

'Why, what happened this time?'

'Ah the bloody thing whips your money and gives you a drink, but then forgets to give you a cup to drink it out of.'

'That's ingenious,' O'Flaherty said, smiling.

'Ingenious it might be,' said the policeman, 'but I'm tellin' you now, everyone in the station from the chief inspector down has just about had enough of it.'

'Fair enough,' O'Flaherty said, 'let me out of this queue and I'll drive in and see to it in a jiffy.'

'You do that,' the policeman said, 'only let me look in the back of your van first, OK?'

'It's OK with me, if it's OK with you,' O'Flaherty said and allowed the policeman to look and poke about. When he was done, he shut the back doors of the van and banged his hand on the steel top as a signal for O'Flaherty to move off and pull into the back of the RUC station. He soon parked, and within minutes had entered the reception of the RUC station. Then, in his blue overalls with the Crankey badge across them, he set down his toolbox, got down on his hands and knees and with a screwdriver set to work taking the back off the drinks machine in the corridor. The machine was situated just outside the door of the interview room. Through another door and further along the corridor was the empty desk of the custody sergeant.

No one else was around and all was quiet for the moment as the personnel of the RUC station trusted O'Flaherty to do his job and get on with the fixing of the vending machine. The Manhattan was a five foot upright machine, and was the height of sophistication in its class for coin-slot vending machines. It dispensed hot tea, coffee and chocolate with extra white and extra sugar as a bonus if preferred. Then there were cold drinks too, such as lemon and lime, blackcurrant and cola. His tools spread out and door off at the back of the machine O'Flaherty gave a good impression of tinkering about with the inside pipes, switches and mechanisms of it for a while.

However, after some five minutes, he looked up and down the corridor furtively and listened for the sound of any footsteps coming along. Satisfied no one was coming, he opened the door of the interview room and went inside. It did not take him long to spot what he was looking for and that was an electrical point. It was situated behind a set of heavy wooden cupboards, and a table that a bank of tape machines rested on. Taking out the plug he inserted it into the double-plug he took from his pocket and put that back into the wall socket and switched it on again. The wall socket was well hidden behind the table and cupboards just like the trailing wire from the tape machines, so that no one would know it was there, not unless they got on hands and knees like O'Flaherty and crawled behind the table.

O'Flaherty was pleased with his little ruse and he smiled to himself and straightened up from his bending position. Just as he did so, he heard footsteps hurrying along the corridor and, flapping momentarily, he wondered what he should do. Thinking quickly he sat down at the table in the middle of the room and got out his cigarettes and matches. He was shaking a little but managed to steady his hand as he lit a cigarette, when the policeman he knew popped his head round the door and entered.

'There you are.'

'Here I am,' O'Flaherty stated.

The policeman said in a sharp voice, 'What are you doing in here? Get out, you know you shouldn't be in here.'

Covering his nervousness O'Flaherty responded, 'The wee place was all alone and so I thought I might have me a fag. Seeing as how I have me a large problem with that there machine.'

'Well you can't nip in here for a fag. Get out and don't let me catch you in here again,' said the policeman, stubbing out the cigarette before grabbing hold of O'Flaherty by the collar and frog marching him out of the room and closing the door behind them. 'Now get on with your work,' the policeman said, hurrying off in the direction of the locker room and toilets.

'What did you come in here for, anyway?' O'Flaherty called after the quickly retreating policeman.

'I was bursting for a pee and wondered where you were,' the policeman shouted back, as he turned a corner and disappeared.

'Just my luck,' O'Flaherty said and kicked the vending machine, venting his anger on it. Standing there tinkering with the machine, O'Flaherty watched a prisoner and his escort walk by from the cells to the interview room. Shortly after, another man in an army khaki uniform went in and the RUC escort came out and went away again. Scanning the area, briefly, O'Flaherty made his way over to the door and bending down, he listened at the keyhole.

'Well Fat Billy,' Captain Dixon said. 'Are you ready to resume after your restful night's sleep?' There was a hint of sarcasm in his voice.

'Meself now, I wouldn't quite have put it that way,' Fat Billy replied. 'But yes, I am to be sure.'

Nodding to himself and satisfied that he had the right man, O'Flaherty moved away from the door and down the corridor sharpish. He walked through the swing doors and past reception, flashing a smile at the brunette sitting behind the sliding glass window.

Politely he said, 'I left somethin' out in the van an' I'm just going to get it.'

'You do that,' the brunette said from behind the glass, thinking to herself that the service repair man of the vending machines was a quaint, funny little fellow.

Losing no time in getting in his van, O'Flaherty opened the glove compartment beside the steering wheel and turned on a small tape recorder, to record the conversation in the interview room between Captain Dixon and Fat Billy. The innocuous looking double-plug that he had added to the plug from the tape machine bank was really a sophisticated eavesdropping device. It was fitted with a transmitter that sent the signal to the miniature tape recorder, which was switched on and recording in his van.

'Good then, let's resume. Coffee and cigarettes, is it?' Dixon was saying like a good host.

'That would be nice,' Fat Billy said, 'on this fine mornin'.'

'Damn!' Dixon announced, 'I just remembered I can't get you a coffee, as the bloody machine is down.'

'Never mind, Englishman. A drag of a decent fag will more than whet me appetite enough to be goin' on with.'

Captain Dixon took out a pack of good quality Park Lane cigarettes and offered Fat Billy one, as he reached across the table.

'You're a darlin' man to be sure, an' so generous,' Fat Billy remarked.

'Here, have the pack,' Dixon said, scooting them across to him. 'It may be my last act of generosity towards you. Unless I get some really useful information out of you, I'm afraid you're going down and it'll be bird in Long Kesh for you.'

Taking a deep drag after Dixon lit the cigarette with his own silver lighter, Fat Billy commented. 'As I told you last night Captain Dixon sir, I'll shop the lot if that's what it'll take to avoid prison an' bein' separated from my family.'

'Good, that's what we like to hear,' Captain Dixon said, relaxed and leaning back in his chair.

'How is the boy?' Fat Billy suddenly asked, tipping the ash off his cigarette into the tin tray provided.

'Your grandson?' said Dixon, as he took out his pen and began to write up his notes.

'That's right?'

'Didn't they tell you anything?'

'In this place with these devils thinkin' I killed several RUC men, begorrah you must be jokin' sir?'

'Don't worry, he's all right. I didn't let Pinky and Perky get their hands on him, if that's what you're thinking,' Dixon said, alluding to the two interrogators. 'In fact, I questioned the boy and he's probably having breakfast at home, about now.'

'Thank Christ for that,' Fat Billy said, 'I've been sittin' up half the night worryin' meself about him.'

'How about your injuries? All healed now are they?' Dixon asked out of polite interest, looking at the bandage on Fat Billy's head.

'The head wound needed ten stitches and me ribs are bruised, but the shoulder wound the doc said I was very lucky with.'

'How's that?'

'He said I was lucky on account of the bullets passing through the fleshy part of me body and not hittin' any important bones or muscles. I guess I have the luck of the Irish, after all.'

'I guess you do. Where was that and how long was your stay?'

'The Royal Victoria Hospital in Belfast for six glorious days, then they needed the bed.'

Captain Dixon kept it light, finding over the years that this had always been the best way to handle a talker like Fat Billy, so he kept the tone polite and sociable, knowing that if he came down too hard Fat Billy would clam up out of sheer cussedness and Dixon would be nowhere.

'Any good-looking nurses there?'

'Any?' Fat Billy asked in surprise. 'Just 'bout all of 'em were the picture of Irish beauty an' made this old heart flutter whenever they walked by.'

Smiling, Dixon said, 'It's always nice to have a change of scenery. And now to business, Fat Billy.' He laid his pen down. 'How exactly did you get these injuries and who inflicted them on you?'

'Well sir, the head wound and the bruised ribs came from that mad ol' bastard of an RUC constable. He came in to me place in a foul temper an' jus' started on me for no reason.'

Captain Dixon pointed out, 'I think he had a reason, the killing of the two RUC men caught unawares by the IRA assassin that played possum in the middle of the road.'

In a wheedling tone Fat Billy replied, 'Ah, to be sure, but that was not me fault, I told 'em what I knew, that's all. It wasn't my fault if they were lookin' in the wrong place, now was it?'

'How about the fact that to the IRA you are supposed to be giving us, the security forces, misleading information?' Pointing his expensive pen at him Dixon warned, 'You wouldn't be pulling a fast one on us now would you, Fat Billy, and playing both ends of the string? For if you are, God help you.'

'Me, now would I?' said Fat Billy, wide-eyed and innocently. 'Honestly, Captain Dixon, the thought never entered me head, so it did.'

'I just hope for your sake, that is so.'

'It is.'

'When did you know they were coming?'

'I received a call fifteen minutes before they arrived, 'bout the time me grandson went to the cathedral to make the contact.'

'What time was that and who was the contact?' Dixon picked up his pen and began to write some more.

'Somewhere around 12.30 p.m. and the contact was Mairead O'Connell.'

'Did you happen to hear the call sign of this Active Service Unit?'

'Yes I think it was Tricolour-7.'

'How many were in the ASU and describe what they were like.'

'There were four of 'em, all young and in their twenties. Liam O'Connell was in his early twenties but could pass for older. He was tall and dark and the leader of the ASU. While his sis' was older but equally as tall with brown hair an' good looks. She was Mairead O'Connell. And the other two were younger. All arrived in a black hearse,' Fat Billy said, stubbing out his second cigarette and lighting another with Dixon's lighter on the table.

'Padraic Duffy was thin and scruffy and Sean Maguire blonde and athletic in build.'

'What was the registration and what had they come for?'

'Don't know it. They came for guns and ammunition. It seems there were none in Crossmaglen, so help me.'

'What guns?'

'Romanian-made AKM Kalashnikov rifles.'

'Some of the good stuff then,' Dixon remarked. 'None of the rubbish. How many rounds of ammunition do you suppose there were?

'Several thousand.'

'Anything else?'

'An RPG-7 rocket launcher and grenades.'

'I dread to think what they were going to do with that,' Dixon said seriously. 'Were they responsible for the two dead the RUC constable accused you of?'

'They were,' Fat Billy said. 'Liam O'Connell boasted to me as much.'

'Did he tell you anything else?'

'He did, but what's it worth?'

'A two hundred packet if it's good. Or a five year minimum stretch for membership of the IRA.'

'There's goin' to be an attack on Loughgall RUC station some time shortly, several ASUs are involved in it.'

'You know this for a fact?'

'Liam O'Connell told me from his very own lips.'

Putting his pen down, Dixon said, 'Then I hope for your sake it is good information, because then the money is yours. Otherwise...?' He left the question in the air, and they wrapped it up. Dixon called for a guard and the escort came hurrying down the corridor to collect Fat Billy.

Soon after Fat Billy and Captain Dixon had vacated the room, O'Flaherty entered and quickly retrieved his double-plug and stuck it in his overalls pocket. Poor old flapping O'Flaherty had had the devil of a job trying to eke out the time he spent on repairing and servicing the Manhattan. So he wandered about, using his eyes and ears observed everything he could, just waiting for the end of the interrogation as the world and his mother walked by and moaned and groaned about the machine being out of order.

When he had finally been able to retrieve the transmitter, he packed away his screwdriver set and ampmeter and other equipment in his toolbox and made a hasty retreat from the RUC station.

Sitting in the van behind the steering wheel, he lost no time in opening the glove compartment and taking it out and rewinding the tape in the machine. Pressing the play button so he heard the words, 'As I told you last night, Captain Dixon sir, I'll shop the lot if that's what it'll take to avoid prison an' bein' separated from my family.'

Disgusted at the traitorous statement, O'Flaherty turned the machine off, just as there was a knock at the window. Turning to look, O'Flaherty saw that it was that nuisance of a policeman who had upbraided him about having a fag in the interview room.

Shit, not him again, he thought, trying to cover his nervousness, as he wound the window down to see what the policeman wanted.

Amused, the policeman said, 'You looked like a startled rabbit, just then.'

Trying not to let either his nerves or his anger show O'Flaherty said, 'It must be 'cos I was really concentrating on the music, you know.'

'I know,' the policeman said with enthusiasm. 'I love listening to music too, when I'm not on duty, that is. What's the tape you've got there?' he asked, referring to the one in the small machine sitting quite plainly on O'Flaherty's lap.

'Oh that, it's the Beatles, *Sgt. Pepper*.'

'Oh pity,' the policeman said, 'if it was that sexy Kate Bush I was going to ask if I could borrow it at all.'

'Well it's not I'm afraid and so...' O'Flaherty said a little aggrieved at the intrusion and nuisance value of the friendly policeman. 'But if I get me hands on a tape of hers then I'll surely let you have it.'

'Thanks very much, Michael,' the policeman said, and leaving O'Flaherty alone, he entered the RUC station for his tea break.

Not wanting any more close calls with anyone in uniform, O'Flaherty put the van in gear and the tape recorder away and drove out of the car park and through the gates and out of Markethill, before there were any more surprises and he had a heart attack.

A short way down the road O'Flaherty pulled the van over and on an old scrap of paper drew a rough diagram of the RUC station at Markethill and its personnel deployment. Though only straight lines and squares it was accurate, if a little misleading to the untrained eye with certain lines being labelled wires A, B, C and D. This was to confuse anyone finding the paper by mistake, while the numbers were the actual amount of persons to be found in respective locations. This and the tape he put in a brown envelope and licked the ends down.

Starting the engine up and driving on, it was not long before O'Flaherty came to the crossroads where the B3 he was travelling on intersected with the A28 road to Armagh. Getting out, he did not take long to walk over to the wooden signpost at the intersection and folding the brown envelope up he stashed it in a hollow at the foot of it. Then, having made his 'drop', he drove home to Richhill to have a nice cuppa to calm his nerves.

Everything that O'Flaherty did for the Republican cause was completely independent of anyone and any meeting. His instructions were transmitted over the phone, and as for who collected the 'drop' he did not know that, either. Had he stayed around he would have seen a motorcyclist stop and collect it.

Within half an hour the scrap of paper and the tape was within the hands of the OC of Armagh city. He was sat in his living room with Liam O'Connell and the rest of the ASU known as Tricolour-7. Spreading the piece of paper out on the glass coffee table, Liam O'Connell said, 'What kind of joke is this?'

'That's a simple diagram of the buildings and layout and personnel deployment of the RUC station at Markethill,' replied Father Behan.

'Is it now?' Duffy said. 'And who is it that got you that?'

'Never mind,' the OC said cagily. 'I told you before that God moves in mysterious ways, so he does.'

'What about the tape?' Mairead asked. 'What is on that?'

'Put it in that there Japanese stereo in the corner and let's find out,' the OC offered.

'It took a moment, for Mairead had to plug the stereo in first and then switch it on, its lights twinkling as it came to life. She put the tape in and hit the play button.

There was a hush, then Fat Billy's voice said, 'As I told you last night, Captain Dixon sir, I'll shop the lot if that's what it'll take to avoid prison an' bein separated from my family.'

'Good, that's what we like to hear,' Captain Dixon said.

'Oh no, it isn't,' Liam said, getting angry like the others in the room.

Part Two
The Soldiers

Chapter Five

The six counties of Ulster which form part of the United Kingdom of Great Britain and Northern Ireland are Antrim, Armagh, Down, Fermanagh, Londonderry and Tyrone. The province is 5,500 square miles in area, barely eighty-five miles from north to south and about 110 miles wide. Right in the middle is Lough Neagh, the largest lake in the British Isles. This huge expanse of water is remarkable when seen from an aircraft coming in to land at the international airport, but even more so at ground level, because the surrounding land is so flat in parts as to make the lough almost invisible.

The course of the meandering Blackwater River flows from before Caledon on to Benburb and between Moy and Charlemont, then past the Argory, a large, neo-classical house of about 1820 and the vast landscape of Peatlands Park and, finally, into Lough Neagh: a journey of over twenty miles.

The angler on the west bank looked up at the grey sky and clouds drifting in from the Atlantic and over Ireland. This they did all year round; he could feel the atmosphere change with the moisture discharge that had nowhere to go and so hung in the air, casting a soft misty light over the flat landscape. He zipped up his anorak and tied his hood up, for if he was not mistaken it was soon going to rain.

The grey sky squeezed the clouds out of the way and sure enough, minutes later, down came the rain in heavy spots and then gathered momentum. That was when the angler on the grass bank took shelter under his black and white golfing umbrella. He reached for his plastic flask and poured himself a cup of piping hot sweet coffee and looked out at the rain. It had increased in tempo and myriad droplets were dancing on the murky waters of Lough Neagh.

The angler was a large-set man, fishing the whole season with the right permit and very experienced. Even so, he had been there for over an hour, it was approaching 12.30 p.m., and he had not as yet had as much as a bite. It was not the preparation or the equipment, it was just that sometimes the fish would not cooperate. Simple as that really, for he had the right tackle of a lightweight fibreglass rod with plenty of nylon line and a good fixed spool reel. The line played out some twelve feet into the water with a barbed hook beneath a coloured plastic float, the float bobbing up and down on the choppy waters.

There was plenty of time for him to catch a fish, all afternoon in fact, and so he was not unduly worried. And now with the rain, well he could not be happier, knowing full well that fish were best caught during the rain or just after, as that was when they went looking for food.

Eating his cheese and pickle sandwich the angler sat on his comfortable fold-up chair and waited patiently for a sign that the fish were taking the bait of maggots. To be extra sure, when he'd thrown the line into the water he had thrown a handful of bait around it; the 'ground bait' that he used to attract the fish. Primarily he was hoping to catch trout, which was related to the salmon, both breeds living in the freshwater of Lough Neagh. He fished for the sport and as a hobby, not so much for the frying in the pan and eating later, though his family would never say no to that. Trout was nice and the better of the two, but he would have settled for herring if that was all that was catchable.

Sitting there dry with the rain drumming on the large umbrella, he ate his sandwiches and watched for the distinctive movement of the float indicating that a fish was knocking the bait with a view as to whether it was going to eat it or not. Just as the angler was about to pour himself another cup of coffee he glanced up and saw the float bob under. Acting quickly, he returned the lid to the flask before grabbing the rod out of its fixed holder. Taking a firm grip, he stood up in the rain. Jerking the line out of the water he lost no time reeling in the fish.

It was a beauty, a female trout swollen with eggs, grey with a pinkish tinge, over two feet long, and about ten pounds in weight. Defiantly it struggled and pulled and fought, but the angler reeled it in to about one foot from the top of his rod and deftly took hold of the fish. Beaming all over his face, despite being sopping wet, the angler removed the hook from the roof of the mouth of the trout and threw the flopping fish in the wicker basket beside him and fastened the lid down. That was great, he thought, and now on to the next.

Fixing the hook back on the line, the angler then put his hand in the wriggling mass in the plastic box and took out a maggot. He fixed the bait to the hook again on the end of the line and cast it out into the lake at the same spot, allowing the line to play out as the hook and bait flew over the dark surface of Lough Neagh.

Then he put the end of the rod back in the fixed holder and sat on his fold-up chair again. This time he had hardly had time to put his bottom on the seat of the chair before, amazingly, there was a definite movement. The angler thanked Lady Luck and shot to his feet, and eagerly grabbed the rod. With a strong jerking movement the rod gave he soon found that this fish was a lot heavier than the last. 'It must be bloody ginormous!' he thought, excitedly. If the last little tussle with the female trout could be explained as a skirmish, then this turned out to be a titanic battle of epic proportions. For a good five minutes he gave his all in trying to land the fabulous catch. He fought and struggled with it until all his strength was gone, his arms and shoulders were numb and his wrists felt like they would give way.

But with one last mighty effort he managed to jerk it out of the water. Despite his rod breaking in half, he whooped as he managed to land the damn great thing. A huge, great, pale monster of a thing that caused him to fall backwards and off his feet.

There was only one thing wrong as he recovered his feet and took a long look at the staring, glassy eyes and the barbed hook jammed in the roof and the bottom of the mouth. To his horror it was a man! A naked man, pale and dead and lifeless. He had caught a corpse instead of a fish.

Shocked and horrified and frightened to move, the terrified angler just sat there a moment, looking at the naked body he had unwittingly hauled out of Lough Neagh. In a panic he suddenly got to his feet and regardless of the pouring rain he scrambled up the wet grassy bank. He fumbled in his pocket for his car keys, and opening the door got behind the wheel of the green Cortina.

Shutting the door, he started the engine and turned the car round in the middle of the road and drove off in an easterly direction towards the Discovery Centre at Lough Neagh, on Oxford Island.

The Discovery Centre was a distance of less than ten miles away. In his panic, the angler in the Cortina got there in record time and pulled into the car park with a squeal of brakes. He jumped out of the car and ran towards the barn-like building of wood and glass, where he hastily mounted the steps and burst through the door and up to the counter along the far wall with a prominent cash register.

The till girl was a young woman, tall and thin with a mop of brunette curls. She was serving a middle-aged couple in duffel coats at that moment, visitors to the area on holiday who were spending their money and buying some glossy nature and wildlife books that they had chosen after first walking around the polished wooden floor and browsing and looking at the leaflets and models and souvenirs and books on display on the glass shelves for some time.

Eager for a sale, the till girl would not be put off by anyone barging in and so, when the angler collapsed on the counter and said in a breathless voice, 'I want to report—'

The till girl snapped his head off, saying, 'I don't care what you want, please get off the counter and in the queue and wait your turn like all the others.'

Looking around, the angler was nonplussed by the situation, and seeing no one even remotely near the counter exclaimed, 'What others?' The till girl ignored him and took the glossy books out of the hands of the middle-aged couple. Swiftly looking at the price of them she rang up the till and said, 'That'll be three pounds and seventy-five pence, thanking you.' She gave the middle-aged couple their change from a fiver and popped the books in a plastic bag with 'Lough Neagh Discovery Centre' on the front, then gave it to the husband. He took the bag and the couple headed for the door and their exit.

Turning to the angler the cashier now said, 'And how can I help you?'

'I want to report a dead body,' he replied in all seriousness.

Slightly suspicious, the till girl said, 'Now, come sir, it's a little late in the day for such practical jokes. Come back on the first of April when all the other pranksters try their luck.'

'But it's not a joke,' the angler said, 'I really have found a dead body.'

'Really?' she questioned, still not believing him. 'Where?'

'About eight miles down the road, where I fished it out of Lough Neagh.'

'And you're not joking?'

'I'm not joking.'

'Oh my God, what shall I do?' she asked, all flustered.

'I think you'd better phone the police and the emergency services,' he said.

He waited as she dialled the number and getting through said, 'Police? I want to report a dead body.'

At Markethill RUC Station, Fat Billy was ensconced in his small, cream-walled box cell with high windows and steel door. But he did not mind too much as he sat there on the concrete plinth with a tray on his lap, polishing off his dinner of faggots and mushy peas. He was enjoying it too, what with the lashings of thick Bisto gravy and the brick-like peppery faggots. These were locally made in a butcher's up the road and so they were bigger and more wholesome and tasty than any to be got out of a packet in the supermarket.

Soon after he finished his dinner the constable came for the tray, opening the cell and taking it from Fat Billy.

'Any afters?' Fat Billy asked cheekily.

'Think yourself lucky you got that,' said the constable as he went to lock the cell door and the custody sergeant hurried up to him.

'Don't lock the cell,' the custody sergeant said. 'Instead, take the prisoner upstairs to the computer room, where Captain Dixon is waiting for him.'

'Will do, Sarge,' the constable said and gave the tray to a woman PC passing by. 'Take this away will you?' he said to her.

Taking it from him she said, 'OK, but what did your last servant die of?'

The constable ignored this comment and escorted Fat Billy

upstairs. When they entered the computer room there were several women in uniform at the computer keyboards doing their job, entering and receiving information from the database.

'Ah, there you are,' Captain Dixon said, spotting Fat Billy enter. 'I have asked you in here so that you can help us with our enquiries and maybe identify those personalities of Tricolour-7, the IRA Active Service Unit.'

Swaggering in, Fat Billy said, 'I'll do that,' in a cocky tone. 'Anythin' to help Her Majesty's Army an' security forces an' you, Englishman.'

Displeased with this new-found cockiness from Fat Billy, Captain Dixon said assertively, 'I don't need to remind you that you have no choice in the matter, do I?' Pausing, 'And that if you don't comply, there's always prison for you to go to.'

Back to his wheedling tone, Fat Billy remarked, 'I've cooperated so help me, Mary an' Joseph, so what would I be goin' to prison for?'

'Just a little matter of GBH and a stabbing of an experienced RUC man and the killing of an RUC recruit, that's all,' Dixon reminded him.

'Oh that well, begorrah you know it wasn't me. Didn't I tell you so jus' this mornin', so help me God.'

'You did and I believe you, but there are lots of others that don't; and it might be out of my hands to help you if these people get their way. So don't run away with the illusion that it's all over, because it isn't.'

'I'm hearin' you,' Fat Billy said, sounding a little more compliant. 'You know I'll do anythin' you ask, don't you?'

'I do, but let's just get this straight and out of the way now, or else you can go back to your cell and rot for all I care,' Dixon said, sounding hard. 'Is that clear?'

'It's clear an' I'll behave meself, only don't be too harsh on me, these old bones you know, they—'

'You can cut out the sorry act as well, or the same thing will apply.'

Turning his sad eyes on Dixon, Fat Billy said, 'You're a hard man, so you are, Englishman.'

'That's a clever remark, right there,' Dixon said. 'Hold that thought a moment and tell me this: who is the hardman out of the ASU known as Tricolour-7. Is it Padraic Duffy, Sean Maguire, Liam O'Connell or Mairead O'Connell?'

'Which one is the hardman you're askin' me?' said Fat Billy, scratching his head in thought.

'That's right,' Captain Dixon said, repeating himself as if to a backward child. 'Which one is the hardman out of them all?'

'Why, all of 'em,' Fat Billy said, amazed that Captain Dixon did not see the logic of it, hardman being the IRA term for cold-blooded killers.'

'All of them?'

'That's right, Mr Army Intelligence, all of 'em, an' that's why so far they have not been taken or killed. Did it not occur to yous?'

'No it did not, I must admit.' Slightly amazed, Dixon asked, 'Even the woman, Mairead O'Connell?'

'Especially her,' Fat Billy said. 'She's pretty as a picture an' tall as the loveliest tree, but she'd still shoot you dead as soon as look at you, so she would.'

'She sounds lethal,' Captain Dixon said, 'but she can't be all that bad?'

'Take it from me, she is,' Fat Billy said.

'Where did this aggression and violence come from?'

'When she was a child, her father was accidentally killed by a soldier an' she never ever forgot it. That's where the violence came from. You and your kind put it there, Englishman, with your occupation of this Emerald Isle an' the restrictions you imposed on the ordinary folk that live here in Ulster and Northern Ireland. Imprisonin' us for utter generations with your rules an' your restrictions an' your legislation from the Great British Parliament an' the tidy bureaucrats of Whitehall.'

'That'll be enough of that talk,' Captain Dixon said. 'Any more and you can go back to your cell.'

'That's the trouble, Englishman, you get a hold of us an' you ask us to be truthful an' then when we are, you don't like it an' send us away again. It's not only us Republicans that need to be able to face the truth, but you too.'

This statement hit a raw nerve in Captain Dixon. Looking at

the guard he said, 'Get this man back to his cell and out of my sight and do it now.'

Just as he said this the uniformed RUC chief inspector, a church-going Protestant of forty-five, with sharp features and appearance and an arrogant manner, entered the room and immediately collared Captain Dixon.

'What's he doing in here?' the inspector demanded, pointing at Fat Billy.

'I said he could come in,' Dixon explained.

'William Shanaghan is a known IRA volunteer and has been for decades. He could pass on any amount of information after being here for any length of time.'

'I doubt it,' Dixon countered. 'You see this man Fat Billy has been on the books of Army Intelligence as a known informer ever since the late '60s.'

Angry at this knowledge having been withheld from a senior RUC officer, the chief inspector demanded, 'Why was I not told of this?'

Not cowed in the slightest by this outburst, Captain Dixon replied coolly, 'I'm telling you now.'

'This is outrageous,' the chief inspector said, fingering the pip on his uniform. 'Remove this man immediately,' he ordered, pointing to the guard and referring to Fat Billy.

'I was just about to have him removed for insolence and insubordination in any case,' Captain Dixon said.

'See you do,' the chief inspector snapped, 'and your superiors will be hearing from me,' he added, as he opened the door and left.

Less than two minutes later, the chief inspector rushed back into the computer room and looking at Captain Dixon said, 'The communications room has just received a call from a member of the public; they've found a dead body in Lough Neagh.'

'Do you think it could be one of the three from the missing patrol?' Dixon asked him.

'It very well could be,' the chief inspector said, 'I'll notify my driver and we can go in my car.'

Looking at him, Captain Dixon said, 'I've got a much better idea. Follow me,' as he pushed past the chief inspector.

'Where are we going?'

'My room.'

'What for?'

'To call up a Navy Wessex helicopter, that'll be quicker than any car.'

Captain Dixon was right and within minutes of his call a Wessex helicopter in camouflage colours was touching down on the grass at the back of the RUC station. The door quickly slid back and the navigator helped Captain Dixon and the chief inspector to climb aboard. It took to the sky, its great rotor blades scything the air as the noisy machine flew over the countryside and headed for the Discovery Centre and Oxford Island on Lough Neagh. It didn't take long, as the distance was short as the crow flies.

When they landed they found that although there was the odd grey Hotspur of the RUC and a few constables; they were completely outnumbered by soldiers and green army vehicles as the 'Red Caps' took control and cordoned the immediate area off. Captain Dixon and the chief inspector made their way across the ground and over the road and down the bank to the edge of the lough. Ten minutes later and the two men had seen the dead body and looked over the spot where it had been pulled from Lough Neagh. The chief inspector got angrier and angrier as it became clear that it was the army issuing orders and not the police. Turning away from the lapping water and the shrouded body, the chief inspector announced, 'This is totally outrageous. What do they think they are doing?'

'Doing their job and taking control of the situation, I expect,' Captain Dixon replied.

'But how can they? This is definitely police business.'

'I don't think they would agree,' Captain Dixon corrected him, 'for it is, most definitely, army business.'

'And how do you make that out?'

'On account of the fact that the man the angler pulled out of Lough Neagh was an army man and we got here first.'

'Yes, how did you do that?'

'Easy, the Royal Military Police attune their radio equipment to the RUC's frequency and listen to their calls, and then race to the scene before your flatfoots can even think of moving,' Captain Dixon, announced proudly.

'That's disgusting and humiliating,' the chief inspector replied.

'Maybe, but it's also efficient,' Captain Dixon pointed out.

'You know what RMP should stand for,' the chief inspector asked, aggrieved at the cheating ways of the army in the silly competition between them and the RUC.

'No, what?' Captain Dixon said, smiling.

'It should stand for Royal Meddling Police.'

'And they would respond equally, that the RUC should be known as the Royal Useless Constabulary.'

'That's not fair,' the chief inspector said, 'our boys do a really good job in difficult circumstances.'

'Then don't pick on the RMPs or you might bite off more than you can chew,' Dixon said, as he walked off and the chief inspector trailed after him.

Looking at an RUC constable setting up a barrier across the road, the chief inspector asked him, 'Has the Royal Victoria been notified? Is there an ambulance on the way, and have frogmen been alerted to the situation and a pathologist called?'

'I don't know, sir,' the young constable said, as he temporarily stopped doing the barrier.

'Begging your pardon sir,' a sergeant in the 'Red Caps' said, 'but I have taken the liberty to do all that, and if you and the captain would like to you're quite welcome to take this Land Rover and go down the road and talk to the angler being held at the Discovery Centre for questioning.'

'Thank you, sergeant,' Captain Dixon said, 'that will be most helpful.' He and the chief inspector climbed aboard and the captain started up the engine, released the handbrake and moved off down the road.

'I still say this should be police business,' the chief inspector said, enforcing the point as Captain Dixon remained silent on the short drive.

It was 9 a.m. on the morning of 25 November, and the OC of the Armagh Brigade, Father Behan, was in the front room of his bungalow with those members of the Tricolour-7 ASU who were still under his roof. But he did not have the pleasure of their company until they had washed and changed and met in the kitchen, where they had all enjoyed a hearty breakfast of fried eggs, bacon, fried bread, baked beans and tea, all served up by the priest's ever-faithful housekeeper. After breakfast, they repaired to the front room, where they sat in the chairs and settee. The OC was reminding them of their briefing the night before, and how they had heard the traitorous Fat Billy condemn himself out of his own mouth. 'Now, are you all clear about tonight and have you got it in your heads?'

'I have,' Maguire said, sounding confident.

'Me too,' Duffy replied.

'And you?' asked the OC of Liam.

'Sure have.'

'And you?' to Mairead.

'I have and it will be a sight to see and a tale to tell all volunteers in years to come.'

'That it will,' the OC agreed. 'But how did Fat Billy ever find out about the assault on Loughgall though, that bothers me.'

'That's easy,' Liam piped up. 'I told him.'

'What in heaven for?' the OC asked in surprise.

'I told him as at the time. Despite my sister's reservations, I had no real evidence or suspicion to go on that I shouldn't.'

'True enough, I suppose,' the OC said, 'but maybe next time you'll be a little bit more circumspect before you open your mouth to strangers.'

'At the time I didn't think he was a stranger,' Liam said in reply to the gentle rebuke. 'I thought he was one of us.'

'Needless to say,' Mairead interjected, 'that the Loughgall operation will be called off now.'

'Yes, I can safely say that. Postponed until a later date, at least.'

'That's a pity,' Maguire said, swinging his legs.

'Such a shame,' Duffy said, as he scratched his arm.

'But our little fling tonight… Well, that should more than make up for it,' Liam suggested.

'Just about,' the OC said, with a smile. 'Just about and a wee bit more.'

'Only a wee bit more,' Mairead agreed, smiling too.

'You could say that,' Maguire agreed.

'Wow, is it going to be poppin' tonight or what?' Duffy said cheerfully.

The time was 8 p.m. and it was windy, with a pitch black sky, and desolate along that stretch of the B135. More than that, it was raining, as the black hearse stopped and Tricolour-7 all piled out. Moaning and groaning with picks and shovels in their hands, Liam, Duffy and Maguire set to work digging up the road. The pick was hard work for Liam. As he swung it above his head, time and again, he felt the pull on his shoulder and upper arm muscles.

'That's it, me boyos,' Mairead urged, 'and put your backs into it,' as she stood in the middle of the road, the moon making a brief appearance from out of the dark clouds while she kept watch.

Liam joined in with Mairead, 'Bet you never thought you'd have to work so hard for the Cause, did you?' he bantered, torch in hand.

'This is hard work for sure,' Duffy said, the sweat pouring off of him as he hefted the shovel. He stopped and handed Mairead his parka, to stop him sweating so profusely.

'Ah, your trouble is you're not fit,' Maguire said, as he wiped his sweating brow on his rolled up shirt sleeve and dug in some more.

Standing there torch in hand, lighting the ground for the workers and looking out for anyone coming, Mairead, like every woman, had a sadistic streak in her. She just loved seeing the men of the ASU actually working. Not willing to miss this opportunity for the world she observed critically, 'You'll have to dig a lot deeper and a lot faster and put your backs into it a lot more than that if you want to get it done by midnight!' as she wound them up.

'Ah, shut up,' Duffy retorted, puffing and leaning heavily on the shovel in his hands.

'Yeah, give your tongue a rest,' Maguire added as he got on with the hard physical work too.

Even Liam thought she was coming it too strong after a while, and remarked irritably, 'If you think you can do so much better, there's the pick, go ahead and try!'

Refusing the handle of the tool and pushing it away, Mairead replied cheekily, 'No, it's all right, dear brother of mine. It's so seldom I see you men work, that I'll just stand here an' enjoy the pleasure of the rare sight, indeed.'

Later on, the ASU of Tricolour-7 moved forty yards down the road and on the bend began digging another hole on the other side of the road. Working steadfastly, planting the objects in the holes and then covering them again so that they did not look like they had been disturbed, it took around an hour. Finally they were finished and, pleased at their handiwork, they drove off in the hearse, tools aboard, to find a hide to rest up in.

They drove to a gully reached by a dirt track that ran off the road behind some rocks. The gully was no more than ten feet wide, but was the perfect hiding spot as they were concealed from anyone looking from the road. High sided banks of scrubby grass gently sloped either side of the vehicle. Atop the banks were low wooden posts and wire fencing with bushes and bare scrawny trees interspersed here and there. It was the perfect spot, as they drank from their flasks and ate the sandwiches the housekeeper had prepared some hours before.

It was cold and it was dark on this night as the grey Hotspur Land Rover travelled from Newtownhamilton to the army base at Crossmaglen on the B135 road. Only its headlights lit up the snaking tarmac road, as they drove through the silent countryside.

It was 10.05 p.m. and in the vehicle were RUC Constable David Smith, forty, RUC Reserve Constable Lawrence McBride, twenty-four and Major John Andrews, forty-six, of the British Army. David Smith was clean-cut and round-faced and had two teenage daughters. Young Lawrence McBride was spotty and thin with a long nose, and had just got engaged to a fanciable young woman that he had been 'walking out' with for over three months – ever since she had turned his way and batted her beautiful 'blues' at him and served him with a pint of Guinness Extra behind the bar of the Three Hounds public house in Newtownhamilton.

Major John Andrews on the other hand, was a happily married man of some twenty years' standing, with a son in the Royal

Engineers and a fine daughter who was a trainee nurse back in Worcester, where he hailed from. The major had a small moustache above his upper lip, and greying sideburns and a stiff military bearing. Even so, the two RUC constables found he was quite a nice chap when they got to know him. All three had stopped off for a drink before the end of their shift at the Three Hounds allowing McBride to have a little chat with his fiancée in between serving customers. Now all three were on their way to Crossmaglen and the remote army base there, to report in.

Behind the wheel of the Land Rover, Smith concentrated on the twisting and, turning road and striking up a conversation, said to the major, 'That's better. Nothing like a couple of pints to set you up for the evening ahead.'

'I like a pint too,' McBride said in the back, 'but that Guinness Extra, well it packs a bit of a wallop.'

'Sure does, but it's lovely all the same,' Smith commented.

'I don't take much to Guinness myself,' the major said. 'A little too heavy for my taste. Give me a good old shot of Scotch whisky any time.'

'You mean Irish whisky?' McBride corrected him. 'Don't you, Major?'

'No, I mean Scotch whisky like I said, more smooth and fiery than the variety made on these isle.'

'Are you sure?' McBride said, looking just a little puzzled.

'Scotch whisky will make a man of you and put hairs on your chest,' the major said, digging McBride in the ribs playfully.

Picking up on the conversation, Smith said cheerfully, 'Yeah, a Scotch whisky or any whisky, eh Major? Especially when someone else is payin'.'

'I told you, I left my wallet back at the base,' the major said grinning foolishly with the drink working its magic inside him.

'And how many times have we heard that,' Smith piped up.

'I know,' the major replied, 'but this time it was true.'

'Don't give me that,' Smith said. 'Just admit it, you like a free drink or two.'

'Oh all right,' the major said. 'Where's the harm, that's what I say.' The four whiskies were giving him a glow and a happy feeling inside.

'That's right, where's the harm, eh?' McBride said, slapping the major on the back.

'Typical officer material if you ask me,' Smith said, half-accusingly, 'Always on the cadge.' He turned the wheel and entered a bend in the road.

It was at this point that the Land Rover arrived at the spot halfway between Crossmaglen and Newtownhamilton on the B135 road. That was when the Land Rover drove over a hard object in the road, and the landmine concealed beneath exploded upwards and outwards as Maguire, hidden in the bushes alongside the road, tripped the electrical connection on the handset. The detonation ran the length of the command wire, ripping the Land Rover apart and blowing out the doors, roof and floor.

A loud bang heralded death and destruction to those in the vehicle, the fiery explosion casting limbs and human flesh and pieces of the Land Rover for a hundred feet or more. A few seconds later the wreckage lay strewn over the road and surrounding countryside.

Looking on from the concealment of the gully, Liam and Mairead cheered and stamped their feet, greeting the chaos with the pleasure of a job well done.

A minute later they were rewarded by the sight of another vehicle about to receive their second present. It was a black Morris Minor 1000 that came around the bend: the same thing happened as the wheels of the car touched the landmine and Duffy exploded it. The driver of the small car was a midwife on her way to a cottage in the outlying countryside and a mother who had been in labour over twelve hours.

This time the devastation was even worse than before, as the force of the explosion blew the tiny car and its occupant into mere fragments. After the deadly explosion there was nothing left of either the car or the midwife, Kathleen Harrison, who was fifty and a grandmother with two grown-up sons of her own. She was a woman well known, well respected and well loved by all those who came across her in the small, sheltered community of Keady. As one tearful mourner later put it, 'She would be sorely missed for her goodness and charity and cheerfulness of spirit.'

When the members of Tricolour-7 looked at the road, what

they saw made their blood run cold. Far from the security forces they thought they would hit as they came from the opposite direction to the aid of those in the Land Rover, they had mistakenly taken the life of a defenceless and ordinary civilian instead. One of the thousands that had been shot and blown up and killed in the Long War over the years by both sides; caught in the crossfire and paying the price for being in the wrong place at the wrong time. And for Duffy not being able to see too well, in the driving rain that had started up again.

In the late seventies the British Army was virtually restricted to foot-soldiering operations in South Armagh. If they were not in the town patrolling, then they were in the 'cuds' – countryside, doing the same thing. Just them and the mud and the rain, their rifles and their bergens, to keep them company as they trudged on cuds patrol for as long as the task took, wearing wellington boots instead of regulation boots in the mud. A regular routine was being picked up by Puma helicopter and taken out for four days living in the field. There were no military vehicles to back up these patrols, as too many had been taken out by culvert like the Land Rover had.

It took at least five minutes before anyone showed up on the road and discovered the two scenes of utter devastation. When they did, it was a four-man 'brick' patrol of the Royal Anglian Regiment, loosely spread out in formation, who had been engaged in searching along the sloping fields and stony ridges above the road. They had heard the first loud bang and saw the Land Rover explode into flames below them, which shocked them. They had never heard the quick, sharp, piercing bang of high explosives before at their tender age. Strong was only eighteen and he knew that he would never ever forget the sound. It would be indelibly etched on his memory for all time. For a moment, they all doubted their eyes and ears, then it sank in, shortly after. East Acton said, 'Bleedin' Jesus, did you see that?'

'Not a pretty sight,' Strong said, as he like the others tried to avert his eyes.

'Bloody ghastly,' Man United remarked, as he looked down at his feet and carried on along the ridge, hurrying now, just like the others.

'Makes me sick at the thought of it,' Spud said, he being the fourth member of the 'brick'. He was called Spud as he loved to eat potatoes: boiled, chipped, fried or mashed, and the name stuck.

Then, to their utter disbelief, came the second explosion and through a gap in the hedgerow they saw the horrific sight of the Morris Minor turn into a fireball, blown apart before their very eyes, with each and every piece scattered to the four winds. 'We'd better get down there, and fast,' East Acton commented.

'Yeah I think you're right,' Man United said in agreement.

'Well I don't, I think we should hold our horses a moment,' Strong said, trying not to panic into anything rash. He took a deep breath and tried to keep cool and calm and collected, despite his emotions screaming out at the cruel, sheer waste of human life.

'There's never a bleedin' helicopter around when you want one,' East Acton blurted out. 'That's the bleedin' trouble with bein' out here in the bleedin' cuds.'

'You're right,' Man United said again, but hedging his bets remarked, 'I daresay the ruperts (officers) know what they're doing.'

'Forget all that,' Strong said, and looking at Spud with the radio he instructed: 'Get on the net fast and call up a helicopter. Tell the operations commander what has happened and give our grid reference, and wait for instructions, got it?'

'Got it,' said Spud, the 'nig' or new boy, as he unpacked the radio and was soon pulling out the aerial and in communication with base. The only trouble was, all that base was interested in was, 'Are there any casualties?'

'Yes there are casualties,' Spud said, correctly, into the handset.

'Are you sure?' came back the answer.

'Yes we're sure,' Strong said, grabbing the handset from Spud.

'How do you know?' the voice at base questioned politely.

'Because they're splattered all over the road by now,' Strong remarked angrily. 'That's how!'

Chapter Six

When Strong, Man United and East Acton got down to the road they found that the two explosions were worse than they feared. Blood, bone, metal fragments and personal effects were strewn over a wide area. All that was left of the smoking Land Rover was its holed chassis and shredded tyres, while the Morris Minor was not even that, but then it was not armoured like the army vehicle.

Taking command again, Strong said, 'I think we ought to take up position in the road and stop and search all vehicles and quiz the drivers if they saw anything suspicious along here in the last twenty-four hours. Or know anything that can help the authorities to identify who did this, what they look like and where they came from.'

Happy for Strong to take the responsibility, Man United, Spud and East Acton fell in with what he wanted, knowing if it all went pear shaped, then it would be Strong hauled over the coals by the colonel and not them.

The three of them had not long taken up their positions in the middle of the road, with Strong and Spud facing south towards Crossmaglen and Man United and East Acton facing the north and Newtownhamilton, when to their surprise a black hearse approached. Their training to the fore, the others covered Strong as he approached the driver's side of the Austin Princess as it slowed to a halt. SLRs in their arms, they stood tensed and ready, with their fingers on the triggers.

Recognising Liam behind the wheel, Strong asked, 'Where is your undertaker friend today?'

'Him?' Liam said. 'Alas, the poor man has a terrible dose of the flu, and so I had to come out instead.'

Quite relaxed, Strong commented, 'I must say you're getting pretty regular on the runs around here.'

'Ah well, you know what they say,' Liam commented, quick as a flash and misquoting: 'Time an' death stop for no man.'

Strong did not have a reply, and asked instead, 'What is in the back?'

'The usual – dead bodies and coffins and formaldehyde.'

'I see,' Strong commented, 'that does sound boring. Nevertheless I think you'd better open it up so as I can have a look, don't you?' as he leant his weapon against the side.

'Help yourself,' Liam said, 'I don't expect they're going to bite.'

Getting out the car and walking round the back, Liam obeyed as Strong said, 'Give me a hand will you?' as he lifted the tailgate. Selecting the coffin to the left of the other two, Strong said, 'Let's get it off and lean it up against the side of the vehicle and have a look, shall we?'

They did that, but just as Strong reached for the lid, it flew open and out jumped Mairead O'Connell, like something out of a grotesque jack-in-the box. Listening to what Strong had said, she had kicked off the lid and jumped out the same time, sending Strong stumbling backwards. Before he could recover Mairead had the Walter PPK in her hand and pointed it at the head of Strong, who struggled to his feet and just stared at her.

'Who are you?' Strong said, and then, before he could stop himself: 'You're beautiful, really beautiful.'

Liam, with his Tokarev in hand, then leaned across the roof of the hearse and gestured to Man United and East Acton, 'Put down your weapons and throw them aside and sit there with your hands on head, if you know what is good for you.'

The two other members of Tricolour-7 had now popped out of their coffins. Mairead looked at Duffy and Maguire and said, 'Shall I lie to him?'

'It's up to you,' Maguire said, hefting a Kalashnikov.

'I wouldn't say nothin',' Duffy said, 'if I was you.'

'Ah, damn it all t'hell!' she said. 'That thick big-mouth Fat Billy will probably have tol' everyone, anyway.' Standing erect and tall with her chest thrust out she declared to Strong: 'I am the famous Mairead O'Connell.'

'What did you tell him that for?' Duffy asked anxiously.

'Well for one thing,' Mairead said, 'he looks so damn cute and the other, he's the first man that ever tol' me I was beautiful.'

101

'That's why you told him?' Maguire said, shaking his head. It never ceased to amaze him, the recklessness of her behaviour and her female vanity.

'You are too,' Strong babbled again, like a silly, lovestruck teen, instead of a streetwise and hardened soldier.

True, she was everything he said she was: an absolute vision of loveliness and she stood there, tall and slim and towering over him with her black coat open showing off her fabulous figure with her shapely thighs, tight red jumper, leather mini skirt and long legs in black tights; she was a dream and a nightmare all in one, with her red mane of hair swirling in the breeze.

For whether he understood it or not, or whether he liked it or not, Martin Strong was in love with the IRA. To Strong she was the loveliest and the sexiest thing he had ever seen; but he did not realise that after this fleeting encounter with her she would stay in his mind and heart, and linger in his memory like an unsolved puzzle. There was nothing he could do for he was in love with her, and as amazing as it sounds her face would haunt him every waking moment until they met again.

'Beautiful?' Man United questioned. 'She's an IRA terrorist for God's sake! What's got into you, Martin?'

'God knows,' Strong said, 'as I don't.'

'She wants bloody shootin' that's what she wants,' East Acton offered. 'And you think she's beautiful. You must be sick,' he said in disgust to his friend.

Which he was of course, Strong was lovesick and deaf, dumb and blind as a lot of people are who fall helplessly in love with someone completely opposite to them.

'Shoot me,' Mairead reminded them, 'and your friend I promise you will bite the bullet before me,' as she pushed him before her, gun to his head.

'You wouldn't shoot me, would you?' Strong asked in a hurt voice.

'No I wouldn't shoot you, just clobber you instead,' she replied, as she hit Strong on the back of the head and, grabbing his shoulders, laid him on the grass verge.

'What did you do that for?' Duffy asked, as irritated by her behaviour as Maguire.

'Nothing he was just gettin' on me wick, that's all,' Mairead said.

'You sure?' Maguire questioned, equally suspicious of her motives as he saw how affected she had been by Strong's kindness and words of love.

'Sure, I'm sure. Now take out their boot laces and tie them all up.' This they did, with the addition of a little masking tape over the soldiers' mouths to keep them from calling out. Then they were dumped in the bushes alongside the road, left behind as the hearse drove off with the full complement of ASU Tricolour-7 on its way to Markethill – with the addition of four SLRs now in their arsenal of weapons.

The top floor of Markethill RUC Station held the offices of both the RUC uniformed branch and the detectives, as well as the operations room, computer room and communications. The ground floor comprised the reception, assembly hall, cells, debriefing room, locker room, toilets, washroom, armoury and canteen. This was the set-up at Markethill, and this information had been learnt and burnt into the memories of the members of Tricolour-7, thanks to the intelligence supplied by Michael O'Flaherty and his simple but detailed wiring diagram of position and personnel.

Ever since that mission, O'Flaherty had been listening out and gossiping with RUC men discreetly, finding out when was the best time to hit the station. That turned out to be anywhere between the main shifts; preferably in the evening after ten thirty when the evening shift had dispersed. At that time of day there would only be a skeleton crew manning the station, before the morning shift arrived for work at six thirty and the place filled up again.

All that day the Tricolour-7 members had talked over their plan in the confines of the OC's bungalow. They went over the proposed order of attack, and the detail of O'Flaherty's diagram with a fine-tooth comb discussing all the possibilities until they were sick to death of talking and bursting to get into action.

They could see the bright lights of the RUC station as the car pulled into a bushy clearing off the side road. Liam and Mairead got out. Standing lookout, Mairead kept watch as Liam climbed on the roof of the hearse. He reached across to a telephone cable stretching between the tall poles that carried it, and fitted a box over it. Then, when fitted, he flicked a switch on the side of the box that neutralised the live current in the cable, enabling Liam to reach into his pocket, take out a pair of wire-cutters and cut the cable without fear of an electric shock. Climbing down again, Liam remarked, 'That should put paid to that.'

Mairead added as they got back in the vehicle, 'And won't they have a shock.'

It was a Friday night, and there were an unlucky thirteen on the premises at the RUC station at Markethill. Some of them were stragglers looking forward to the start of the weekend, who had not yet vacated the place, while others were on night duty.

Upstairs, in the offices, a lone detective sat at his desk with his lamp on, trying desperately to catch up on his pile of paperwork. The computer room was shut and empty, while next door in the communications room sat a female dispatcher, her microphone before her. Downstairs, there was the brunette officer behind the glass partition in reception downstairs. Also on that level was the custody sergeant behind his desk in the corridor, and two prisoners in the cells around the corner from him. They were a smelly old drunk and a young teenage tearaway, who had been caught in the act of breaking and entering and had not long since been charged.

There was also an RUC man on the toilet, caught short before he went home, with his trousers round his ankles. Another was stripped to the waist in the washroom, having a quick wash and shave with a safety razor in his hand. He stood before the mirror on the wall, sprucing himself up before he left for his girlfriend's house. There was another RUC constable in the locker room changing out of his uniform and into his plain clothes. Sitting in the canteen, having a late meal of hot steak and kidney pies and chips they had cooked themselves, were two new recruits eating something hot before trudging back to their lodgings. Finally, outside, a uniformed officer manned the crash barrier and his colleague the lookout position as watched through the viewing slit in the wooden structure alongside the front gate.

Upstairs, the lone detective pored over the paperwork and scribbled notes, wishing he had done the sensible thing and cleared off home with the rest at shift's end when he had the chance. Looking at his watch, he saw it was 10.55 p.m. and yawning, he rose from his chair and stretched his body and arms. Having been sat there for hours, he decided to get himself a coffee and a breath of fresh air.

Passing the communications room on the way to the stairs, he popped his head round the door and said to the female dispatcher, 'Fancy a coffee?'

'Yeah, I'd love one,' she replied. 'Do you want the money?'

'No, that's OK,' the detective said, 'we'll settle up when I get back.'

'Fine with me,' she told him. 'White with plenty of sugar.'

'And I thought you were sweet enough,' he answered, flirting with her.

'I bet you say that to all the girls,' the dispatcher said.

'No,' the detective said, shaking his head and smiling. 'Only pretty female dispatchers with great legs on the night shift.'

'Careful,' she said, smiling at him and turning around in the swivel seat and showing off her legs. 'I might just forget you're married and have my head turned by all these compliments.'

'No chance,' he said, smiling, and walked towards the stairs.

Moments later, she called out anxiously, 'Tom, Tom, quick!'

Rushing back in the room he said concerned, 'What is it, Mary?'

'I don't know,' she said, the phone in her hand. 'But it's gone dead. I was going to call my mother before she went to bed and now, I can't.'

'Give it here.' The detective replaced the phone, then picked it up and listened to nothing. 'You're right,' he said surprised. 'It's dead.'

Just then there were two loud bangs downstairs. The dispatcher ran into the next room. 'Now the lights to the computer display have gone out! I've switched it on and off and hit all the right keys, and still it won't respond.' As she finished her sentence, all the lights went out.

Outside the RUC station, the black hearse pulled up at the barrier and the uniformed constable walked up to the vehicle. Before the constable could say anything Liam wound down the window and said, 'We're lost officer, can you help us?'

'Not really,' the constable joked. 'You see we deal in live bodies, not stiffs.'

'But you're a stiff,' Liam remarked, 'so you are.'

'How do you make that out?'

'Easy,' Liam explained, with the door open and the Tokarev pistol in his hand. 'I shoot you and you become one,' as he pulled the trigger and fired into the face of the constable. He was dead before he hit the ground. Shocked at the sight of what he witnessed from the lookout position, his colleague rushed out, gun in hand, and started firing wildly. The tailgate of the hearse went up; Duffy stuck his head and trusty Thompson machine gun out and cut down the other uniformed constable in a hail of bullets. Then the four members of Tricolour-7 taped the torches to their army SLRs and donned their black balaclavas.

Straight away, Duffy then pulled the pins on three grenades, one after the other. He tossed the first two through the long windows of the downstairs floor, the explosions blowing out the glass and brickwork of the debriefing room, as well as that of the canteen to the side of the building. The second grenade also had the effect of disabling the junction box on the wall and all the electrics, plunging the station house into total darkness as a result.

Cheered by the successful start, Tricolour-7 carried on with the attack plan as Liam reversed the hearse and Duffy rolled a grenade towards the steel gates, the explosion blowing a gaping hole in them. He rejoined the others in the car and Liam put his foot to the floor; the Austin leaped forward and rammed the gates through the swirling smoke and dust and broke through into the compound that was the RUC station at Markethill.

The Austin screeched into the car park at the back of the station and with a squeal of tyres came to a halt. Tricolour-7 jumped out and raked the building with automatic fire as, led by Mairead, they strode towards the building. Not believing his eyes, the detective upstairs moved away from the windows and rushed down the stairs to look out the narrow front windows. He stared out at the magnificent but frightening sight of the young, beautiful terrorist walking towards them weapon pointed and torch shining. The detective was joined by the custody sergeant and loosing off a few shots, they ducked the automatic fire and simply stared in awe.

'Christ, she's beautiful!' the detective announced as Mairead suddenly stopped and opened her coat and took out an RPG-7 rocket launcher and loaded it.

'Jesus, she's lethal too!' the detective exclaimed, 'Get down and duck for God's sake.' He pushed the custody sergeant to the ground as Mairead took aim and fired in their direction. A whoosh, and then there was a loud bang and part of the brick wall collapsed on them, crushing them under the rubble as Tricolour-7 came on at the run.

Maguire was using his commandeered SLR to spray all the upstairs windows and Duffy the downstairs with his SLR, too. Then they entered by the front door and before the brunette could scuttle away Mairead was on her. Having abandoned the rocket launcher for the SLR strapped to her shoulder and now in her arms, she shot up all the reception in a short, sharp burst, leaving the desk holed, the glass shattered and the brunette slumped over the floor.

Duffy then hit the locker room and riddled the lockers with automatic fire as the man changing hastily grabbed his clothes and, pulling the door shut, jumped inside out of harm's way. Maguire hit the toilets next, and the washroom. He shot the defenceless man on the toilet, leaving him in a pool of blood, while the RUC man shaving heard the cacophony and gunshots and forced open a window. He jumped out and fled for his life, running across the car park and towards some houses close by, his safety razor still in his hand.

Mairead ran upstairs looking for her next victim and easy target, and had a high old time kicking open the doors and shooting up the various offices, destroying the expensive equipment in the computer room used for communications. With fierce bursts of automatic fire Mairead sprayed a deadly tattoo of bullets around the room, leaving the computers sparking and wrecked as the high-velocity firepower tore into all and sundry.

But she did not find Mary, the female dispatcher. She had heard Mairead coming a mile off and promptly slid back the door of a metallic cupboard and hid inside. Making herself small and very quiet, she trembled and jumped at the sound of the viciousness and wanton destruction Mairead was deploying all around her. Then she heard Mairead walk out, and breathed a sigh of relief.

Downstairs, Maguire and Duffy both headed for the canteen, with Duffy being the first to enter the area and poke his head around the door. The two recruits that had been eating had taken cover, realising the station was under attack after the grenade was tossed through the window. They were sheltering behind the high-sided but damaged serving counter that had taken the full brunt of the grenade as it blew out the ceiling and walls. Despite the destruction they had stayed put and waited to see what would happen. Moments later, as Duffy came unsuspectingly into the room and shone his light round the corner, one of them leaned out and shot him in the leg and stomach. His colleague did the same and finished him off with shots to the chest and upper body. Dropping his weapon, Duffy fell to the ground clutching at his side and mortally wounded.

Having spent their weapons, the two recruits stood up; pleased with their handiwork, just as Maguire stepped into the room. He cut them both down where they stood. It was so quick and deadly that they never really knew what hit them, the SLR on rapid fire as it chewed them into bits.

'Take that and take that, you fuckin' coppers!' Maguire said angrily, as he saw his fellow IRA volunteer dead in front of him. Their bodies, riddled through and through, gave Maguire a sense of satisfaction, but not much, as he dragged Duffy's leaden, warm body out of the room. A real sense of loss struck Maguire as the realisation of what had happened sunk in.

Meanwhile, Liam headed for the cell area and, looking through the slit in the door but not seeing Fat Billy, he questioned the drunk. Pointing his weapon and shining the torch in his face, he asked brusquely: 'You see a man called Fat Billy in here?'

'Whatsh yuh shayin' chief?' came the slurred reply, as the drunk helped himself to a bottle hidden in his sock.

'Ah, you're no good,' Liam said in disgust, as he could smell the drink from where he stood outside. He closed the slit back up and moved on to the next and opened it. 'Have you seen or heard of a man called Fat Billy?'

'Not me,' the tearaway said, as he swung his legs and sat on the concrete plinth looking bored. 'But you can let me out if you like.'

'Nothing doing,' Liam said, and closed up the slit and opened the next. He saw only an empty cell, and kicking the door in frustration he left and joined the others. But not before he had vented his anger and blasted the doors, corridor and the custody sergeant's desk with his SLR!

The rest of the unit were in the hallway and making quite a bonfire out of a heap of discarded rubbish from the waste-paper bins in the various rooms and offices. They added the SLRs for good measure and poured several cans of petrol all over the place then set fire to it. Outside, they stuck a rag in the petrol tank of the hearse and let that blaze just like the fire now engulfing the RUC station. Then they stole an unmarked Cortina and made their getaway, heading out of reach of the security forces, over the border to Dundalk.

The ferocious assault on the RUC station at Markethill took less than five minutes from start to finish. It was a typical IRA attack, callous and brutal with indiscriminate killing. Hearing the crackling of flames, Mary clambered out of the metal cupboard she was hiding in and stumbled down the stairs and out of the burning building; but not until she had freed the prisoners, letting them out of their cells after they called out in fear of death. They stood outside, like her, coughing and spluttering as a paramedic took care of them. The fire brigade were hosing the fire down with several tenders sent to put out the blaze, after a 999 call by a householder who overlooked the station.

On leaving Markethill, Liam drove the unmarked RUC car like the wind as far as Keady, a short distance of some eight miles where they left Duffy's body with a family of IRA sympathisers. They transferred quickly to a lime green Vauxhall Viva outside a local grocer's shop, left for that purpose. From there the remaining members of Tricolour-7 ASU lost no time in taking the A29 to Newtownhamilton and out again, along the stretching A29 that intersected the B30 running from Camlough. Here Liam suddenly turned off the main road and took one of the many signposted border roads not on any map. From there it was a safe and straight run right into Dundalk, a friendly but small industrial fishing town in the Republic.

'Damn it! We missed him,' Liam said, letting out his feelings of anger and bitterness at not catching up with Fat Billy.

'Not only that,' Mairead reminded him, 'but we lost one of our own this time.'

'Yeah, another martyr to the cause,' Maguire said, as they rode on in silence, each with their own thoughts.

The first two years of Kenneth Newman's as chief constable of the RUC saw a growing effectiveness on the part of his reformed Criminal Investigation Department in getting to grips with the terrorists. Many of the crimes being cleared up at this time dated back to the early days of the Troubles. The use of the corrugated iron-walled compound inside the Army's Palace Barracks, Holywood, a few miles away, had ended with internment. The powerhouse for the police operation consequently became a group of prefabricated huts at the back of Belfast regional headquarters in Ladas Drive, Castlereagh, formerly occupied by the army. Later, on 1 November 1977, another holding centre was opened at Gough Barracks in Armagh, where there were twenty-four cells and nine interview rooms. These cells were sparsely furnished, windowless rooms, with just a chair and a bed. Equally, the interview rooms were austere, with a table and a desk and three or four chairs in each.

It might have been quiet in the Vauxhall Viva with the IRA volunteers, but not so at Gough Barracks. For here in an interview room were the chief inspector from Markethill and Captain Dixon. Though it was after midnight and nearly into the next morning, neither man had been able to get any sleep yet, their minds sifting through the facts and intelligence that they were collating from eyewitness reports and police and army on the spot.

'That was a stroke of genius you getting us out of there when you did,' the chief inspector said in gratitude. He, Dixon and Fat Billy had moved out of Markethill Station and transferred to Gough Barracks only a matter of hours before the ASU attack on Markethill.

'Just call it a funny feeling. I just thought Loughgall, why not Markethill?' Dixon said to the chief inspector. 'More's the pity we had to leave them poor sods behind to take the flak.'

'Casualties of war,' the chief inspector commented. 'You of all people should know that.'

'I do, but it doesn't make it any less palatable,' Dixon said. 'Do we have any reliable information as to how many casualties, and who is dead and who alive in this bloody fiasco?'

'Yes, we do. Eight dead and five alive.'

'Can we piece together how they died?'

'One was shot at the barrier and one in the lookout position. Two recruits having a meal in the canteen were shot and two men were killed by falling masonry, when a wall came down. The receptionist was shot and a man in the toilets.'

'So who survived then?'

'The female dispatcher, two prisoners, one man shaving in the washroom who managed to escape and raise the alarm and one man who hid in his locker until it was safe to come out.'

'And terrorists?'

'One dead, that they must have taken with them. There has since been a verified sighting of them and the body in Keady, shortly after the attack.'

'How about the station, has it been burned to the ground?'

'No, it seems the fire service was called just in time. Though badly burnt and gutted, it has not been put out of action for good. It should be operational again within a matter of weeks rather than months.'

'Good, at least we have salvaged something out of this.'

'Something very interesting turned up though.'

'Oh, what?' Dixon questioned.

'The fact that survivors with second-degree burns and smoke inhalation taken to the Royal Victoria have told of lines of communication being cut and the power supply hit all to order, before and during the assault.'

'Which points to detailed knowledge of the station and a lot of prior knowledge and know-how...'

'Exactly,' the chief inspector said, 'not the usual hit and run and hope for the best job.'

'This was thoroughly planned and well executed, and by an IRA ASU more professional than lucky.'

'I think we'd better get Mr William Shanaghan in here again.'

'I think you're right,' Dixon agreed. 'I think a talk with Fat Billy at this hour is just about due, don't you?'

Within minutes, Fat Billy was sat there in front of them. 'T'be sure, this is a fine time of night t'be havin' me here,' he said in a tired tone, his head in his arms on the table.

'It's morning, actually,' the chief inspector pointed out.

'I don't know if you know,' Dixon began hesitantly, 'but Markethill was hit by an ASU earlier on this evening and we have reason to believe it was Tricolour-7 that did it.'

'With all the commotion around here an' panic an' pandemonium, t'be sure a blind man couldn't fail to notice that somethin' had happened,' Fat Billy said. 'But as I tol' you, my information was that it was Loughgall to be hit, and not Markethill.'

'Could you have been sold a dummy?' the chief inspector questioned him.

'It's always possible, but I have no idea whether that's right or not.'

'Have a look at these pages and tell me if you see any members of Tricolour-7 on them, and what you know about them.'

The pages were known officially as 'terrorist recognition aids': usually photo montages containing mugshots of terrorist suspects and a brief description about them or why they were wanted.

The documents, of the lowest 'Restricted' security classification under the Official Secrets Act, had been compiled by the RUC's Criminal Intelligence Unit, then passed out in their thousands to police and soldiers on the streets over the years of the Troubles. Colloquially they were known as 'bingo lists' and the people on them as 'players'. Without these documents it would have been futile to deploy patrols and carry out checks for terrorists, for the security forces would have had no idea whom they were looking for.

'He's one,' Fat Billy said after flicking through half a dozen pages.

'Padraic Duffy,' the chief inspector said to Captain Dixon, setting aside the sheet. 'There's another, Sean Maguire,' Fat Billy said and again the chief inspector ringed the mugshot with a red pencil. 'And Liam and Mairead O'Connell.'

'You're positive that they are the members of Tricolour-7, the ASU?'

'T'be sure I am, on me mother's grave, so help me.'

'This Mairead O'Connell,' the chief inspector asked, 'does she have red hair?'

'Red hair? No begorrah, just plain old brown hair.'

'You're sure?' Dixon emphasised, 'As we've been getting a lot of reports of a woman terrorist with red hair, could it be her?'

'Not the las' time I saw her, so help me,' Fat Billy commented.

'How about a wig? Could she be wearing one?' pressed the chief inspector, as anxious as Captain Dixon to get to the bottom of it.

'Not to my knowledge, that's all I can say,' Fat Billy said with an open-handed gesture that meant, 'who knows?'

'You're sure now?'

'T'be sure, I'm sure. Can I get some sleep now?'

'I suppose so,' Dixon said and called out: 'Guard, take him away.

'Are you goin' to charge me or keep me in custody some more?' Fat Billy enquired, before he was escorted back to his cell.

'Provided you turn Queen's Evidence on the shootings at the Shamrock pub and sing like a canary about Tricolour-7, we'll keep you in the manner you've become accustomed to at Her Majesty's pleasure,' the chief inspector answered.

'Otherwise?' Fat Billy questioned in a worried tone.

'Otherwise,' Captain Dixon suggested, 'we'll release you without charge and let your former friends come to their own conclusions about you.'

'But that would mean they would stiff me for sure.'

'Quite so,' the chief inspector said with finality, 'so you'd better not let us down, had you?'

When Fat Billy had gone off to his cell with the RUC escort the chief inspector said: 'You know of course, that William Shanaghan began his illustrious career in the IRA by being caught red-handed in a surprise raid on his mother's house in Armagh, by the RUC in 1937? They netted themselves quite a sizeable haul that day of guns, ammunition and sixty-nine sticks of gelignite.'

'It's all in the case file on him,' Dixon said, and stifled a yawn. 'Is there any point to this?' he countered.

'Only this,' the chief inspector replied. 'You seem to be taking an awful lot for granted to do with this man, and that he's turned over a new leaf?'

'He has, trust me,' Dixon remarked wearily.

'Oh I do,' the chief inspector said, 'I just hope that trust does not turn to regret, that's all.'

'It won't. We've got him and he knows it.'

'Let's just hope for your sake that is the case and not vice versa. For habitual criminals like him are notorious liars, and will do and say anything, in my experience, to save their hides. I would not like to see all your hard work blow up in your face,' he added, with an underlying tone of sarcasm.

'I bet you wouldn't,' Dixon said in response, and passed off the comments as part and parcel of the competitiveness between the army and police. Getting back to the matter at hand, he asked, 'How about "dabs" and ballistics on the weapons in the assault?'

'As far as we can ascertain from the shell casings, the bullets were from SLRs, 7.62mm standard army issue, and both fingerprints and weapons were largely destroyed by the intensity of the fire.'

'Is that it?'

'No, there were also bullet wounds made by a Tokarev pistol and an old fashioned Thompson 9mm.'

'Is that the same Tokarev pistol used to shoot the two RUC men outside the RUC station at Markethill?'

'Could be, we'll know more later on.'

'So for this attack they were using mainly commandeered weapons; and so they probably jumped some army patrol somewhere?'

'Seems likely,' the chief inspector said. 'I can't see anyone just handing them over, otherwise?'

'First priority will have to be to find that patrol,' Dixon urged.

'I couldn't agree more, but where?'

'Tell the search teams near that double-whammy landmine explosion earlier on, to have a damn good look in and around that vicinity.'

'Well, the army did tell us that shortly after the explosions a "brick" in that area had radioed in and reported about the incident.'

'That'll be them, then. Find them and we might be halfway home to nailing these clever bastards in the ASU, Tricolour-7.'

'I'll get right on it,' the chief inspector assured Captain Dixon.

The phone rang, and Dixon picked it up. 'Special Investigation Branch. Yes, yes, good. Right, hold them until we can speak to them,' he said, and put the phone down.

'What was that?'

'A red-cap reporting to say they've found the patrol, tied up in the hedgerow off the Newtownhamilton Road.'

Putting his peaked cap, on the chief inspector said to Dixon, 'So what are we waiting for?'

'Will I call up a helicopter?'

'Do it. The quicker we see them, the quicker we get some answers.'

'And the quicker we find out if it was Tricolour-7 and a female with red hair?'

'With any luck.'

'Luck doesn't enter into it, my old sergeant used to say: forty per cent of police work is legwork and forty per cent getting the facts, ten per cent the eyewitness and ten per cent a nose for their modus operandi – method of operation.'

'Yes, and don't forget that essential one per cent extra,' replied Dixon, putting his red cap on.

'And that is?'

'An instinct for who your dealing with,' replied Dixon, as he reached for the phone.

'Very impressive,' the chief inspector wryly. 'Sounds to me like nothing more than the essential characteristics of a good detective in the RUC.'

Not debating the fact, Dixon smiled, 'You're probably right.' He was beginning to dial for that helicopter when the phone rang again, this time on the chief inspector's desk. Picking it up, the chief inspector turned around and looked at Dixon and said, 'It's for you.'

'Who is it?' Dixon spoke into the phone.

'The ballistics department at Knock, Belfast.' This was the police headquarters just outside the city.

'Yes, and what have you got for me?'

'Good news I hope,' the ballistics expert said, 'for the rifling on the bullets match the others perfectly,' he said quite excited.

'Slow down a moment,' Dixon said. 'I haven't a clue what you're on about.'

'We've been analysing the bullets from the shooting of the two RUC men in the road the other week. Now to all intents and purposes these correspond with the latest bullets passed to me within the last couple of hours from the attack at Markethill.'

'What bullets are these latest ones?' Dixon demanded to know.

'Those within the hour rushed to me from the autopsy of the constable shot at the barrier. Both sets of bullets are a perfect match, with the same rifling of two twists to the right.'

'Is that good?' the chief inspector asked, never having understood the peculiarities of this particular science, as he listened in on an extension line.

'Yes,' the ballistics expert said. 'It means they can all be perfectly matched to the exact gun they were fired from.'

'How is that?' Dixon chipped in.

'I shan't bore you with the technical jargon, but suffice to say, each gun is unique and has its own individual rifling. It's as distinctive as a person's fingerprints. If you get hold of the gun we'll be able to prove beyond reasonable doubt, that this is the one.'

'Good,' said Dixon and put the phone down. He redialled for the helicopter. The gun the ballistics expert was talking about was the 7.62 Tokarev pistol that Liam O'Connell used in both sets of killings.

Chapter Seven

Crossmaglen was such an inaccessible and dangerous place for the army that simply everything was flown in by the helicopters. People, food, ammunition and letters, everything, even the toilet roll. One local joker remarked, 'If the IRA on the housing estate next door ever knocked that one out then it would be curtains for the British squaddie and Crossmaglen.

Belying its importance, the helipad was nothing spectacular, simply a set of wooden slats outside the camp sangars on to which the helicopters swooped in quickly and efficiently. By far the most daring were the Navy boys in their Wessexes, and more importantly they were always on time, especially when picking up a patrol from out in the field.

One duty a squaddie did not mind 'bagsing' was that of doorman in the sangar. Easily done, it was no hardship to open the door just enough for those jumping off the helicopter and running to squeeze through. This particular morning it was Captain Dixon who leapt out and ran inside out of the pouring rain. Being friendly, he said, 'Not a very nice morning, I'm afraid.'

'Bloody typical of this country if you ask me,' replied the soldier, returning Dixon's salute.

Dixon replied, 'Er, yes, I suppose so,' and hurried along.

He had arrived at the army base to initiate action on the ASU Tricolour-7 and to lend his expertise to the imminent arrest and detention of said members of the IRA. Glad to be doing something positive at last, he could not wait to get to the briefing.

Held in one of the garden sheds, it was a quick affair presided over by the multiple commander. Pointing at the men involved he said, 'You're to patrol the town centre, you the left and you the right, while the other patrol stays out and does the house search. That means you Strong, East Acton and Man United and Spud. When it's done, you will come in and the others will carry on patrolling.'

Dixon handed each of the four men in the 'brick' patrol their 'bingo-lists' as they looked at the photo montages on the pages.

'Who are we looking for?' Strong asked.

'Primarily those members of Tricolour-7 that you briefly met last night,' Dixon explained.

'Led by the great Mairead O'Connell,' East Acton commented sarcastically.

'And Liam O'Connell,' Man United said.

'And I recognise Duffy and Maguire too,' Spud said, as he added his two-pennyworth.

'What are they wanted for?' Strong asked, staring at the ghastly picture, reminiscent of those used in passport photos and thinking that it did not do justice to the beauty that was Mairead O'Connell in the flesh.

'It would be simpler to tell you what they were not wanted for.'

'Killing?' Strong asked, dubiously.

'Killings in the plural,' Dixon remarked.

'Mairead too?' Strong asked, still not really able to believe that this beautiful woman he was infatuated with was such a 'hardman' and killer.

'Her especially,' Dixon said, flatly.

'Really?' Strong said, still unable to keep the disbelief out of his voice.

'Really,' Dixon said. 'Why?'

'Oh nothing,' Strong said, going quiet.

'Nothing really,' East Acton commented. 'Just the fact that he's sweet on her, that's all.'

'Yeah, he's in love with a terrorist,' Man United said gleefully.

'I am not,' Strong strenuously denied, but they all knew it was true and Dixon filed away that tidbit of information in his memory to be used another day.

'Well you be careful,' Dixon said, 'all of you, and remember she may be beautiful but she'll plug you all the same.'

Speaking up, the multiple commander said, 'Remember it's a war out there and be cautious at all times,' as he dismissed them.

This operation was to be no great shakes, just another house search like hundreds of others carried out by the regiment.

Assembling by the main gate, the four-man patrols each took turns in coming forward and loading their weapons in the bay provided. Then on the radio the guard commander quickly informed Baruki Sangar that the patrols were ready and waiting, for it was their job to cover and protect the patrols as they came out.

'Here we go,' Strong said, as they tensed themselves for it.

'Yeah, ain't it bleedin' great,' East Acton said, in his cockney twang.

'Give that girl with the big tits a squeeze for me,' Man United said, laughing and smiling, trying to relieve his tension.

'Yeah and tell my mother I love her,' Spud said, as they got ready to go out in the cold and damp weather. Each man wore a nylon flak jacket and had written his blood group on it, while East Acton had done a private deal and cadged himself a little something extra – for under his combat jacket he wore a nice, comfy duvet jacket as well.

Moments later, each patrol 'bomb-bursted' out on another tedious patrol; it would consist of three hours in the town, back for four, and out yet again for another three hours.

The reason they bomb-bursted out and ran like blazes was simple: when the gates were open the troops were particularly vulnerable at that point, to either a sniper, or a bomb or a grenade attack. The IRA after all were not stupid, they knew no matter how safe and secure the soldiers in the army base, that they had to come out some time.

Town patrol was a four-day affair in which the troops wore boots rather than wellingtons. It was also a twenty-four hour period in which there were constantly three patrols in and about the town. However, unlike in the 'cuds' there were two Saracen armoured cars that stayed on constant duty and in the town. They were covered in armour mesh which protected them against rocket-propelled grenades penetrating the armour. The soldiers colloquially called them 'cans' and they never went outside of the town, but ferried troops around from position to position as required.

Newry is a cathedral town, population some 23,000 and was well placed at the head of the 'Gap of the North', a pass between two ranges of hills through which the men of Ulster sallied forth to harry the tribes of Leinster in the days of the Fianna legends. The strategic position of the town meant it was destroyed in the wars for the control of the North. The name Newry comes from a yew tree said to be planted by St Patrick himself.

It was early dawn and cold and damp when the troops made their way out of Crossmaglen along the B30 leading to Newry. Quietly and cautiously, with protection from the Saracen armoured car, they proceeded on foot to a housing estate by the Newry Road on the edge of the cuds. In the Saracen the crews had a boring job of just sitting, or in the gunners' case standing, manning the turret-mounted machine gun.

As they marched along, weapons in their arms, the troops concentrated on the job at hand; especially Strong, Man United, East Acton and Spud, with their new SLRs loaded and ready for action. The air was cool and the atmosphere was quiet, not even a bird singing or a car backfiring, as they approached the housing estate.

'Jesus, it's quiet,' East Acton said, as he broke the silence in a hushed voice.

'Sure is,' Strong agreed, as he kept alert and expected anything to happen as they turned the corner and entered the predominantly Catholic estate. Passing the brick wall of the first house, they saw a young kid who suddenly scuttled down a back alley between the shabby two storey houses. He was a 'dicker' for the IRA, a lookout who soon after alerted the reception committee, whoever they were. The troops were tensed and alert as they made their way further into the road, in full view of the houses, passing the parked cars.

'That's torn it,' Strong said, but even as he said it his brain was still going over the bingo-list he had looked at and had in his pocket. It stated that Mairead O'Connell was twenty-four years old and a school teacher at the school in Crossmaglen, while her brother Liam was twenty-two years old and was the caretaker there. Nineteen year old Duffy and twenty year old Maguire were both unemployed.

Too young, it seemed, for war: just like the soldiers Strong, East Acton, Man United and Spud. But the players seemed to be bottle-fed on the violence and attrition, indoctrinated from knee-high to a grasshopper into the Cause and were willing volunteers from their teens.

The patrol and the can moved further into the seedy estate, where the houses formed an L-formation with an unkempt central grass square completing the picture. It was in one of these houses that Mairead O'Connell was resident, according to the bingo-lists in their pockets.

The can pulled up outside a dirty brick house. It looked no different from any of the other houses as Spud walked up to the front door along the concrete path, his SLR cocked and ready. He rapped on the door.

A scruffy looking urchin answered the door. He looked Spud up and down like he was a bit of shit and said, 'Yeah, what do you want?'

'Is Mairead O'Connell at home?' Spud asked him politely.

'No one here of that name,' the child said, and shut the door in Spud's face before he could step over the threshold.

While Spud did this, Strong was in a doorway several houses down. He was 'ballooning', making himself a non-static target as he stood up, then crouched and then moved again, covering that side of the street and road. Man United covered the rear of the can, kneeling behind the wheel as East Acton did the same at the front. All three troops covering Spud at the door with their arcs of fire should he make contact with a player.

Pausing for the others to get in position, Spud waited for the signal from East Acton. When he got it, Spud went into action, spurred on by his irritation at the kid's attitude. It was the same boy that had been seen diving down the alleyway earlier on, which should have taught him something. But Spud angrily knocked the glass out of the door with the butt of his SLR. Then he stepped back, took a run at the door and gave it a damn good kick. The glass was nothing, but when he kicked the door the frame gave: that was when the contact was made and the explosion signalled, too late, that the door was booby-trapped. There was a loud bang as the explosives blew Spud and the door to bits.

For a moment time stood still and everything stopped. The rest of the patrol looked at one another in shock and utter disbelief. The front lawn was covered in glass and debris and blood and the pieces of Spud's mutilated body. It was just unbelievable that it had happened to one of theirs. For a moment everybody forgot their training and looked around in bewilderment for someone else to take charge. They need not have worried as soldiers and another can appeared on the scene from all directions. Suddenly it was pandemonium and everyone was shouting and screaming at once. Doing the decent thing, the platoon sergeant stepped forward and covered the remains with his combat jacket.

Spud was a grisly sight as he had lost his head and arms and legs in the force of the blast. He was dead, there was no doubt of that, and what a horrible way to go. All those who had seen the explosion were sick to their stomachs.

The can was covered in blood and pieces of flesh. The soldiers in the can had screamed when the explosion went off, and needed reassuring and calming down. Up on a nearby hill, at the small row of shops, the greengrocer hurried out and stared in horror.

Motorists on their way to work abruptly turned round and went in the opposite direction. People opened their doors in curiosity and hurried inside again or walked away from the scene. Each one with their body-language signalled the same story, that they were not going to get involved. For they had lived through the Troubles and seen it all before, the violence and the men behind it that they did not want to know about.

All around the shocked Strong, East Acton and Man United, people were getting on their radios and shouting orders. There was no doubt about it, the patrol was downright scared, for this was the first time they had really come face-to-face with death and the stark possibility that it could happen to them too. Now they knew the real price of peace in Northern Ireland and what it cost in human sacrifice to achieve it.

The QRF (quick reaction force) was alerted almost immediately and they tore out of the base and soon put up roadblocks all over the town, but to no avail. It was too little too late and poor Spud paid the price for one moment of anger and one moment of hot-headedness that cost him his life.

Then, as the saddened troops did their best for their dead

mate, a few locals came out of their houses and shouted things like: 'Ra one, Brits nil.'

One wild-eyed, bearded fellow brandished his fist and shouted, 'Serve you fuckin' Brits right. Now, maybe you'll leave us alone you fuckin' bastards!' as a hostile crowd formed.

They were cheering and heartily glad that a soldier was dead, a British squaddie. Their gladness and cheer was a bitter pill for Strong and East Acton and Man United to swallow. They wanting to vent to their anger and turn their SLRs on the crowd and shoot them down in cold blood where they stood, so incensed were they with their eager display at the death of this comrade-in-arms.

When Strong had joined the army it had all seemed such fun, and a game, right up until Northern Ireland. Now, it was no longer a game but a very serious business. One in which Strong did not just want to get even, but kill one of them. An eye for an eye, the oldest and bitterest of emotions. He wanted revenge – on the killers, the bombers, the schemers, the instigators and planners of the IRA. He wanted revenge on the whole sorry organisation and prayed to God he would get the opportunity.

The freckle-faced Spud, or Derek Fowler as he was christened, was eighteen and from a good family in Hertfordshire. His parents would never see the sense of policing Northern Ireland, nor the rhyme or the reason for their boy's death in such circumstances. They would grieve, hard, and ask God, 'Why?' every single day of their lives. Spud didn't have to die but someone in the IRA decreed he should.

Strong would remember forever the smell of his burning flesh and the thick blood that he was soaked in, like the others, as he helped carry the combat jacket and tenderly placed Spud's remains on the helicopter from Bessbrook. But most of all, Strong would see him and be haunted by the memory of Spud standing there in the loading bay, when he said, 'Yeah and tell my mother I love her.'

The look of Spud standing there would be a permanent reminder to Strong of what he had to do and how ruthless he had to become in this long war to combat the IRA menace. Now, for the first time, he had real determination and cast-iron will, and knew what direction his life should take. From that moment on he would become a changed man, fired by the revenge he needed to extract for his dead comrade's life. He hoped that in some way he could allay the fears and doubts of blame he had about that moment, the nagging thought that somehow he was responsible. That he could and should have done more, possibly even warned him and shouted quickly and loudly to him, 'No – stop!'

It was later on the morning of the 26 November when Captain Dixon returned. It was about 9 a.m., and lighter and brighter but still cold and damp as he walked into his office at Gough Barracks, Armagh.

Spotting him, the chief inspector hurried after him and shut the door as Captain Dixon threw his cap on the light-grained desk and fell into his wooden chair wearily.

'So you're back?'

'Evidently,' Dixon said, not really in the mood for a row.

'And where have you been?'

'Out, where else?'

'But where?'

'Just out,' Dixon said evasively.

'Shall I tell you where you've been?' the chief inspector said, his temper rising.

'Why, have you turned all clairvoyant on me since my absence?'

'No, not clairvoyant. Let's just say that you're not the only one with a nose for trouble, shall we?'

'Go on then, tell me. Where have I been?'

'To brief the Royal Anglian Regiment on the members of the ASU Tricolour-7 and to arrest and detain them.'

'Very good, and why should I do that?'

'I don't know why, you tell me? After all, we had a deal or so I thought, didn't we?'

'You had the deal as I recall, all I had was empty words and a lack of action.'

'A lack of action, yes, because this was a police matter and needed handling with kid gloves and not the army's clod-hopping size twelves.'

'Yeah, the size twelves step on toes I grant you, but they get the job done.'

'Oh, is that what you think?'

'It is.'

'Well, let me tell you that all you succeeded in doing was to antagonise the locals on that estate and make things ten times worse.'

'Ten times worse maybe,' Dixon said in a pig-headed tone, 'but it had to be done to get the job done.'

'You call that getting the job done, when the birds had flown the coop and all you succeeded in doing was to get a soldier killed unnecessarily and cause a riot into the bargain?'

'Like you said, casualties of war.'

'Casualties of war, yes. But even so, there is a right procedure and a wrong procedure in doing these things and yours was quite plainly the wrong one.'

Both men had laid bare their petty rivalries and dislike for each other's methods and service and were by this time shouting at one another.

'Why, because the army responded almost immediately? Instead of taking everyone's sensitive concerns into consideration before acting at all?'

'No, because with a little more thought and tact and a little more cooperation it could have been handled so much better, and a young man might not have lost his life needlessly.'

'More sensitively, you mean?'

'If you like, yes.'

'And what could you have done so much better than the army?'

'For a start they are our people and we understand them better, and know how they think and react. And more than that, we have been patrolling these streets long before the army was called into these Troubles, and have the expertise to handle these situations with all the social proprieties. Now, all you've done is to exacerbate an already far from ideal situation.'

'You say a soldier died?' Dixon said as he went quiet and forgot their petty rivalry. Seeing for once that a flat-footed copper in RUC uniform was right and actually making sense, he looked up at the fuming chief inspector bent over him and said, 'I'm sorry. It won't happen again.'

'You mean that?' the chief inspector queried.

'Yes, I mean it.'

'Good. So the next time we agree on with closer cooperation between the RUC and the army, you'll stick to your side of the bargain?'

'I said so, didn't I?' Dixon said, only slightly aggrieved at the chief inspector's harping on.

'Good,' he said, and marched out, as Dixon got up and turned on the television. He was in time to catch the mid-morning news.

Standing in front of the wreckage strewn all over the road and surrounding area, Dennis MacMourne began, with mike in hand: 'Around 10 p.m. last night along this deserted stretch of the Crossmaglen Road, there were two controlled explosions of landmines, set off almost at the same time. One blew up a Land Rover patrol consisting of three men – one RUC constable, a reservist and an army major. While the other, moments later, on a bend on the same road only yards away in the opposite direction killed a fifty year old midwife, Kathleen Harrison.'

'Do we know who was responsible?' the presenter said in London.

'It was almost certainly the IRA, the security forces seem to think.'

'And the reason for the double explosion?'

'Almost certainly the second mine was intended to blow up those who would come along this road from Armagh to assist and help from the RUC. The security forces were soon alerted by a foot patrol who were in the area and saw the explosions, and reported it to their headquarters.'

'Are there any clues to go on as to who the individuals responsible might be?'

'The RUC are not saying at present as they are awaiting the results of the forensic report.'

'I see, Dennis,' the presenter said. 'And are they the same IRA that later on attacked the RUC station at Markethill?'

'Well, that Andrew,' MacMourne said, 'is the million dollar question on everyone's lips here at the moment. From those I've talked to on the scene here from the RUC and security forces the feeling is that it probably was. However, until they have evidence to prove that point, I am informed that they are keeping an open mind on the matter. They will be interviewing all those who survived the attack, and all those in and around the village who might have seen something suspicious beforehand or know something about the events leading up to it.'

'I believe you are in fact soon to be leaving there and travelling to Markethill, is that right?'

'Yes, that is right,' Dennis MacMourne said. 'As soon as I can I shall be bringing you a further report, later in the day, on the attack on Markethill.'

'Thank you, Dennis.'

Dixon switched off the TV and sat down again. He, like Dennis MacMourne, was wondering if the two landmine explosions and the attack on Markethill could possibly be the work of one single unit, Tricolour-7. Could it be them, or was he barking up the wrong tree?

Just as he thought that, the chief inspector marched back in the room, looking pleased with himself and like the cat that got the cream.

'What's got you so pleased?' Dixon enquired.

'Oh, nothing. Just the fact that detectives have been talking to that army patrol and to a soldier who stated that a female terrorist with red hair admitted she was, "the famous Mairead O'Connell", quote and unquote.'

'Well, that is news,' Dixon said, brightening and not feeling half so tired. 'And was it a wig?' he asked.

'Who knows?' the chief inspector said, with a thin smile. 'Your guess is as good as mine.'

Armagh is the smallest county in Northern Ireland, with an area of 512 square miles and a population of 25,000. Situated to the south of Lough Neagh, the topography is very similar to the southern uplands of Scotland, but at a lower level.

A Bronze Age site, Emain Macha, dating from the third or fourth centuries BC, was a religious centre for the district surrounding the current site of Armagh, which took its place in the early days of Christianity. The legend is that St Patrick founded the town, and the Church of Ireland cathedral is said to be on the site of the church he founded.

Miles out along the B77 road, on the outskirts of Armagh city, lay a quaint little stone cottage in a pretty setting among the rock walls and hedgerows out in the wilds of nowhere. It nestled among twenty-five acres of good pasture, off the beaten track and up a long dirt road. There, out in the fresh air of a pleasant but cold early December afternoon, was the farmer Mick O'Shaughnessy to be found, tending to his sheep with his shepherd's crook in his hand. Of stocky build, he was five feet ten inches tall and fifty-five years old, with a ruddy complexion and wispy brown hair that just about covered his bald pate underneath. At the moment the breeze was blowing his hair about and it looked rather a mess. Dressed in an open-neck white shirt, an ill-fitting brown jacket and wellington boots, he gave the impression of a rough-and-ready chap, which he was.

But he was not concerned about his appearance, for he was out in the emerald green fields to do a job. Right now, that was to get the sheep in before it got dark. The sheep were cute looking, with their black faces and legs and smooth, creamy coats. They were of the Suffolk variety that had been exported to almost every country in the world, so popular were they as a breed.

Opening wide the cross-barred gate, the farmer let his black and white border collie into the field and told the appropriately named dog, 'Get them, Blackie.'

The dog needed no further instruction and nipped inside, smartish, and immediately set to the task of barking and rounding up the dozing sheep. The animals were none too pleased at the interruption to their chewing the cud or basking in the pleasant sunshine in the ditches and hedgerows. Blackie snapped at their heels and prodded and poked them with his cold nose and got them on their feet and moving. He was a good dog and had fulfilled all the potential the farmer had expected, after much patience and hours of painstaking training. O'Shaughnessy had bought him as a puppy two years ago, and he was well pleased with the result of his work.

Darting this way and that across the sheep, and laying down and heading them off and turning the stubborn animals with short sharp runs, Blackie managed to dominate the Suffolks. He soon got them out of the field and marching into the three fenced pens to the left of the sturdily built cottage, with its smoke curling charmingly out of the chimney on the thatched roof.

Blackie and his farmer owner had begun to bring the sheep in from the farthest pastures before they lost the light and it grew cold, gradually working their way towards the nearer ones and home. Two hours later, they were glad to be putting the last of the sheep to bed in the fenced pens and feeling relieved to get it over, when a lorry, its headlights blazing, turned into the dirt road and began its approach to the cottage.

Five minutes later the headlights lit up the outside of the flint and rock of the cottage as the lorry turned towards the door and came to a halt. Shutting the last pen and looking at the pleased dog, the farmer said, 'Come on, Blackie. Let's go and see who our visitors are,' and he and the dog raced off towards the cottage and the lorry parked in front.

By now, the driver had killed the lights on the lorry and all three occupants had got out. Running up breathless to the lorry, with Blackie jumping up and down excitedly and licking the faces and hands of the visitors, the farmer said, 'There you are, and do you see who it is that has come to see us?'

'I've got eyes, haven't I?' his wife said, a bosomy, wide-shouldered, grey-haired but presentable woman. She stood with a shawl wrapped round he shoulders, in the doorway, with the light spilling out as she gestured for them to come on in.

'Come in, me darlings,' the wife said, 'out of the cold and dark.'

'Don't mind if I do, Mary,' the driver said. They went inside, followed by the farmer who shut the door behind them.

Some distance away, well hidden in the dark and hedgerows, and silent as the grave, was a brick patrol and their leader, Corporal Daghert. He was a short, feisty little character of some five years' experience as a British squaddie.

'Looks like the reports from intelligence were right, Corp,' Strong said. He was lying there flat on the damp ground, feeling the cold seep into every pore in his body. His SLR lay cocked and ready in front of him.

'Never mind intelligence,' Daghert said, 'this is our op and we're gonna get the recognition due us.'

'Yes, Corp,' Man United said in full agreement, looking forward to surprising the terrorists in the stone cottage below them. He was keyed-up and ready to go, as were the others, looking forward to meting out some retaliation on the terrorists.

East Acton passed the night vision glasses back to the corporal after looking at the images of the men that got out of the lorry, everything in the dark being visible but coloured green as you looked.

'They certainly look like three cut-throat bastards if ever I've seen one,' East Acton said, dryly.

'Never mind all that crap,' Daghert said. 'Who is for going down there and watching and listening at the windows?'

'I'll do it,' Man United piped up, eager to get moving. His body was pumping pure adrenaline in high expectation.

'Good man,' the corporal said. 'You do that then, and keep your eyes and ears peeled and signal if they are coming out.'

'Will do, Corp,' Man United said, and getting to his feet kept low and moved off quickly down the ridge.

'When he's in position in five minutes I want you to go down there and fire that big old barn. Got any matches?'

'No, Corp,' East Acton said, then helpfully. 'But I expect there'll be something down there I can light up the place with.'

The corporal warned, 'Don't leave it to chance, ever. We can't afford the luxury of not being prepared. Take these and do it.'

He handed East Acton a box of red-headed Swan Vestas, known to all squaddies everywhere as 'fire-lighters', for the fact they would strike up on virtually any surface.

'Got you, Corp,' East Acton said, and then looking at his watch he made sure, as did Strong, that he had synchronised his timepiece to that of the corporal before he moved off.

'You and Strong have got five minutes to get in position and then I want that barn hit ASAP, got it?'

'Got it,' chorused Strong and East Acton as they stood up and moved off. East Acton was to fire the barn and take up a position to the side of it, while Strong was to hide beside the dirt road and take out the vehicle and its occupants, should anyone decide to flee in it.

The corporal followed hot on their heels and took up a position inside the nearest of the fenced sheep pens. It was a good vantage point but hardly an ideal position to coordinate the attack, should it become necessary after he had confronted the terrorists and given them the chance to give themselves up. Lying flat in the mud with milling sheep knocking into him and voicing their displeasure, he settled under the lowest part of the fence, his weapon pointing towards the lorry and the cottage and anyone that ventured to come out.

'Come on, lad. Get on with it,' Daghert said to himself, as he waited anxiously for East Acton to do his part and fire the barn.

He was not the only impatient one, as Man United crouched flat against the wall of the cottage listening at the partly open window while Strong crouched behind a rock along the dirt road, where it turned into the yard outside the cottage. It was his job to cut off all hope of an escape route along the road and to stop anyone trying to do so. Like the others he waited anxiously to get on with it, ready to fight if he had to.

Inside the barn there were rusty old farm implements like rakes and hoes and scythes hanging on nails inside the door, as well as heavy bags of feed and piles of hay and several cans of petrol. East Acton homed in on the fuel and lost no time in sprinkling the cans' contents all over the place, before striking a match and dropping it on the petrol-soaked hay. He watched the yellow and red flames rise up and grow, before briefly looking around, running out the open door and taking up his position.

It did not take long before the smoke and flames were spotted by one of the men sat around the heavy wood table with the farmer and his wife.

'Jesus, will you look at that?' he said, as he pointed and got everyone's attention round the table. 'The barn's on fire!'

The three visitors were all rough customers in their thirties. One was tall and lanky, the second short and stocky and the third fat with a heavy build.

The farmer jumped up and shouted, 'Jesus, mother of Mary and isn't he right?'

The fat one turned to the farmer and said, 'Where are the weapons, may I ask?'

'They're in the barn beneath the hay and the floor, so they are,' the wife said.

'Then let's get out there and put out the fire quick!' the short one said, 'before the damn thin' gets out of hand.'

He and the others grabbed several buckets out of a storage cupboard beneath the kitchen sink and, filling them at the tap, they ran out the front door. This rather amused Man United as he signalled to the others with his hands that the targets were coming out of the cottage.

It took several minutes, but with the help of the buckets of water and a hose that ran directly from the taps the fire was soon put out. The brick patrol concealed in and around the yard did not have long to wait before the men started uncovering the Armalites and other weapons and bringing them out of the barn. They loaded them directly on the lorry under a false floor that they then covered with bags of feed and potatoes grown in the fields the sheep were not in.

It was as they were finishing off their handiwork that the corporal called out, 'This is the British Army. Stand where you are and put your hands on your head. Do not move.'

'To hell with that!' the fat one said and ripped up a section of the false floor not yet completed; he grabbed a handful of weapons and clips threw them at the farmer and his wife and the other two men. Hitting the dirt they threw themselves under the lorry and inserted the ammunition clips.

Soon all hell broke loose as the farmer and his wife jumped up and sprayed the area around the sheep pen and the corporal. Man United broke cover but was winged almost immediately by a stray bullet dropped his weapon. O'Shaughnessy and his wife quickly ran back into the cottage and shut the door, and began knocking the windows out to shoot from.

The short one did not favour the odds, being right in the middle of the battle as the patrol opened up and returned fire with 7.62mm bullets flying all around. He hastily hot-footed it across the yard, firing from the hip a short burst from his Armalite as he ran into the gloom of the barn. His fire caught Man United in the legs.

'Forget about him for the moment,' the corporal shouted, as he slithered under the crude fence of the sheep pen and ran hell for leather for the other side of the cottage.

At the smashed windows were O'Shaughnessy and his wife, firing rapidly out of them as red-hot lead kicked up the ground around every step the corporal took until he reached the wall of the cottage, seconds later. He kicked open the door to the cottage and fired the M79 grenade launcher he had in his hands. A fierce explosion was heard and then smoke and dust billowed out as all went silent inside, the room blown up and the occupants left dead.

'You bastards!' the short terrorist shouted, and ran back out of the barn firing angrily and rapidly as East Acton stepped out from the shadows behind him. The IRA man ran for the corporal, who clung to a corner of the wall and ducked behind it as rapid fire tore chunks out of the stonework. But before he could reach the corporal, East Acton riddled the terrorist thoroughly from behind and the man fell to the ground, his weapon still smoking.

Now there were just the two left in the cab of the lorry. 'For God's sake start up this thing an' let's get out of here,' the lanky one said to the fat one, as he turned the key in the ignition and started up the engine.

Tensed and ready, Strong saw the lorry careering fast towards him as the corporal aimed his second grenade. East Acton was firing at the lorry's sides but without much impact, as they were reinforced with steel sheets. But the grenade was far more effective, the explosion ripping off the back of the vehicle as it headed right for Strong, who fired a deadly tattoo across the windscreen and took out the fat one driving. He fell forward, his body slumped over the steering wheel, with his head stuck out of the broken glass. His passenger next to him did not wait for his turn, but jumped from the flaming vehicle while it was still moving. Falling awkwardly he limped across the field as the vehicle's petrol tank exploded and it was blown to bits.

Minutes later, Strong caught up the lanky terrorist and ordered, 'Give up your weapon and come quietly,' as he stood over him.

'Not likely,' the man replied. He reached for his weapon and pointed it at Strong, who had no choice and no compunction in shooting the terrorist where he sat, on the rocky ridge, under a hedgerow.

There was no remorse and no regret as Strong checked his handiwork then headed back down the ridge towards the cottage, and said quietly to himself, 'That was for Spud.'

Chapter Eight

'I am standing here outside Markethill RUC Station, where last night there was a particularly sudden and vicious attack perpetrated on the personnel contained in the gutted building behind me, as you can see,' Dennis MacMourne said, as he opened his report speaking into the microphone in his hand. He stood out in the cold and damp in a thick padded anorak, the hood up around his ears and tied under his chin as the rain tumbled down.

'Do we think it was the same IRA gang that set off the explosion on the Newtownhamilton road?' came the question from the studio.

'Oh almost certainly,' the BBC correspondent said. 'From the eye-witness accounts and reports from survivors it now seems a safe bet that it was the same unit responsible for both attacks.'

'And what about those press reports that a member of the gang is a red-headed woman? Can that be confirmed by any of the survivors.

'Yes, it has been confirmed, I am reliably informed that more than one source has identified her as such.'

'And so, the RUC and security forces are confident that it is the same Active Service Unit they are dealing with?'

'They are confident in that respect, yes.'

'And that the woman they wish to interview is one of the prominent members of the gang – if not the leader?'

'Yes, that is so.'

'Really, that is interesting,' Andrew Simmons said back in the London studio, as he failed to keep the fascination out of his voice at the thought. 'Do the RUC have any fresh leads as to who they are and where they might strike next?'

'Well Andrew, all I can say is that they tell me they are sure of their haunts and their identities and have been talking to known associates of theirs, but as yet they have not been able to interview those in question. But even so, they feel the suspects are on the run and that it is only a matter of days before their arrest and detention.'

'In the morning papers over here,' Andrew Simmons said, 'there is word of an army patrol being captured and their weapons being used in the assault, is that correct?'

'That is correct, yes. And what is more, the attack on the station was very unusual in being a direct frontal assault, instead of a hit-and-run, which is the usual method of this kind of attack.'

'Which suggests what?' Andrew Simmons asked, picking up on something being left unsaid.

'Which suggests, Andrew, from the precision and quickness of the attack, that this gang had specialist information.'

'By specialist information you mean what?'

'That this gang almost certainly received inside information.'

'Thank you, Dennis, as always,' Andrew Simmons said politely, 'but we'll have to leave it there. And now back to the studio and the rest of the news.' The pictures switched from Northern Ireland back to the London studio.

Not interested in anything else, Dixon turned off the TV and looked at the chief inspector. 'Who the hell writes that stuff? "A matter of days before their arrest" – pure fiction that is, and better fantasy than a Disney film.'

'I know, I know,' the chief inspector agreed. 'But you've got to admit it does show us in a much better light than it would otherwise.'

'Oh, it does that all right,' Dixon agreed. 'Only problem is that it is inaccurate and not much help except to Mairead O'Connell and her little gang, who I bet are laughing their socks off at that little charade.'

'Maybe so, but you've got to think positive.'

'I'm thinking positive,' Dixon said gruffly, 'only trouble is it isn't helping very damn much.'

'We know for a fact that one of the gang has been shot and is possibly dead.'

'Possibly, but can we be certain?'

'A QRF has been sent to Keady to locate and identify the body and question the locals that saw Tricolour-7 drop him off. Which I must say was nice of them.'

'They had no choice, since he was hit and beyond a quick repair he would have been no use to them and so they had to drop him off, before he became a deadweight and a liability that held them up.'

'In that report MacMourne said they were on the run. Do you think so, or do you think they might be holed up with known accomplices, family, relatives or what?'

'Or what,' Dixon said, as puzzled as the chief inspector. 'One thing is for sure, whatever happens they sure like giving us the run-around.'

'That is for sure. So what do we know?'

'We know,' Dixon said, 'that they are Mairead O'Connell and Liam her brother. They are twenty-four and twenty-two years of age respectively, and Padraic Duffy and Sean Maguire are even younger. If they are as clever as the press are making out, and not just lucky at making monkeys out of us, what would they do?'

'If I was them I would stay clear of known associates and family, as they'd know that would be the first place we'd look.'

'Which is why we have drawn a blank so far, right?'

'Right, so where do you go from there?'

'Across the border and out off the island to the USA or Great Britain, where else?'

'The USA would seem a bit extreme, but the mainland, well that's something different. Provided they had help and false passports they could go almost anywhere.'

'Almost anywhere yes, but you put your finger on it, the mainland is the better bet, as then they could pass back and forth; and where is the best place to go from?'

'Either the ferry terminal in Belfast or the airport?'

'That's right Chief Inspector. So we want an APB – All Points Bulletin – issued to customs and all ports of entry and exit officials.'

'An APB for what exactly?'

'Send copies of the bingo-lists to them and insist that they identify any and all redheads, both male and female, to be detained for further questioning by both of us at the nearest police station or barracks to the place in question.'

Scratching his head, the chief inspector said rather puzzled,

'You mean women only, surely?'

Dixon reminded him, 'You told me not to take anything for granted. So I'm not.'

Rising to leave, the chief inspector said, 'Good. I'll get right on it.'

Dixon sat back and sighed; fiddling with his gold-nibbed Parker pen he said, 'At last, some bloody action!' then fell asleep at his desk.

'That wasn't right jus' leavin' him like that,' Maguire said.

'We had no choice,' Mairead said, sat in the front of the lime green nippy Vauxhall Viva that was plunging down the narrow, winding border roads at considerable speed. The bumpy and uneven surface was no more than a dirt road in places, which made driving quite an achievement in the dead of night and without street lighting.

'It still wasn't right,' Maguire went on, incensed by the way they had dumped their fellow comrade, like some useless sack of spuds not needed anymore. 'I know he was thick as a brick, but still, he was loyal and a good volunteer,' he went on. He was getting on the nerves of both Liam, driving, and his sister Mairead next to him who said, 'Quit your bellyachin' Maguire or you'll be left behind too.'

Aggrieved, Maguire said in response, 'Oh, I see, now you run this ASU, do you?'

'No,' she said, and Liam replied, 'No. I do.'

Backing his sister he added, 'Now I'm tellin' you, stop your bellyachin' or you can get out here an' now, is that understood?'

'Fine,' Maguire said defiantly, his AKM Kalashnikov in his hands, cocked and ready. 'So stop the car an' let me get out an' I'll take my chances on me own.'

Trying to bring a little common sense to the proceedings, 'Don't be so stupid,' Mairead said, 'you wouldn't last five minutes on your own and you know it.'

'Maybe so,' Maguire retorted, 'but I'd rather be on me own than listen to you two barking orders at me day an' night.'

'Put the gun away, there's no need for that,' Liam commented.

'Sure there is,' Maguire went on, 'I am sick to death of being ordered around by the likes of you an' your bitch of a sister.'

'Thanks very much for the compliment,' was all Mairead could think of.

Liam simply added, 'And thanks for the vote of confidence, I must say.'

It was at that moment that the vehicle hit a bump in the road, that jolted the suspension and made all three hit the roof of the small car as it went down the rough track and through the sloping fields either side. Seizing her chance, Mairead slapped Maguire round the face and swiftly disarmed him. Pointing the weapon in his face, she said coldly and in no uncertain terms, 'Now you can either come with us and do as we say. Or I can stiff you here and now and leave you to kick up daisies, which is it?'

Bursting into tears, Maguire said, 'Shoot me now, I don't care.'

'You don't mean it, I know,' Mairead remarked. 'You're just upset by the death of your friend, we know that. But remember we owe it to our dead comrade to carry on the long war an' take as many of the British bastards with us to hell, as we can.'

'I know an' I'm sorry,' Maguire said, as she handed him a tissue. He wiped his eyes and blew his nose. 'It won't happen again.'

With that, Mairead gave him back the automatic weapon and the sheepish and saddened Maguire took the rifle from her and went silent. But there was no time for remorse as Liam shouted out, 'Shit, soldiers ahead!'

'Kill your speed and lights and head for the farmhouse over there,' Mairead said, pointing over to the right. Liam braked hard then backed up and turned right up the track leading to the house. Nearing the farmhouse, all three got out of the car and pushed it energetically into the farmyard and into a barn, easily breaking the lock on the door. Hiding the Viva inside, they waited out the time nervously as the brick patrol skirted the outlying stony, ridged perimeter of the place. Within half an hour the patrol had moved on, having thoroughly searched the thick thornbushes, hedgerows and fields. Seeing no lights on in the farmhouse cottage, for it was after midnight, the corporal did not see fit to disturb the residents in their beds and decided to leave well alone.

As soon as the soldiers were in the distance, outlined against the skyline, the three ASU members rolled out the car and pushed it far down the dirt track before daring to start it up again. Then they lost no time, and were soon on their way in the direction Dundalk, putting both the police and army behind them, with any luck, as they did so.

Dundalk, from the Irish 'Dún Dealgan' – Dealgan's Fort – was made a borough in 1220 by King John. A Franciscan Friary was founded by John de Verden in 1240 and a survival of this is the high, square building known as Seatown Tower. Two more recent monuments worth seeing are the sixteenth century memorials to the Bellew and Field families, and also that to Robert Burns' sister Agnes, which can be seen in the churchyard. But sightseeing was far from the thoughts of Tricolour-7 as they approached Dundalk.

The hill was a steep one that carried them down into the coastal town and more traditionally 'hardened' Republican territory. Liam had some difficulty watching his speed and had to keep his foot on the brake pedal. The little car struggled to hold the road as it headed down into the heart of the town and the dockland area in particular, passing the huddled together cottages clinging to the hillside.

'Look, there's the sea!' Maguire exclaimed, like some little boy who had never seen the water before.

The moonlight was shining on the inky black sea as the waves vigorously lapped at the rocks and sheer white cliffs around the headland and the high walls of the breakwater. The waves rolled far inland and up the sandy beach. Facing the sea, a line of unassuming guest houses and arcades sat quietly along the seafront.

It was close to one in the morning when the Viva came to a halt on the quayside. The area was silent and deserted and not very well lit-up, and all the premises locked tightly shut. The visitors got out of the car and locked it up, then headed for the nearest alleyway. They threaded between the backstreets, heading for a pub which was still open with blazing lights on. It was old-fashioned in style, with wooden detailing and painted black and white. Above the door hung a sign that creaked in the breeze of a man in a sou'wester with a net in his hands in a small boat. The place was named the Fisherman's Tavern.

Liam stepped up to the door and knocked loudly. A voice bellowed in response, 'We're shut, go away!'

Looking at Mairead, Liam said, 'Ready,' and both of them took a run and kicked the door hard, Liam knocking it off its hinges and crashing to the floor. Liam, Mairead and Sean stepped over it and entered the premises.

'Come in, why don't you?' the little, frightened barman said in a small voice, as he poured out another smooth Irish whisky into a shot glass.

'I think me an' me friends will be doin' jus' that,' Liam said, accentuating the Irish brogue and sounding a touch thick.

'Didn't you hear me, at all?' the man propping up the bar said in a confrontational mood. He was forty-six with luxuriant growth of red hair and beard, and a blue sailing cap on his head. He was wearing a blue blazer with a button missing and a thick, knitted Aran sweater. He was in a disagreeable mood and did not like his drinking being disturbed as it had by these unwelcome visitors. 'I tol' you we were shut. Now put the door back and jus' piss off and leave me an' my good friend here to continue our conversation and good cheer.'

Ignoring the inherent threat of violence, Liam said, 'I am here lookin' for a man named Quinn.'

'I'm Quinn,' said the man propping up the bar. He downed his whisky in one gulp, then looked at the barman and demanded gruffly, 'Another.'

Standing his ground and ready for anything, Liam looked at Quinn and the barman and remarked, 'I wouldn't do that if I were you.'

'Oh and why not?' the barman asked, as he became apprehensive and paused with the bottle in his hand.

'This man needs to be sober, as he's going on a little trip,' Liam explained.

'That's news to me,' Quinn said, unconcerned.

'Oh and where is that?' the barman said, his growing apprehension meaning that by now he did not know who he should listen to.

'Nowhere special,' Liam said mysteriously. 'Just around the coast until I say stop.'

Not liking the authoritative tone of Liam, 'Like hell I shall,' Quinn replied, 'and who do you think you are, tellin' me what to do?'

'I am Liam O'Connell in command of ASU Tricolour-7, that's who I am,' Liam said, pronouncing his credentials.

'Well, Liam O'Connell, or whoever you are,' Quinn said, in an ugly mood. 'I'm not goin' out in that boat and not you or the Head of the Army Council can make me.'

'That's where your wrong,' Liam said, as Quinn raised another glass to his lips. He took out the Tokarev pistol, and shot the glass out of Quinn's hands as he raised it to drink.

That was the last straw as far as Quinn was concerned, and bellowing and furious like a bull in a china shop, he charged at Liam. 'You bastard, I'll have ye if it's the las' thing I do, so help me!'

Agilely, Liam sidestepped the charge and tripped up Quinn who fell down heavily. Then, grabbing Quinn by the hair Liam smacked his head into the wooden floor and left him unconscious. It was all over in a matter of seconds, the tall, sober and sharp Liam, out-smarting the overweight and inebriated Quinn with ease.

This made the barman somewhat uneasy as Liam and the others stepped up to the bar.

'Er, you're not goin to, er, start on me, now are you?' he said, with the bottle in his hand shaking.

'No, take it easy,' Liam said with a friendly smile. 'We want no more trouble, just three large whiskies if you please.'

A few minutes later, there was a groan from the prostrate body of Quinn as he came round.

'What about him?' the barman said.

'Oh, don't mind him,' Liam said. 'He's comin' with us.'

Quinn groaned again and rubbed his head, and sat up as the barman said nervously, 'What shall we do?'

'I don't know about you,' Liam commented, 'but this is what I'm goin' to do.' Picking up the ice bucket off the end of the bar he walked over to Quinn and threw the freezing contents in his face.

'That should do it!' Mairead said and laughed.

'I reckon so,' Sean commented, as he gulped his whisky down.

Still a little groggy, Quinn grabbed at a chair and sat on it, rubbing his head as he looked at Liam across the table and said, 'Now, don't tell me, I have you to thank for this large lump on me head.'

'That's right,' Mairead said before Liam could reply.

All his faculties back in working order, Quinn demanded, 'And who might you be?'

'I'm the sister of the man that had to teach you a few manners, like taking your hat off to a lady,' she said, as she placed his sailor's cap on the polished table.

'Oh, I'm sorry about that,' Quinn said all apologetically. 'Only it was the drink don't ye know.'

'I know,' Mairead remarked, looking at her brother who nodded.

'Our father was a drunk too.'

'I hope you're not runnin' away with the thought that I am drunk.'

'Not now, anyways,' Sean said, looking at Quinn. 'But you were.'

'You certainly gave that impression,' Mairead piped up.

'That you did,' Liam said, 'but that is not the issue here—'

'Wait a moment,' Mairead said in her usual suspicious tone, 'can he be trusted?' She indicated the barman.

'Sure he can,' Quinn said, 'he's flesh an' blood so he is. He's my brother-in-law, God help him.'

'Good,' Liam said. 'Now all we want from you is some assistance to get round the coast and dropped at Belfast Lough.'

'Belfast Lough, is it!' Quinn questioned. 'Hell, it might as well be the dark side of the moon.'

'No, not the dark side of the moon,' Mairead repeated, 'just Belfast Lough, that's all!'

'It's all right for you people goin' on,' Quinn said, 'you jus' don't realise what it is you're askin', that's all.'

'Yes we do,' Sean said, as concerned as the others that Quinn would get the message and help. 'Belfast Lough.'

'Yes, yes, Belfast Lough, I hear you,' Quinn remarked, irritated by their pressing the matter. 'You can go on about it till the cows come home. But the fact of the matter is that Belfast Lough is a tricky place in the daytime, but at night, well, it speaks for itself.' He paused, then added, 'Then, there's the tides to take into consideration and the rocks. Well, as you can see, it jus' can't be done, so it can.'

'I appreciate that,' Liam said. 'But no matter the excuses, you will take us one way or the other,' he said, the Tokarev in his hand.

'Surely, what would you be needin' that thing for. Only desperate men want to go out on a cold and windy night like this.'

'That's us,' Sean Maguire remarked. 'You hit it on the head first time.'

'That's right,' Mairead agreed. 'You got it in one. We're desperate enough to ask you.'

'And I'm jus' desperate enough to make you,' Liam said, cocking the pistol.

Quinn hesitated in doubt and fear, and then said, 'Put the pistol away. I'll do it, so help me. Though the saints preserve me, I don't know why.' Then, looking at them all, 'Is it so bad you have to do this in the dead of night? What about the mornin' and drivin' there?'

At the end of his patience, Liam grabbed Quinn by the throat and, putting the pistol to his head, said grittily, 'I guess you've got about three seconds to reflect on the right answer and what it will be. For the mornin' will be too late and as for drivin', well none of us fancy drivin' through a countryside thick with hundreds of police an' soldiers lookin' for us. So are you with us, or not?'

'I'm with you,' Quinn uttered, as he jumped to his feet and in a strong do-or-die voice said, 'After all, a man has only one life and it might as well be served in the way of the Cause.' With a wink of his eye at Mairead, he added, 'An' besides, it'll be somethin' to tell me grandchildren, around the ol' fireside.'

'That's the spirit,' Maguire remarked.

'Talkin' of spirits,' Quinn said, looking at Liam, 'How about one large whisky to be goin' on with?'

'Oh, no,' Mairead said, taking him by the arm and leading him towards the door. 'You've had quite enough for one night.'

'She's right, you know,' Liam said, putting the pistol away.

Seeing he was not going to get his way in their company, Quinn said, 'I guess you're right, so let's be havin' you,' as they all went to walk out.

Before they did, Liam said, 'One thing, barman. You're comin' too.'

'Me?' the barman said, looking both frightened and nonplussed. 'But my lips are sealed and I wouldn't say anythin'.'

'I know you won't,' Liam said in an assured voice. 'That's why you're comin' with us,' and they all made their exit.

Strolling towards the quayside from the pub and through the alleyways, Quinn caught sight of the lime green Vauxhall Viva. 'That your car?' he asked Liam.

'It is.'

'What's in it, then?' he asked, turning to Mairead.

'Oh, nothing much, you know. Just spare tyre, road maps, guns and ammunition.'

'Lose it,' Quinn said succinctly.

'Where?' Maguire said.

'In the drink,' Quinn offered equally as succinctly.

'But why?' Liam protested.

'Is it hot?' asked Quinn.

'I guess so,' Maguire said.

'Then t'hell with it, you'd better lose it, before the sky falls in on all of us.'

'Very well,' Mairead said and seeing the logic, all three pushed the car off the jetty and into the water.

'Satisfied?' Liam asked of Quinn.

'It's a start anyhow,' Quinn said, as he and his barman brother-in-law headed for a small boat moored further on. It was a ketch, a fifteen foot, two-masted cutter-rigged coasting vessel. There were two berths below, made into bunks and sleeping four in very low and cramped conditions.

The three members of Tricolour-7 ASU climbed aboard the ketch as Quinn cast off the mooring rope and he and the Barman put up the sail and checked the rigging.

Liam said, 'So you're happy to go through with it then?'

'Put it this way,' Quinn explained, 'I don't fancy a bullet in me brain if I don't.'

'Good man,' Maguire said cheerfully.

'What's the accommodation like?' Mairead enquired.

'It's not the Ritz if that's what you're thinkin',' the barman said flatly.

'I bet it isn't,' Mairead said, none too enthusiastic.

'But then beggars can't be choosers as me old mum used to say,' the barman added.

'Ain't that a fact, so it is,' she said, and Maguire and her went below.

'We do appreciate this,' Liam said in an almost apologetic tone. 'And I'm sorry for—'

'Don't you go worryin' your wee head now,' Quinn said, amiably. 'Just go below and catch some shut-eye with your friends an' we'll have you there in no time at all.'

'Don't you want a hand?'

'No, me and me brother-in-law there have done it before. So thanks, but no thanks.'

Minutes later, as the watch Liam was wearing showed 2.05 a.m. Liam settled in his own bunk below deck.

The little ketch, named *Sea Breeze*, sailed out of the dock and out into the Irish Sea. It turned to starboard for a few miles before then taking a port tack and hugging the coastline as in the dark, the small ketch set course for the mountains of Mourne and Ardglass, then Donaghadee and on to Belfast Lough and the dropping-off point.

It would take a good few hours to cover the forty miles or so, but Quinn would easily get them to Belfast Lough and land them by the time of first light.

Captain Dixon was so tired, having been up all night collating intelligence and information from the two mine explosions and the attack on Markethill RUC Station, that when he got a chance, it was not surprising that he fell asleep. So tired was he that he did not even know it had happened as he sat at his desk, his head in his arms, his mind and body glad of the rest from the eternal pressure and hassle of dealing with the death and misery and havoc that Tricolour-7 wreaked in their wake.

When the girl from the Records Department brought in a cup

of coffee and set it down on the desk and stirred the spoon in the cup, Captain Dixon bolted awake and alert as his senses told him something was wrong.

'Ah, you're awake at last, good,' the chief inspector said, as the girl closed the door behind her and left them alone.

Coming to a little more and yawning as he put the cup to his lips, Dixon had a good sip and suddenly exclaimed, 'Christ, it's hot!' He nearly burnt his lips, and put the cup in its saucer hastily. 'Christ, I know you don't like the army round here but do you have to resort to such underhand methods to get rid of us.'

Ignoring the banter, the chief inspector said, 'Will you get serious a moment?'

Putting on a suitably serious look Dixon said, 'All right, I am. So spit it out.'

'They've found the green Vauxhall Viva the ASU exchanged for the armoured Cortina they dumped. An angler out for an early morning's fishing off the quay at Dundalk caught his hook on it.'

'Good for him,' Dixon said, 'and lucky for us. Let's pay the man a visit.'

'By helicopter?'

'What else?' Dixon commented. 'It's the only way to travel.'

'Good as done,' the chief inspector said, having dialled the number Dixon handed him on his notepad.

'Don't you people know any other sport over here but hooking dead bodies and hot cars,' Dixon commented. 'Doesn't it ever occur to you to try fishing once in a while?'

'Sometimes,' the chief inspector said.

Looking at the large, coloured map on the back wall of his office, Dixon was tracing the route from Armagh city to Dundalk in County Louth. 'About twenty miles. That shouldn't take too long.'

'No, it shouldn't,' the chief inspector agreed. 'Helicopter will be here shortly.'

'Better service than the buses around here,' Dixon remarked.

'Better by far, I'd say,' the chief inspector said, joining him at the map.

'Time to shed the cloak of secrecy and inform the press, radio and TV boys that these three are all now wanted for murder.'

'Good idea,' the chief inspector remarked. 'Especially as, heading out from Dundalk, they could conceivably pop up anywhere next, isn't that so?'

'That's true,' Dixon agreed, 'but I'd still put a fiver on them making their way to Belfast and doing what we thought earlier.'

'You think so?'

'I know so,' Dixon said, with a thin smile on his lips.

'By the way, while you were comatose we've had a report that the dead terrorist was Padraic Duffy,' said the chief inspector.

'Now all we need are the others.'

'Trouble is, they've got a several hours head start on us.'

'Don't think I haven't thought of that,' Dixon said, as both men put on their caps and went out the door.

Northern Ireland is a place that has cities not much larger than some small English towns, and many towns are not much larger than an English village. And so, Belfast truly stands out as a relative metropolis.

Some half a million people live there, a third of Northern Ireland's population, within ten miles of Belfast City Hall. Walking around the city today you find the place has a greater air of prosperity than maybe the political commentators would have you believe, the centre being full of cinemas and restaurants, with theatres and art galleries aplenty. Shopping arcades ring with the gay, tuneful music of buskers with fiddle and bodhrans or a lone tin whistle. A large statue of Queen Victoria dominates the front of city hall and gazes regally down Donegall Place into the main shopping area. The central shopping area is pedestrianised, except for buses and those cars used by the disabled. Pay and display on-street parking is confined to an area behind city hall and around of St Anne's Cathedral.

It was here that Liam, Maguire and Mairead O'Connell sat in a stolen black Ford Zephyr. They had easily broken into the car with the aid of a metal coat-hanger, just one of the things to come out of the arsenal of Mairead's handbag. Maguire had slipped the bent wire between the gap in the door and the rubber seals and with a hook on the end, tripped the door lever. Seconds later all three got in the car, after making sure the parking attendant was not around and no one was looking.

Sat there, Maguire in the back remarked out loud, 'So what do we do next?'

'We do what we were told as per instructions,' Liam said, sounding a bit put out.

'Which was?' Mairead said. 'I'm that tired that my memory is goin' and I feel a bit thick.'

'To make contact at city hall,' Liam said, as if it was the easiest thing in the world for three people on the run from the police and security forces to do.

'Just like that?' Mairead said, not so assured as Liam.

'Yes, just like that.'

'Oh, right,' Maguire said, feeling a little uneasy about walking the streets there as a known felon and without his Kalashnikov, now in the drink with the Viva.

'And the name?' Mairead pursued.

'The name is Councillor Grew of Sinn Fein.'

'Is he? I've never heard of him,' Maguire said.

'Me neither,' Mairead said.

'Well that's the name, now are you goin' to sit here and argue about it all day, or are you goin' to see him?'

'I'll see him, don't worry, keep your hair on,' Mairead said, as she got out of the car after a quick study of the Belfast street map contained in the glove compartment.

Taking a deep breath to calm her nerves, Mairead walked out of the car park with never a glance backward at Liam and Maguire, who would vacate the car soon after. Acting more bright and breezy than she felt, Mairead lengthened her stride and tried to act as normal as she could under the circumstances. Down Donegall Street she walked, took a right and stepped out the tail end of North Street and then entered the High Street and went right along Castle Street. She passed the post office before entering Donegall Place and straight after, Donegall Square North, a jaunty walk that took a good half hour. She smiled at a couple of British soldiers at a checkpoint along the way, who waved back. Mairead felt a lot better in herself and more confident after that.

149

Part Three
The Intelligence

Chapter Nine

Without pausing for thought, Mairead strode to the entrance of city hall and went inside. The city hall is rather a splendid building that dominates Donegall Square. White Portland stone makes up the main facade, which is 300 feet long, with a striking copper dome rising 173 feet above the busy traffic. When Belfast was declared a city in 1888 the city fathers soon set about demolishing the white Linen Hall of 1784 and built a city hall worthy of their new civic status. Knighted on its completion in 1906, the architect, Brumwell Thomas, then had to sue the corporation before he got his fees. In a grand ceremony in 1921, George V opened the first Northern Ireland Parliament there at city hall.

Filled with wonder and awe, Mairead wandered around the place free as a bird. She gazed at the grandiose interior of colourful Italian marble, an oak panelled banqueting hall, a large industrial mural and an enormous crimson Smyrna carpet in the great hall. She was just admiring the room, when a man walking by stopped, then paused before entering.

He was fifty-five years old, in a smart grey suit with a white shirt and blue tie, with pleasant features and silver hair.

'What do you think you're doing?' he asked challengingly, as he tapped Mairead on the shoulder and she turned around.

'Just looking,' she said wistfully.

'Well you can't,' he said, taking her by the elbow. 'Now, let me show you the way out madam.'

'But I can't go,' Mairead said, looking perplexed. 'Not until I know more about all this,' she said, as she spread her arms and broke free from his grip.

Hastily he recounted, 'This room is 120 feet long and was destroyed by a German bomb in Spring 1941, when nearly a 1,000 Belfast citizens were killed in the Blitz. Happily it was rebuilt in time for Queen Elizabeth II's visit in 1953, her coronation year.

What more did you want to know?' He went to grab her again.

'But I can't go!' Mairead insisted, and pushed him away.

'And why not?'

'I've got to see someone, that's why.'

'And who might that be?' he questioned, looking at her rather dishevelled appearance, the big bags under her eyes and her tarty clothes of leather boots and miniskirt, not believing a word she said.

'I've come to see Councillor Grew,' she said, and added confidentially, 'on very important business.'

'Oh, really,' he said, standing there wondering what was the best way to get rid of this tiresome girl.

'And why should I bother to see you at all?' he questioned, looking at the cheap brunette before him.

'My name is Mairead O'Connell and I'm a member of the ASU that hit Markethill RUC Station and caused two controlled explosions on the Newtownhamilton Road, the other night.'

'So what are you doing here?'

'I've come to ask for your help, so I have, for me an' the others.'

'Why should I do that? You bloodthirsty fools killed an innocent woman. A midwife no less.'

'Yes, I know and we're sorry, but it couldn't be helped. So help me, there have been a lot of innocent lives lost in the years of the long war an' by God, there'll be a lot more before it is over.'

'Well, I can't help you. I've got to think of my reputation, and there's talk of the Party entering into negotiations with the British Government. So I can't help, and there's an end to it.'

Calmly, though she was hopping mad at the councillor, Mairead said, 'I know that Sinn Fein means "*Ourselves Alone*", but we don't intend to be. If you don't help, then I'll just have to let it be known that when the chips were down you refused to help a volunteer in need.'

'Don't do that, for God's sake!' Grew said ashen-faced. 'Think of the damage it would do to my reputation, and—'

'And the lack of votes next time, eh Councillor?'

'Just so,' he said, and in a more friendly fashion put his arm round her waist and showed her out. 'So what is it you want, and who gave you my name?'

'Father Behan gave me your name, and what we want is money an' a sure-fire escape route off this island, if you please.'

'Hallo Mum,' Strong said, shouting above the din of the hustle and bustle of people rushing by and buses revving up as they came in and out. He eventually got through after dialling the number, but he was struggling to make his voice heard and that of his mother as he jammed the receiver in his ear. Then, when he heard her voice he put the money in the slot of the payphone.

'Hallo Martin, is that you?'

'Yes, it's me, Mum. Just thought I'd ring and see how you were.'

'I'm all right son, your father's got another chesty cold, but other than that we're just fine.'

'Good Mum. Look, me and some mates have had an idea and we'll be staying on here a while longer.'

'How much longer love? As we're looking forward to seeing you home, and besides, I've baked some cheese straws and made a Victoria sandwich cake, your favourite.'

'Not much longer, it's just the weekend in Belfast to see some of the sights.'

'Are you eating properly?'

'Yes, I am Mum. And no, it's not a glorified pub crawl, on my honour it's not,' he said laughing as he pre-empted the next question. How suspicious mothers were of their sons when away from home.

'Have you got enough money, and does this mean you're not coming home then?'

'Yes, I have and no, silly, it doesn't mean I'm not coming home. How could I stay away with a lovely cake to look forward to?'

'Well, when then?' she asked.

'I'm coming home on Monday and I'll phone you when I get to King's Cross, all right Mum?'

'You're not showing me up by not wearing clean underpants, are you?'

'No, Mother, will you stop it. You're embarrassing me in front of everyone as I'm calling from a public phone.'

155

'Well, have a nice time and come home soon. We love you and miss you.'

'Yes I love you too. Oh, there go the pips. Give my love to Dad and Bonnie and I'll see you. Bye.'

He ran out of coins and put the receiver down on its cradle. Hefting his kitbag he walked away from the red booth and out of the Europa Bus Centre towards Sandy Row.

Standing outside, it was not long before he hailed a taxi and threw his bag on the back seat. He looked at the driver and said, 'To the youth hostel, if you please,' as he patted the leave pass in his pocket.

Turning around, the craggy faced taxi driver said, 'Well, you're a polite passenger, so you are.'

'My mother always taught me that it did not cost anything to have polite manners.'

'And she was right,' the taxi-driver said, as he turned the wheel and the taxi pulled away from the kerb and headed along Sandy Row to the youth hostel adjacent to the Donegall Road.

By 10 a.m. Strong had checked in and signed the register. He stowed his kitbag and gear in the roomy but simple facilities and quickly freshened up and changed. Soon he was back on the street and headed in the direction of the Dublin Road. He walked into Howard Street, turning right into Donegall Square South and from there along into May Street, where the Presbyterian church was located on the corner.

This was where Martin Strong began his sightseeing, after a little information and a visitor's guide was kindly loaned to him by the small, neat woman who sat behind the desk in the hallway and signed him in at the youth hostel. A few inquisitive questions and she had soon pointed him in the right direction.

What he had told his mum about his other mates was a small white lie. He did not like doing it, but knew how she worried about him, and so he had been forced to do it for her peace of mind. The truth was stranger than he liked to admit. For although he was a stranger in a hostile land, he still had an overwhelming urge to know more about the Irish, and so, he had decided to stay on in Belfast this weekend and do just that.

In 1829 the May Street Presbyterian Church was built for the

Reverend Harry Cooke, a formidable Victorian who campaigned against the theological errors of the time. Cooke's statue stood at the top of Wellington Place in front of the well-proportioned facade of the Royal Belfast Academical Institution, where Lord Kelvin's father taught mathematics. Kelvin, 1824–1907, was the man responsible for the absolute scale of temperature, the Kelvin scale. He also made a fortune from his submarine cable patents. His birthplace in College Square East has been demolished but a statue stands inside the gates of the botanic gardens. This sort of thing did not interest every young man he knew, but Strong had taken an interest in history and the past ever since his parents had taken him to the Victoria and Albert Museum as a little boy.

The Institute itself was opened in 1814 as an interdenominational school. The poet-physician William Drennan, 1754–1820, saw the school as a place, 'where the youth of Ireland might sit together on these benches and learn to love and esteem one another.' Son of a Presbyterian minister, Drennan helped found the United Irishmen Society and was inspired by the spirit of free thought sweeping through Europe. He was the first person to call Ireland the Emerald Isle.

Strong walked away feeling enlightened and as usual fascinated by the past. He was heading south down Durham Street and then Sandy Row, and passed the youth hostel without stopping. Taking the left at the intersection where it forked, Strong strode down University Road and into Queen's University.

Anyone will tell you, if you cared to ask them, that the area around Queen's University is good value for moderately priced restaurants, art galleries and theatre. The Queen's Restaurant was one of those moderately priced establishments, and it drew Strong inside like a moth to a flame, after he'd looked at the glassed-in menu and price list outside. The smell of freshly fried cod and chips made his mouth water as he looked at his watch, and to his surprise he realised it was 12.30 p.m. Strong had been so interested in all he had seen and read about, that the morning had just flown by and now it was lunch time. He went inside the busy restaurant and found a vacant but clean table close to the kitchen. In no time at all, there was a waitress at his side, complete with white apron and pad and pencil in her hand, who asked him, 'Are you ready to order, sir?'

'Yes, I'll have cod and chips and two pieces of bread and butter and a cup of tea, please.'

'Will that be all?' the waitress asked.

'Yes, thank you,' Strong said politely.

Writing out his order, the waitress was soon back with his bread already buttered and on a plate. Then she went away again and returned with his cup of tea, before bringing the big piece of cod and heap of chips some minutes later.

Picking up the tomato ketchup, Strong liberally doused his fish and chips with it, and was just taking a large bite out of one of the buttered pieces of bread when there was a sudden commotion A man rudely shoved into a girl on his way out and caused her to fall across the table as Strong was eating. The poor girl got tomato sauce on her coat and in her hair, and mashed chips on her face. She did look a sight as Strong handed her a napkin and said, 'Here, use this,' as she looked close to tears.

'Yes, I think I will,' she said, happily accepting the napkin. She looked at the young gent, Strong, and said, 'Thank you, very much,' dabbing her face and lips and coat with the napkin and putting it down again.

'That's OK,' he said, then quite surprised himself as he offered: 'Would you like to sit here?' indicating the chair across from him at the table.

'Are you sure?' the girl said, in a lovely Irish brogue and sat down.

'Yes, I'm sure,' Strong replied.

'I was going to have what you've got,' the girl said, 'but I guess you could say I have, anyway.'

That broke the ice for them, and both the girl and Strong laughed. 'Have it, anyway?' Strong urged.

'No, I don't think I shall, I'll have a steak and kidney pie an' chips instead.'

'Sounds good to me.'

'Doesn't it,' the girl agreed.

'One steak and kidney pie and chips,' the waitress wrote down, 'and anything to drink?'

'Yes, I'll have me a coke.'

'Right, coming up,' the waitress said, and bustled into the kitchen.

As she sat there, the blonde girl opened her white PVC coat and crossed her long legs, showing off her matching ensemble of white miniskirt and white sheer tights, with white knee-length boots and handbag to match. Strong looked at her and briefly thought she was the sexiest girl he had ever seen.

Minutes later, the waitress brought her steak and kidney pie and coke and both were at ease in each other's company as they ate.

'I apologise for that man,' Strong said, 'it was very rude of him.'

'T'be sure, you'll do no such thing,' the girl said. 'Some people are jus' naturally ignorant and he's one of 'em. So forget it, I have already.'

As they ate and Strong drank his cup of tea and the girl her coke, she asked him, 'So you're English then? And where do you come from?'

'Oh, nowhere very special, just a town called Borehamwood in Hertfordshire. Where they make the Saint and Baron TV series at Associated British Studios.'

'Roger Moore,' she said dreamily. 'There's a beautiful man for you.'

'He is rather good looking,' Strong added, 'better than me.'

'Oh I don't know,' she said, 'I think you're quite a good lookin' fella yourself, so you are.'

'Thanks,' Strong said, taken aback by the compliment as no female of his acquaintance had ever said that before.

'You're welcome,' the girl remarked.

'Are you a student around here?'

'I should be so lucky,' she said. 'No, just a tourist like yourself after taking a half day off from me job at the pub.'

'What do you do?'

'Oh, nothin' much, I'm just a barmaid that's all, at the Crown. So what are you, a civil servant?' She finished off her coke and put down the empty bottle.

'No, close, I'm a soldier in Her Majesty's armed forces.'

'What regiment?' she asked, suddenly very interested.

'The Royal Anglian Regiment, no less.'

'Never heard of 'em.'

'Not many people have.'

'I see,' the girl said, 'and do you like the army?'

'It's OK, more interesting than civvy street and you get to see the world at the taxpayers' expense. I mean, that can't be bad, can it?'

'No, I don't expect so,' she said and rose out of her chair and stood up. 'Look, let's pay our bills and get out of here, shall we?'

'Why not?' Strong said, and that is what they did.

Stood outside the restaurant, her handbag in her hands she said, 'My name is Brigit Nolan, what's yours?'

'My name is Martin Strong,' he responded, 'and what shall we do now?'

'How about we go back into the city centre and see some of the things listed in this book,' she said, referring to the visitor's guide she had taken off Strong.

'But Brigit,' he protested, 'that's a long walk back there and it's going to take some time.'

'I know, but we've got all afternoon,' she said enthusiastically, and looking at his watch added: 'Look, it's only 1.15 p.m. So what do you say?'

'Oh, all right, but if I get tired…'

'And I thought all you soldiers were supposed to be fit,' she teased.

'We are, we just don't like going over the same ground, that's—'

'Stop moanin', you'll love it, an' besides you've got me to share it with.'

'That's right, I have,' he said brightening and they walked off hand in hand together. They strolled back down University Road, then the Dublin Road and into Donegall Square. He was not fully aware of it yet, but he was falling for Brigit and she for him.

'I love your clothes by the way,' he said, 'they are real groovy.'

'I got them in a boutique near here,' she said. Then, 'You can drop the hip act, it's not necessary with me. I like you jus' the way you are.'

'You do!' Strong said, really surprised.

'Yes, I do, casual but smart.' Looking at his short-cut hair, clean appearance, his Levis and blue two-tone zippered windcheater, 'You'll do for me,' she said, and planted a kiss on his cheek.

'What did you do that for?' Strong quizzed her.

'Nothing, I jus' felt like it, so I did,' she said, as they arrived outside of city hall, where, behind the railings, was a statue of Sir Edward Harland, who came to Belfast from Yorkshire as a young marine engineer in the 1850s and became the city's leading shipbuilder. Moving on, the pair of them looked at a marble figure commemorating the tragic loss of the *Titanic* in 1912.

After that, they both walked on a little further and came across the dashing nobleman, complete with handlebar moustache and cocked hat in the little temple on the west side of the building. Strong read from the visitor's guide: 'He was the first Marquis of Dufferin, who among other things, was Governor of Canada, ambassador to Moscow and viceroy of India. The statue was unveiled in 1906 and, together with the city hall, speaks volumes about Belfast and its past imperial pretensions.'

'Pity I didn't bring a camera,' Brigit said, 'I could have taken a picture or two of us posin' next to all this history.'

'I'm just as bad,' he remarked, 'I didn't think to bring one either.'

'Never mind,' she said hesitantly, 'you are enjoyin' it, aren't you?'

'I am,' Strong answered, 'but more than that I am enjoying seeing it with you.' He amazed himself at this forthright expression of his feelings.

'Good, I am glad,' she said and kissed him full on the lips, to which he eagerly responded.

'What was that one for?' Strong smiled, unsure of the demonstration of affection she showed him.

'Because I wanted to again,' Brigit replied.

Suddenly filled with happiness, 'I loved it,' he said, and threw his arms around her and kissed her again.

The afternoon came and went so quickly for the couple, who were having fun and enjoying their new-found friendship while the sun went down and the dark crept up on them. Finally, it was the time to say goodbye, with Strong returning to the youth hostel and Brigit having to turn up for work at the Crown Liquor Saloon. But she was not content till she extracted one last lingering kiss from him, and the promise he would come for a drink at the Crown and be there when the bar closed and she got off work.

Strong walked away from Donegall Square West, which was taken up by the huge Scottish Provident building, interesting for its proliferation of stone carvings of lions' heads, queens, dolphins and sphinxes, while ropes, the spinning wheel, loom and ship represented the traditional industries that made Belfast prosperous. As he walked she called out after him, 'No talkin' to any strange women, now!'

'No, I'll be a good boy,' he answered with a smile.

'You'd better be,' Brigit reminded him, as he disappeared down the road.

Cosy, atmospheric pubs are to be found all over Ireland, but in Belfast some of the best are to be found in the narrow passageways called 'entries' in the High Street area. Just opposite the Grand Opera House in Great Victoria Street is one that was much frequented by John Betjeman the poet, it is called the Crown Liquor Saloon, and was formerly part of a Victorian railway hotel. It is a charming place, what with its stained and painted glass, and panelled snugs lit by the original gas lamps, restored by the National Trust.

The place was brightly lit with the hanging lamps over the bar and the interior sparkled as Strong lingered over his pint of Guinness. His gaze fell on the liquor behind the bar, and the shiny brass pumps before him. It was quiet now, as the customers had been shown the door, and he only waited for Brigit to finish the washing-up behind the scenes and come and join him.

It was nearly 12.20 a.m. when she emerged, and she looked at him and said, 'Drink that up and we'll go.'

'Go where?' he questioned, as he drained his pint glass.

'Upstairs, where else?' she said, and grabbed his hand. They climbed the back stairs and soon stood outside her room, where they had a long lingering kiss before entering the simply furnished room. There was a single bed against the wall, and she turned on the bedside lamp.

'It's not much,' Brigit said, shutting the door behind them, 'but it will do for our purposes.'

Going all shy on her, Strong looked at his feet and said, 'I think there's something you should know. I've never had a girl and I don't know what to do.'

'So you're a cherry boy it is, t'be sure. Well, never mind me lad,' she said reassuringly. 'I'll show you what to do an' you'll be jus' fine.'

'Are you sure?' Strong said, not wanting to disappoint this obviously more experienced girl, as she pulled the curtains closed.

'You like kissing me, don't you?' she said, her arms round his neck.

'Oh, yes,' he said shyly.

'Then kiss me, as long and hard as you can,' she said, before her lips met his. Breaking off, Brigit said, 'Now you sit down there,' pushing him on the bed, 'an' I'll give you a right royal treat, so I will.'

In the dim light and quiet of the room she undid the buttons on her white blouse slowly and parted the garment, showing him her big breasts encased in their full white bra-cups. She slipped the blouse off her shoulders and on to the floor. Then, she deftly undid her miniskirt and stepped out of that and let it fall at her feet.

She teasingly shook her breasts at him before she undid the catches on her bra and let each breast gradually fall out of its cup, until the bra too, fell at her feet and she stood there and asked, 'Am I as beautiful as those English girls then?' as she finally removed her panties.

'More so,' he said, totally entranced by the most beautiful sight of her naked, so stunningly beautiful that she took his breath away as she leaned over him and guided his hands to her pendulous breasts.

Minutes later, they were both naked in the lumpy bed and Brigit was touching and kissing him and building a raging desire in him. So that, when the moment came, he had no choice but to do what came naturally, as they pleasured each other through a long and oh so sweet night.

The next morning was lovely and bright, contrary to belief it does not always rain in Northern Ireland, it just seems that way. As the sunshine showed through the chinks in the curtains, Strong awoke to find that Brigit was gone and he was tied up with masking tape round his ankles and wrists and mouth. He was firmly bound and gagged and could neither go anywhere nor call out as he was attached to the bars on the bedstead. Not until 9.30 a.m. was he freed, when the maid coming to make the bed opened the door and screamed as she saw the astonishing sight of him naked on top of the bed.

Getting help, they soon freed him and he dressed again. As he did so, he reached for his watch off the cupboard next to the bed and found a note there. Picking it up, Strong was in for another shock as he read, 'Thanks for a lovely night. Love, Mairead O'Connell.' When he saw that familiar name, the whole extraordinary business made sense. So it was she, and now he really was in love with the IRA.

When Dixon got the call, he and the chief inspector were up to their armpits in redheads detained at virtually every army barracks and RUC station in the province.

Receiving the call at the customs office in Belfast's International Airport, the chief inspector soon arranged for a car to take them into the city centre and drop them at the Crown Liquor Saloon.

When they arrived twenty minutes later, all the staff and guests were assembled in the main bar and the chief inspector and Captain Dixon immediately quizzed them. Soon after, Dixon said, 'I'm just popping upstairs to see the lad.'

'You do that,' the chief inspector remarked, 'and I'll just have a word with the proprietor and see what I can learn from him.'

It did not take long for Dixon to climb the stairs to the top and enter the room, that overlooked the back alley and rubbish bins which were piled high and attracted the stray cats in the neighbourhood, hungry and looking for a meal. Turning from the window, he looked at Strong who was sitting on the bed looking disturbed and worried as he stared into space.

Flashing his warrant card he said, 'I am Captain Dixon of the Army's Special Investigation Branch. I'd like to ask you a few questions.'

'Ask away,' Strong said in a couldn't care less tone. Then he added, 'Are you going to put me in the glass house for what I've done?' he added, in a small, meek voice.

'No, I don't think so,' Dixon replied. 'Whatever makes you think that, lad?'

'I didn't know who or what she was, and I didn't think it was Mairead O'Connell.'

'Believe me,' Dixon remarked, in the way of a man of the world. 'It's never wrong for a man and a woman to love each other – just the circumstances.'

Looking up at Dixon, Strong said, 'But it's wrong to love a woman in the IRA, isn't it?'

'That's for you to decide. It's not my job and it's not the job of the law, either. No one can say who you should or shouldn't love. It doesn't work that way.'

'But it is wrong to love her, isn't it? She's a murderer and a violent terrorist.'

'Not with you, obviously.'

'That's something I can't understand. Why me? Why her? It just doesn't make any sense.'

'The best love affairs never do. It's just the old story of attraction, that's all. But in this case you really would be advised not to get involved.'

'I know. But I can't get her out of my mind and I want her here and now, but there's this guilt about it all. I can't shake it. And what's my mum and mates going to say when they find out that I slept with the IRA?'

'Nothing son,' Captain Dixon said, more tenderly than he thought he could be. 'They won't hear it from me, and you're not going to tell them, now are you? So there's an end to it.'

Droning on, Strong commented, 'I keep seeing her lovely face and that voice, and feeling that body that sends shivers down my spine.'

This was a little too personal for Dixon, and embarrassed he said, 'Yes well, er, that's for you to know. Tell me, is she as beautiful as they say?'

'More so,' Strong remarked, with a far-away look in his eye.
'What colour was her hair?'
'Blonde.'
'Was it real?'
'What do you mean?' Strong said, looking accusingly at Dixon.
'Was she wearing a wig?'
'I don't know. All I do know is that she didn't like me touching her hair, so I stopped it.'
'Tell me, why does she always leave you tied up?'
'I don't know. I think she does it to stop me following her.'
'No other reason, like maybe she enjoys being in control, or that it's some act or game and that she likes making a fool of you?'
'No, no, she wouldn't. Oh, I don't know,' Strong finally conceded.
'One last thing,' Dixon commented, 'did she happen to mention anything about the others of her group or where she was going?'
'No, nothing.'
'I thought as much. So she treated you like a mushroom then: fed you on shit and kept you in the dark.'
'I suppose so,' Strong said, a forlorn figure, quiet and still.
'It begs the question,' Dixon commented, 'did it never occur to you that it was the same girl?'
'No, never,' Strong replied. 'She looked and acted completely different.'
'Just one more thing trooper,' Dixon said as he turned Strong's face up towards him. 'Bear this in mind, that if this had been any other girl you'd be jumping for joy and thinking that all your birthdays and Christmases had come at once. So I advise you to think of this little sordid episode in those terms. Don't cheapen yourself by giving her the satisfaction that she used you for her own gratification. Also, don't run away with the thought that you did anything wrong. Christ, most of the regiment is talking about this particular girl and would love to get their hands on her.'
'Maybe, but they are not in love with her, are they?'
'No, and it's something you'll have to come to terms with in time, but you will. Cheer up for God's sake, the chances are you will never see her again.'
'Yes, you're right,' Strong said, rising from the bed.

It was 6.15 a.m. on the morning of 27 November, a cold, grey, chill one, as Mairead, Liam and Maguire walked the pavement and entered the intersection of Howard Street. It was so early that the three had not really given any thought to the forces of law and order combing the countryside and byways for them. Their heads cleared quickly in alarm when they spotted ahead of them a patrol car with two policemen in it. They were two constables who had been on night duty and were soon to return to their station and the end of their shift. The car was parked at the kerbside, meaning they had to go past it if they were to appear normal and not attract attention to themselves.

The pair in the car were an older constable and a young one, learning the ropes. Leaning out of an open window the old sweat asked, 'And where do you lot think you're goin' at this hour?'

'If you're not mindin',' Liam said, 'it's home we're headed.'

'I'm glad to hear it,' the constable said, looking quizzically at their dress.

His partner, the younger man piped up, 'And what's the football gear for then?'

'Fancy dress,' Maguire chipped in. 'You know how it is.'

To further allay their suspicions, and looking them straight in the eye, Mairead explained, 'You see constables, we've been to one of them all-night parties.'

The old sweat then looked at them and suggested, 'Is that right? Well you get along then, and make sure you go all the way home. For these streets are not for the likes of you at this hour.'

'We will,' Mairead said, and leaned in and kissed him quick.

Pleased but surprised, the old sweat remarked, 'And jus' what was that for?'

'For bein' nice an' so understandin',' she said, as they walked off.

'Ah, get on with you,' the constable said, and called after them: 'All the way home now.'

'We will,' they chorused, and headed around Donegall Square North and into Donegall Place. From there it was a short haul to the local car park and the waiting Dormobile van painted red and white with, 'Tommy bites yer legs,' scrawled on the side, after the reputation of the Liverpool FC full-back Tommy Smith who was the hard man of the side.

As they approached, the back door was thrown open and a helping hand extended as all three climbed inside, joining the other three in the back and the driver and passenger in the front seats.

Not being a football fan and not seeing the logic of it all, the ungrateful Mairead complained, 'And whose brilliant idea was this then?'

'Mine, actually,' Liam said, 'but don't thank me, that would be too much to ask. Actually, to be strictly accurate, mine and Grew's.'

'You went and saw him behind me back?' she countered, flabbergasted at the thought. 'Why and when?'

'He wanted to talk to the organ grinder not the monkey, and I did it when you went gallivanting' off for the afternoon.'

'I see,' she said, and went quiet as it was a better plan than she had discussed.

'Now let's jus' all sit here an' get a little shut-eye before we move off, OK,' said Liam as he locked the door tight, and everyone did as they were told, terrorists and genuine Liverpool supporters alike.

At half past seven, the driver of the Dormobile looked at Liam and said, 'It's time.'

'Then let's go,' he replied, and the van pulled out and turned right at the Main Post Office, down the High Street and along Donegall Quay to where the sea ferry terminal was.

Chapter Ten

Belfast, the capital and largest city of Northern Ireland, is situated at Belfast Lough at the mouth of the River Lagan on the east coast of Ireland. The city is the main industrial centre and chief port of Northern Ireland and is busy, to say the least, at all hours of the day and night. So it was with difficulty that the Dormobile made its way through the heavy goods and container traffic both coming in and out of the place.

The van and its driver and seven passengers arrived at the quayside, and though it was not yet 8 a.m., they still had to cool their heels and be patient, joining the never-ending queue of car lorries, vans and coaches to go on the ferry. The queue slowly approached the barrier and the concrete hut with the officials in their luminous jackets, checking the boarding passes and tickets of those wanting to go on the ferry. To the consternation of the three wanted terrorists there were also a few policemen walking around and stopping the odd car and group of passengers and doing a spot check.

Sitting in the small and cramped interior of the van, Maguire was suddenly panic-struck, 'What shall we do?' Going to get up, he said: 'Let's jump out and make a run for it.'

Pushing him back in his seat, Liam said, 'That would be stupid. After all the trouble we've gone to not to attract attention to ourselves.'

Irritated, Mairead could keep quiet no longer and remarked, 'Look Maguire, show a bit of backbone an' think of someone else instead of jus' yourself for a change.'

'Look you,' Maguire said, about to start in on her, when Liam commanded, 'Maguire, get a grip on yourself or we'll all be sunk!'

Laughing in a silly fashion out of fear and nerves, Maguire exclaimed, 'That's a good one. Ha ha ha! So near the Lagan River.'

Twenty minutes later and the Dormobile had moved to the front of the queue and in front of the barrier. Two port officials in their luminous donkey jackets stopped the van and did a quick check: one with the driver up front and the other at the back, as the doors were opened and he popped his head inside and did a quick headcount. 'One, two, three, four...' he said, as he pointed his finger.

'You'll find there is eight of us with the driver,' Liam remarked helpfully.

'Thank you,' he said, 'and are there any redheads?'

'Why do you ask?' Maguire said, shifting uncomfortably on his seat.

'Oh, it's just that there's this flap on about some beautiful redhead of a terrorist.'

'Oh really, and what is she wanted for?' Mairead asked of the official leaning in the van.

'Oh, nothing much, just murder and bombing.'

'Really?' Mairead said, surprised.

'Really,' the official replied. 'Time was they were as ugly as sin and like as not with a scar on their cheek. But now, they are beautiful redheads.'

'All done here,' called the official at the front as he finished his check and glanced over the party of eight's boarding passes and tickets for the ferry.

'Right,' the official at the back said, and slammed the doors. But before he did, he looked at Mairead and smiled and said, 'Who are you supporting?'

'Liverpool, naturally,' she replied, with a smile.

'And who are they playing today?'

'Spurs at home,' Liam chipped in quickly.

'Well, have a good match and I hope you win.'

'So do we,' Maguire said, as the official closed the doors and Liam locked them tight. Moments later, another official gestured for them to move forward.

'Right, you can go aboard now,' he said, and with that the van went up the steel ramp and on to the ferry and stopped behind a coach on the lower deck of the vessel. Inside, there was a collective sigh from the three terrorists.

Liam looked at Maguire and Mairead and said, 'Well, so far so good.' Mairead nodded and Maguire had his fingers crossed.

'After the boat gets goin' I think it'd be advisable for all of you to get out an' stretch our legs. But remember,' Liam said, 'don't go talkin' to anyone and don't draw attention to yourselves.'

'Other than that of course, we can all enjoy ourselves, yes?' Mairead asked in a sarcastic voice.

'Other than that,' Liam agreed.

'Good,' Maguire said, 'I need the toilet.'

'So do I,' one of the genuine supporters said, and went to get up.

'Leave it until the boat starts up, OK,' Liam urged the lad, and no one moved until the ferry did get under way shortly after. The genuine supporter did not know who the terrorists were. But as they were guests of Councillor Grew and had replaced other seasoned fans at the last moment, he knew better than to question an elected member of Sinn Fein.

Once the ferry got going, the driver locked up the van and the seven football supporters, all dressed in Liverpool colours, headed for the upper decks. The genuine fans headed for the top deck and the best view, while the three terrorists went to the toilets and then bought some refreshments. Laden with coffees, a cake and rounds of ham and tomato sandwiches, they sat by the window in the comfortable seats and looked out at the hectic port and the view. The Harland and Wolff dockyard passed slowly by, welders working amid showers of sparks. Then came the sight of brown scummy harbour walls, and a hotchpotch of warehouses, offices and huts. Overhead, tall cranes swung slowly with their loads as seagulls screeched and circled around.

While they were eating they listened to the announcements given by the captain over the tannoy, and especially the routine one about the use of life jackets and safety should there be an accident or the ship about to sink – which was not a pleasant thought for the ordinary passengers, let alone the three terrorists. After a while, and as the ferry chugged further out into the North Channel, Maguire got restless and said to Liam, 'I'm goin' to take a look round the boat.'

'Very well,' Liam said, 'but don't be late back.'

'I won't,' Maguire said, and walked away and climbed the stairway to the upper deck.

'I know you love gallivanting' off,' Liam remarked to Mairead, 'and so, is there anywhere you want to go?'

'No,' she said yawning. 'I feel tired and so I think I'll just have me a nap, instead.'

'Well, I'm goin' for a walk to stretch me legs, but I'll be back.'

'You go,' Mairead urged, wanting to be alone. 'Don't let me stop you. I'll still be here when you get back.'

'If you're sure, then?'

'Yes, go!' she said, and Liam walked away.

By now they were passing the Isle of Man and were a third of the way on their 140 mile passage to Liverpool. The sun had cleared off and the day became wet and grey and dull. The sea was no better as it deteriorated from a mill pond to rough and choppy.

Sitting there relaxed, gazing out of the window, it was only now that Mairead's mind wandered as she no longer was fraught with worry about escape and being caught. For she felt fairly confident that she and the others were safe on board the ferry. So she began to think of other things than just herself, and naturally her thoughts turned to her sweetheart and soldier love.

By the time Martin Strong was freed, Mairead was a long way away at sea. The funny thing was that she was no nearer an understanding than he was of this love affair they had with one another. A soldier and a terrorist, it just didn't seem to make sense. But there it was, maybe it was the fact he was a virgin and so green and thoroughly nice; not yet warped and cynical and bitter about life. Or maybe it was the fact that he just looked so damned cute in her eyes. Whatever it was, she just could not forget him or leave him alone. For keeping her hands off him was a problem, and if he had been there then it would just have all started again, she would have had no choice but to eat him up with a spoon and never let him go until she had drained every ounce of sexual energy from him and had her fill!

It was wrong and it was stupid that she should feel so, but she just could not help herself. She was in love with the enemy and she wanted to shout it from the rooftops. But that was a big 'No No' under the circumstances and certainly not advisable. The others would chastise her for it she knew, but even so, she loved Strong with all her heart, there was nothing she could do and that's all there was to it.

Mairead loved Christmas, the feel of goodness and cheer in the air and, with very few exceptions, the charitable and happy people she met. But most of all, the children were the ones that made it for her. With their little smiling faces aglow and their eyes shining, and their hearts bursting with gladness and excitement, as the great day came ever nearer. What a great time, with everyone looking forward to the festivities and lots of turkey and pud.

But the children, they were the ones, for if not for them she would never have become a junior school teacher in the first place. She found herself reminiscing about the previous Christmas: the hall and class rooms were bedecked with pieces of holly and ivy, and paper chains strung all around, while in the main hall used for gym practice and prayers during morning assembly, stood a tall pine tree complete with bright fairy lights twinkling and an angel on the top.

For hours the children had been getting the classroom ready and now Tommy, the cheekiest, cutest six year old you ever clapped eyes on looked up at Mairead and said, 'What do you think, Miss?'

'It's absolutely lovely,' she said and then reminded everyone, 'Now then children, get in costume and on your marks and let's do one final rehearsal, before your parents turn up later tonight.'

The Nativity play went about as well as could be expected, what with Joseph and one of the three kings forgetting their lines in a momentary lapse. But otherwise it was all right and the children, finished with a flourish and an enchanting version of the carol, 'Away In A Manger': 'Away in a manger / No crib for a bed / The little Lord Jesus / Lay down his sweet head / The stars in the bright sky…'

The children sang it as only little children can, like little nightingales, and brought a tear to her eye and a lump to her throat.

Shaking her awake, Liam said, 'What's up, Mairead, have you been dreamin?'

As she came to, she sat up and wiped a tear from her eye and said, 'I'm goin' to miss the children an' Crossmaglen at Christmas.'

'I know,' he said and gave her a hug as she burst into tears again. 'But it just can't be helped,' as she sobbed into his shoulder.

It was days later and Martin Strong was back home in Borehamwood. After the initial searching questions and eagerness to hear everything he had to tell about the difficult situation in Northern Ireland, everything settled down eventually. Proudly he showed them a replica of a Republican flag, and pictures of him and his mates in combat gear and clowning around in the barracks, TV room and shower, half naked.

The time was only 11.30 a.m. and Strong sat in his front room bored half to death after going for an early morning run, followed by breakfast and a bath and reading the local rag from cover to cover.

Entering the room, his slight-built mother, with her brown hair in curlers, looked at him and began to dust the furniture. The normally active Strong could conceal his frustration no longer and threw down the newspaper with a sigh.

'That's a big sigh,' his kindly mother remarked.

'Yeah, I know, and though I love being on leave, well, it is kind of boring.'

'Why don't you go and see Alan?' his mother suggested.

'Yeah, I could, trouble is it's a week day and he'll be at work at the moment.'

'So he will,' she said and then: 'There's always the dog to take for a walk?'

'I took her up Manor Close earlier on,' Martin said, 'when I got your fags and the *Daily Mirror.*'

'Then I don't know what to suggest,' she said. 'You could always go and meet your father from work, if you want?'

'Yeah, I think I'll do that, I'll go for a walk down Shenley Drive; that should kill an hour or so.'

'You do that,' she said, and then with a pleading voice. 'And do me a favour and take Bonnie for another walk as well. You know how she misses you when you're not here, so spoil her for me, will you love?'

'Yeah, all right Mum,' Strong said, and went into the kitchen and picked up the lead from off the fridge by the back door. As soon as she heard that, Bonnie was there at his feet. The black mongrel dog as pleased as punch and wagging her tail as Strong fitted the lead on her collar and opened the door. The dog was raring to go, and so Strong had to hold her in a firm grip.

Joining him at the door Strong's mother said, 'And when you get back we'll have a good old fry up.'

'Suits me,' he said and they left the house.

The Special Air Service, without Colonel David Stirling, would have been no SAS as we know it. He was one of those unorthodox and independent thinkers that come along once in a generation to revolutionise and re-think the way we do things. In the case of the SAS, he threw out centuries of military conception when he set out his pencil-written proposal from a hospital bed in Cairo. He explained that strategic operations' demand for the achievement of success required a total exploitation of surprise and guile. The bedrock of its organisation was to be the formulation of sub-units of four men. Before that, battalion strength formations, whether airborne formations or commandos, had no unit smaller than a section or troop, consisting of an NCO plus eight or ten men. It was the NCO who had to do the thinking for the rest, noisily bringing up the rear. The SAS would instead have each of the four men in the unit trained to a high level of proficiency over the whole range of SAS capability. In addition, each man was trained to have at least one specialty according to his aptitude. In operations, often at night, each SAS man in his module had to exercise his own individual perception and judgement at full stretch. Stirling deliberately chose the number four to avoid the emergence of a leader in the general sense. This decision had affected regimental thinking ever since. Officers only joined the SAS after facing a barrage of criticism from other ranks and consequently restructuring their thinking about the men they would soldier with. The result of that had been to foster a unique military democracy within the SAS which changed the man from his former class and identity, exchanging it for a caste as binding as any family of which exclusion was the only decision he feared.

The tenets of the SAS as described in the regimental philosophy were as follows:

1. The unrelenting pursuit of excellence.
2. The maintaining of the highest standards of discipline in all aspects of the daily life of the SAS soldier.

They always reckoned that a high standard of self-discipline in each soldier was the only effective foundation for regimental discipline. The SAS brooks no sense of class, not even among the wives. It was the traditional idea of a crack regiment to be officered by the aristocracy, and indeed, those regiments duly won and deserved their great renown. In the SAS they share with the Brigade of Guards a deep respect for quality but they have an entirely outlook.

David Stirling was the man who started it all, a Cambridge educated Scots Guardsman who joined one of the first Army Commando Units in 1940. Stirling, at six feet five inches, was ideal commando material: an enthusiastic climber, and one who had explored the Rockies.

Later, he joined a unit known as Layforce, after its leader Robert Laycock. With the object of capturing Rhodes, Layforce was sent to the Middle East, but this did not work out. Because of operational demands it was scattered from Tobruk, in Libya, to Syria. An Oxford graduate and rowing blue, Jock Lewes of the Welsh Guards was a fellow officer of Stirling in the organisation. With the disbandment of Layforce, forced on them through shortages of ships and equipment, the two men sat and cogitated on other ways of hitting Germany's extended supply lines and fouling them up in the Western Desert.

By chance, a consignment of fifty parachutes on its way to India fell into the hands of Lewes off the back of a lorry in Alexandria. Though neither Lewes nor Stirling were trained parachutists they still rigged up a makeshift static line system, using seats as strong points in the clapped-out Valentia aircraft. This was far from ideal, as it was certain that the parachute canopies would snag the tailplane. It is no surprise then that this is exactly what happened to Stirling, and several tears were made in the canopy as his sixteen stone weight increased the speed of his descent to such an extent that he crashed on to rock-hard ground and injured his back so severely that both his legs were paralysed for some time.

Never one to waste time, Stirling in hospital soon wrote out his memorandum, arguing that strategic raids – deep penetration behind enemy lines – did not need the cumbersome naval backup of full-blown commando assaults. What Stirling proposed was simple and effective; the use of parachutist saboteurs, who would inflict a level of damage on enemy airfields as great as a force of commandos many times larger. And this is how the SAS came into being.

★

At the home of the SAS at Redhill, Hereford, the colonel was beginning his address.

'It is my pleasure, gentlemen, to welcome you to Stirling Lines.' The blossom was on the trees and it was Spring 1981. There were a dozen rows of hopeful recruits sat facing the colonel, over a hundred in all. The colonel smiled sardonically, for at his time of life, he long ago left behind the nervousness that those assembled was experiencing at the beginning of this new venture. A weather-beaten figure dressed in old camouflage windproofs and faded olive green trousers, he wore the famous beret and stood on the stage of the training wing theatre. Like him, the beret too was battered and creased and could have told many a story. He leaned on the lecturing stand and coldly eyed those before him. He was smoking a small Hamlet cigar and seemed very at ease in their company, waiting a moment for everyone to go quiet and hush their whispers. He had a well-chiselled face and unflinching gaze that seemed to penetrate their very being. Now and then, the colonel gesticulated with the swagger stick in his hand, using it to emphasise his point. Now, in a no-nonsense fashion, he started.

'First, let me tell you that this is not going to be a picnic. So put any notions of that out of your head. It will be hard and gruelling for you to earn this,' he said and briefly took the beret off his head with a sweeping gesture and returned it just as quickly. 'And don't think it won't!' he bellowed, as he swiped the lecturing stand and made everyone jump.

'To start with there are three weeks of rigorous selection,

during which you will be subjected to Sickener One and Two. These, I may point out, are aptly named and if you get through those there are another fourteen weeks of continuation training for you to endure. If you're still around after that, there is the parachute course and finally, combat survival training. And by then, you'll think you've got it in the bag, but we have been known to fail someone at the last moment.'

He swiped the lecturing stand again, and puffing on his cigar, he looked down at them and drilled his gaze into them, like hot brands. 'So be prepared to work harder than you have in your life and die a thousand deaths. And then, you may just be one of the lucky ones to be presented with this beret and its famous winged dagger badge.'

There was a murmuring of unease through the assembled men.

'No matter what you've heard, the fact is that the SAS is only as good as the people in it. That's a crucial point. They've got to be of the highest calibre, and special men, that can be called on in a crisis to act swiftly and decisively. Men with initiative, stamina, intelligence, patience and, believe it or not, a sense of humour. For that will come in handy on the most impossible of missions and when you least expect it.'

Flicking his ash in an old piece of shell casing on the stand, the colonel let that sink in as there were more hushed words in the audience. Then he went on, 'The SAS is different and a specialist group within the British Army. We move alone and in small groups – team players are not for us, but individuals who can survive and have the self-discipline to work as a team are.'

More murmurings, and then the colonel rounded off with, 'There has and always will be war, it's the same for every generation and every decade: Kuwait, Brunei, Borneo, East Africa, Aden and Belfast, they are part and parcel of the same world-wide malaise. When the do-gooders and liberals run out of solutions then they call on us, to crack the whip and get things done. No matter the terrain, no matter the continent and no matter the country, colour and creed, we'll be there and have to fight. It will be exciting and a great adventure, but no one will know you as heroes and there will be no fame and fortune. So put all notions of that out of your head. Here there will be no media and no publicity. You will be expected to move silently, do the job and melt away. What you do get is to be part of a unique family that will welcome you with open arms if you have the stamina, guts and willpower to be a part of it. Otherwise, then goodbye and we'll see you around.' With that the colonel walked off the stage and out of the room.

A sergeant shouted, 'Right you 'orrible lot, get yourselves over to the Quartermaster's in ten minutes and pick up your kit.'

Leaving the lecture theatre, Strong and the others made their way across the barracks at Hereford and passed the four-sided regimental clock, tall and gleaming in the sunshine, its bronze and woodwork shown off to full effect. Three of the large bronze panels were inscribed with soldiers' names, who had died and not 'beaten the clock' as the euphemism went. Behind the clock and over the back of the perimeter fence were neat rows of local houses.

The store resembled a free-for-all at a jumble sale, but even so, everyone was quiet and orderly again as they approached the corporal behind the counter. He did no more than glance at Strong and disappeared among the cubbyholes to reappear with an old-fashioned .303 Lee Enfield rifle that had to be cleaned, and a Bergen rucksack; it containing all the items Strong would need for the first phase of selection.

The Bergen was made out of untreated canvas, and in the rain and awful weather it would soak up like a sponge and increasingly became heavier. But Strong would learn that the hard way as no one told him. He opened the metal fastenings and immediately checked the contents. There was a sleeping bag, a patterned web-belt, a poncho for wet weather, two water bottles and carriers, then a cumbersome standard army prismatic compass. As well as that, there were detailed Ordnance Survey maps of the Brecon Beacons and Elan Valley, a brew kit and three twenty-four-hour ration packs all ready for the weekend and the affectionately known Sickener One.

There was a lot of banging and crashing around, and finally Strong came to and could focus with his eyes open. He glanced at his wristwatch. It was a little after 4 a.m. and he did not know if he felt half awake or half dead, as he threw himself bodily out of bed and got dressed and went through the motions of the early morning routine. His brain was on automatic and he didn't stop to think otherwise he would have just turned over and gone back to sleep.

Like everyone else he was outside in minutes and clambering on the nearest of six Bedford three-ton lorries taking them to the location of Sickener One. Heading in a westerly direction, they went north along the A470 tracing the River Wye, onwards to the Elan Valley and ever deeper into the Cumbrian Mountains of Wales. The names seduced you into thinking it was nice and conjured up pleasant thoughts about it all. But as Strong and the others were to find out, it would be anything but pleasant, as the Bedford convoy droned on its way and shook everyone's insides about as it did so.

Finally it stopped and Bill the instructor, the craggy-faced, taut-muscled Northerner more used to the jungles of Malaya than the Welsh mountains threw down the tailgate and told them to get out.

With a feeling of enjoyment in his tone he said, 'Get out boys, for this is where we seriously sort out the men from the boys and the particular weekend sportsmen and mummy's boys and whiners!'

As the men jumped out he grinned and said, 'Well lads, this is where it begins and the only way is up!' as he pointed at a great hill, so steep that it looked almost impossibly vertical.

'Shittin' Jesus,' said a thin-faced Geordie of the group. 'I couldn't have put it better myself.'

Strong clutched at his rifle, gulped and checked his kit and compass, and then set out to climb and sweat like never before. It was three days of physical and mental torture spent in a nightmare of pain, where the corporal, easily hiking over the hills, constantly turned up like a bad penny. He reminded Strong and the others that there were no shortcuts and that it was not just about succeeding in getting from point to point, but cross graining the hills. Which meant the agony of making it from trig-point to trig-point, and not ducking out and taking the more comfortable gentle slopes or a straight ridge linking the two. All the time, there was the corporal snapping at their heels and appearing from out of the woodwork, while making notes and suggesting you gave up. Telling you it would be better by far if you took it easy and dropped out and returned to your regiment, and that there was no stigma attached to those that did. Such suggestions had to be vehemently denied, and a moment's hesitation in pace or a brief halt, could be enough to get you rejected and told to go down to the roadside and wait; for the transport to pick you up.

It was during this primary phase that Strong developed a much needed sense of self-preservation, one that to a certain extent fed on the misery of others, when he saw them limp to a stop, or stop for a fag. That was when he told himself that he was not finished by a long chalk and that he should carry on regardless. That he had to selfishly look after himself and not worry about the welfare of the others. For it was every man for himself and the prize was the winged dagger badge and the famous sandy-coloured beret which he intended to wear with pride.

One scrawny mid-counties individual Strong came upon, exclaimed with his face contorted, 'I've gone and twisted my bloody knee, thanks to that fuckin' great hill!'

'Never mind mate,' Strong said, sweating profusely and jogging on, 'There's a lot more to come.'

Strong felt tired, but he was not yet out of it, as he left those who had dropped out whining behind him. Now the blood pounded in his head and his body moved in rhythm and regular time. Though the questions came thick and fast, and his brain swam and his vision was a blur as he concentrated on the next point. 'Why are you here? Who are you kidding? What are you doing this for? Where the hell are you going? Why do you put up with all this pain and sufffering? Why don't you stop a moment? Who the hell cares if you get through this or not?'

However, the answer was always the same as in the faint and dark recesses of his being he fought back, and his pride and stubborn resolve would not allow him, Strong, to fail. Not unless he died in the process sometimes that did not seem such a remote possibility. With complete and utter tunnel vision Strong trudged on, neither thinking of the future nor the past, but steadfastly and blindly concentrating on the moment for all it was worth. Just on that moment and on every tired footstep and every racking breath and aching muscle before the adrenalin kicked in. When it did, nothing was too difficult and nothing was too hard as his limbs became like liquid, not so jerky, but free-flowing and fluid.

Then he flew along, becoming a superman as the adrenalin surged through him and fuelled his body and made him lighter and quicker, eating up the distance between the points as his steely determination came to the fore. With the difficulty of the situation eased, he put the fear of failure to the back of his mind and gritted his teeth and got to the end of it at last.

Tired, knackered, he was transported back to camp to rest ready for the next day. The reason Strong could get through Sickener One was not only sheer determination, strength and stamina, but also good preparation. For weeks, ever since he had known about the acceptance of his application for 22 SAS, he had been hard at work sounding out people knowledgeable about such things. Consequently, when at home on leave he had been getting up early and doing five miles around Borehamwood.

Going down Bullwalk Road, he would head down the steep path past Bullens, running on past Associated British and turning left up the steep hill past the school, round the roundabout and pounding down the pavement then across another roundabout, and racing through the park, after passing the offices of John Laing construction, and up Manor Way and home again.

A good run that made his thighs ache and the breath rasp in his breast. His heart pounded as he finished each day with another gruelling run early in the evening to build up his physical fitness, doing lots of press-ups and knee-squats and legs and arms together. Eating like a horse, he had been packing away the carbohydrates, taking extra vitamins and eating lots of mashed potato and eggs and bread for energy. On top of that he had become a social pariah upsetting his mates by not going to the Red Lion pub, instead taking the opportunity of lots of early nights and rest and relaxation.

Then he had bought a bottle of surgical spirit, and began soaking his feet in it to toughen them up after every run and to aid against blistering, especially on the soles of his feet and heels.

When he had turned up at Hereford it had not taken him long before he visited the local shops and bought lots of cotton wool and padding for his boots. As well as that, he had visited the NAAFI stores and purchased dozens of Mars bars and pounds of boiled sweets to supplement a diet of extra vitamins and glucose tablets. For the aches and pains he bought painkillers and Ibuprofen ointment; and that is why, half his usual weight and looking a ghost of himself, he passed the initial phases of the selection process.

There was one more day to go, and the last was the worst of them. Day Five of Week Three was the endurance march, still known affectionately as Sickener One, and was the punishing climax to initial selection. An ultimate challenge of supreme strength, stamina, gut-wrenching motivation. A strength sapping forty-six miles of cross-graining the desolate Brecon Beacons, with heavy rifle, four water bottles slung from Strong's belt and a gargantuan 55 lb Bergen scything into his back at every step – and only twenty-four hours to do it!

Strapping on the Bergen, Strong found it almost impossible to move, the bag chafing his shoulders before he even took a step. Over thirty men moved off at first light from the railway station at Talybont, no longer used these days, a location some eight miles due east from the Storey Arms across the great expanse that was Pen-y-fan and its threatening hills. At the end of the hike would be only one Bedford lorry used to deliver the weary back to camp. Even then, there would be plenty of empty seats as more hopefuls were rejected and had to take the next train out of platform four.

The next twenty-four hours were comprised of Strong crossing jagged stones and squelching through horrible peat bogs, flattening green ferns then wading through stagnant pools of water, jumping from one reed clump to another. All this concerted effort caused friction and a razor sharpness as his boots rubbed on his ankles, causing him much distress and pain. Not for the first time he questioned the common sense of the whole thing, and whether to give up, the bile rising up in him from the pit of his being every time he did so, refusing to give in to it. The disgust and the hate and bitterness he felt at the thought of failure acted as the personal salvation of Strong as he fought the persuasiveness of the arguments beating in his brain.

The death of Spud, too, motivated him, being unresolved business as far as he was concerned; and the fact he still felt personally responsible for his death no matter what anyone said. All this deep feeling and emotion meant Strong had no intention of failing, and he made a vow he would finish and go on with the training, so that he could become even better at survival and learn the tools of his trade he would need in his vendetta with the IRA. He would hunt down those who had killed his mate, so that he could properly take his revenge and put to rest this emptiness and the burden that he was somehow responsible for Spud's death.

Chapter Eleven

They were stuck out the back at Gough Barracks, in a dull, grey Portakabin, no more than twelve feet long and six feet wide with two meshed windows admitting light, and a flimsy door at the end. It was not an ideal working environment, as desks and filing cabinets and chairs jutted out into the narrow passage between Dixon's desk and that of the chief inspector. Each found the other tripping over his things and each invaded the other's space involuntarily. To be perfectly truthful, after a month of this confinement and lack of space it was really getting on their nerves.

'I don't see why we couldn't keep the other office we had?' Dixon moaned, as he paced the room in a tense and frustrated mood.

'You know why, that was temporary and only while their own people were away sick and on holiday,' the chief inspector replied, as he sat behind his cramped little desk, his big knees banging on the wooden top.

'Pity they didn't all get the raving lurgy and die then,' Captain Dixon said, somewhat uncharitably.

Over the past three months, since being thrown together with the good captain, the chief inspector had got to know him very well and knew what was really aggravating him, which was the fact that he had not had a break in the case they were investigating on Tricolour-7 the IRA ASU unit and their known accomplices. 'You know you don't mean that,' the chief inspector said, 'and besides, we'll soon be able to return to Markethill when it's ready and then—'

'And when's that?' Dixon interjected, as he reached the door and turned round.

Being precise, 'Are you asking operational or just ready?' the chief inspector wanted to know, while reading a report and making a remark in red ink in the margin. His mind was half on what was before him and half on what Dixon was talking about. The chief inspector was no happier about things than Captain

Dixon was. But was more ready to put up with circumstances than his counterpart, knowing nothing could really be done about it.

Stopping his pacing and looking the chief inspector in the eye, Dixon replied, 'Ready. Well, operational, I suppose.' He leaned over his desk. 'Is there a difference?'

'Oh yes, there's a difference all right. You see it can be ready in a few weeks' time…'

'And operational?'

'Not for months yet.'

'But they said that six weeks ago.'

'I know, so tell me about it,' the chief inspector went on, 'but talking to the builders about the whys and wherefores is like banging your head against a brick wall.'

'That's appropriate.'

'If you don't believe me you're more than welcome to try yourself,' the chief inspector said. 'I'll gladly give you their number and you can call them.'

'No, don't bother,' Dixon said, suddenly disinterested as he pulled out his chair and sat down.

'I wouldn't mind so much, but going over this case just seems to make it worse week in and week out,' Dixon said, in a weary tone, as he picked up a whole load of files from his in tray and spread them out on his desk.

That was the nub of the matter, thought the chief inspector and that was what had really been bothering him.

'Well now,' the chief inspector remarked, 'there I think I can help you out. As I've read those reports cover to cover and inside-out almost and I think I've come up with three suspects for you.'

'Any blondes or redheads among them?'

'If you don't mind me saying it, but I reckon all of that was a red-herring. No pun intended.'

He was referring to the fact that they thought Mairead O'Connell was a redhead, and had arrested over fifty on sight at airports and ferry terminals and border checkpoints, questioning to no avail.

'Very good,' Dixon said, and took a sip of his coffee from the plastic cup in his hand. 'You know what I think, the only person who'd be able to recognise her is that soldier Strong, and when we capture her it will be essential to have him here to identify her.'

'When we do?'

'Wouldn't that be nice,' Dixon replied, taking another sip. 'Anyway, you were telling me of these three suspects you have.'

'Yes, that's right,' the chief inspector remarked, looking at the notes he had made on the pad before him.

'And they are?'

'Father Behan, the Undertaker and Michael O'Flaherty.' He leaned back in his chair.

'Nice try,' Dixon remarked sarcastically 'but we looked at them and decided the frame wouldn't fit.'

'I know, but just maybe we were a little hasty in rejecting them. What do you say?'

'You could be right, so convince me.'

'Father Behan – his Republican views are well known, and he takes every opportunity to spout them.'

'I know, just like your Paisley loves to slag off the RUC and the Brits and the government at Stormont. But it doesn't mean he's a member of the IRA, or in any way, shape or form an aid to known terrorists.'

'No, but he is connected with the Undertaker, who has premises not five minutes' walk from his church, Saint Mary's, and a hearse that is very often parked outside.'

'What do you expect? He's an undertaker for God's sake, it's natural that there's a connection between the priest and him.'

'Yes, I know and I accept that,' the chief inspector pointed out. 'But is it also natural that he should pass off a known terrorist, Liam O'Connell, as his nephew and part of his family at an army checkpoint?'

Sitting bolt upright, Dixon commented, 'When did that happen?'

'It was in a report and came from the interview we had with Strong, after he and his mates had been jumped by Tricolour-7. When their weapons were confiscated and later used in the attack on Markethill.'

'So you're telling me that Strong said he definitely identified him at the time.'

'Not at the time, but certainly later, when he saw a picture of him on a bingo-list and told his interviewer when brought in for questioning.'

So the three could be connected after all?'

'There's a good possibility that is so, yes.'

'What shall we do, then?'

'I suggest a surveillance on all three for a couple of weeks, night and day. And if we don't net any positive results from it, well at least we had a try.'

'And if we're barking up the wrong tree?'

'Then at least we haven't missed out by it.'

Being direct and assertive in his usual manner, Dixon remarked, 'Do it will you?' He crumpled his plastic cup and threw it in the waste bin. 'Get on to your boss and get the necessary authorisation and go ahead. We'll do it and see what crawls out, shall we?'

'Why not? We have nothing to lose by it.'

Looking at his counterpart, Dixon remarked, 'You're right, nothing but our jobs, that's all!'

'Our jobs, or Michael O'Flaherty.'

'Where does he fit in?'

'I'm not really sure, but out of the three he has the most access to all the RUC stations in the county.'

'How's that?' Dixon queried, racking his brain and going over the thousands of words he had read in the never-ending stream of files and reports so far compiled on the case of the Markethill attack.

'Don't you remember,' the chief inspector said gleefully, 'he's the sole Crankey agent for the area.'

'Still none the wiser,' Dixon said, not quite on the ball.

'He's the person responsible for the coffee machines in all the RUC stations.'

'So he is,' Dixon said. 'And if we can connect him to the other two?'

'We can announce to the world that at last these arrests are imminent.'

'Won't that be nice,' Dixon said, 'if we can just nail the tricky bastard.'

'We will,' the chief inspector assured him.

'You're confident all of a sudden,' Dixon remarked.

'It must be working with you that does it,' he said, and both of them smiled at that.

It was 8 p.m. before Michael O'Flaherty finally locked up the shop Richhill Electrics and headed down the main street, to the fine local hostelry and a night with his mates in which there would be much drinking and much reminiscing about the old times.

The two policemen, in plain clothes, sat in an unmarked car just around the corner, but far enough up the alleyway not to be seen by O'Flaherty as he walked by. Both from CID, one was a detective sergeant and the other a constable. In fact, they were the two men, 'Nasty' and 'Nice', that had originally set out to intimidate and question Fat Billy before Captain Dixon stepped in and, much to their annoyance, had taken control of the situation.

The thin faced, calmer one was DS Garrick, and the fatter more volatile one was DC Dougherty. Right now, they were just giving O'Flaherty ten minutes to disappear into the pub. Then, provided the coast was clear, the officers would leave the car and make their move.

As soon as O'Flaherty was out of sight, the two officers lost no time and let themselves in the back gate of the premises of Richhill Electrics. Quickly and quietly they approached the back door, and glanced around looking for a means of access to the place without making a noise or having to break in. There was a small side window open, but alas it was five feet off the ground and at an awkward angle for someone to put their arm through and reach down and turn the handle of the bigger window to the side of the door.

Spotting what he needed, Garrick ordered Dougherty, 'Bring those crates over here and let's see if they are any use.'

Dougherty did that, and Garrick stepped on the two wooden crates, one on top of the other, and got just enough height and leverage before the lighter of the detectives put his foot through the one on top. But that did not matter, as it had given him enough time to reach down and open the side window. He and

Dougherty gingerly climbed inside and stepped down to the floor from the window sill. It took a matter of minutes before Dougherty found the phone in the main shop, unscrewed the receiver and inserted the small bug, and then screwed it back on again. Torch in hand, Garrick helped Dougherty as he did so and then both men briefly searched the place and O'Flaherty's bureau. When they were finished they left as they came, this time Dougherty kneeling down while Garrick stood on the kneeling officer's back as the broken crates were no use any more.

Since then, it had been ten days of constant vigil and surveillance with three, teams of officers involved in a twenty-four hour period. No one had faith they would hit paydirt, and then all of a sudden it happened.

One fine morning about 8 a.m., soon after the previous officers had handed over the surveillance to Dougherty and his DS, Garrick took up the headphones and settled into position in the back room. He was in an empty premises several doors down from O'Flaherty's shop that used to hold a shoe repair and key cutting business until the owner had gone broke and moved away. The dirty windows and white-washed 'Vacant For Sale' notice gave nothing away of the secret goings on inside.

'Here we go again,' Garrick said, sat on the rickety chair and hunched over the large tape recorder monitoring the phone of Michael O'Flaherty in Richhill Electrics.

'Maybe we'll be lucky today,' Dougherty said, with his customary optimism.

'Yeah and maybe pigs will fly,' Garrick commented.

'More tea,' Dougherty said, as he rose from his chair and grabbed the mug off his DS.

'Yeah OK,' Garrick said, as he became more interested in the sounds in his earphones as he heard the phone ring.

A moment later, Garrick heard the phone being picked up and O'Flaherty said, 'Richhill Electrics, how can I help?'

Then a smooth voice announced, 'We need a job done quickly.'

'Wait a moment while I get a pencil,' O'Flaherty said, and Garrick heard him scratching around for one and then, pencil in hand. 'Go ahead with the job.'

'We need a rewiring and unitary circuit job done with a good safe estimate and not too much damage to Mrs Loughgall's house, ASAP. Can you help?'

'Certainly, I'll do that,' O'Flaherty said helpfully. 'Cash on the nail or usual terms?'

'Cash on the nail and will you drop the estimate off at the usual address when passing Markethill?'

'I'll do that, see you then.'

'Good and goodbye,' the smooth voice said, and put the phone down.

O'Flaherty, having received the coded message, was sure in what he had to do. It didn't take long before, tools in hand, he was loading up the small Thames van and locking the door. Sat behind the steering wheel and putting the vehicle in gear he drove off, not realising that the two officers were in an unmarked car and close on his heels. Garrick clicked away with a Japanese Nikon camera taking good photographs of O'Flaherty, the van and its registration, and of him driving off in it as well.

The small Thames van with O'Flaherty driving headed along the A3 road towards Portadown in the north and then joined the B77 in a westerly direction that took him to Loughgall and the RUC station there, a journey of some sixteen miles of unhurried driving.

Loughgall had a population of some 300 and was surrounded by 5,000 acres of apple orchards, most pretty at blossom time between the months of May and June. Situated at the end of an avenue of mature lime trees was the picturesque and gabled mansion of Loughgall Manor. At this time it was a horticultural centre, to be visited on open days and by appointment. The work of the estate included husbandry, sheep mostly, and plant breeding as well as research into fruit and vegetables. The distinctive yew walk was planted over 300 years ago by the Cope family who settled in 1616.

Protestant farmers in 1795 were responsible for, at Sloane's bar, establishing the Orange Order. Nowadays a museum, it was where there was a fight between the Protestant Peep O'Day boys and the Defenders of Catholic persuasion at the Diamond, just outside the village. The museum held a colourful collection of Orange sashes, flags and documents.

Michael O'Flaherty had never looked in on the museum and he did not have the time now, as he carried out his instructions from the IRA hierarchy. The two detectives in the unmarked car did their level best to look inconspicuous as they parked out of sight of the main stream of traffic and yet within view of Loughgall RUC station and the gates, wide open, that admitted both pedestrians and traffic to the RUC station and village.

O'Flaherty was in the RUC station for the best part of an hour before he came back out, got in his Thames van and headed out of Loughgall on the B77 heading south. Then on the outskirts of Armagh he joined up with the A28 that took him east. He stopped at a wooden sign that indicated Markethill and Newry at the intersection of the A28 Newry road and B3 to Markethill.

It was there that the officers took more pictures as they spotted O'Flaherty pull over and step out of the van. Making his way across the road and over to the sign post, he looked surreptitiously around and then put something into the hollow at the foot of the sign post. The two detectives, on foot, carried on observing the suspect from a tall hedge in a field alongside the road where their car was.

Minutes later, and O'Flaherty had turned his van around in the middle of the road and headed back along the A28 in a westerly direction and Armagh. That was when the two officers dared to leave their concealment in the field and recovered the contents of the envelope stashed in the hollow. Getting it out, they photographed the makeshift diagram that looked like it was of an electrical circuit. They did not know the significance of the find but knew it must be of some considerable interest.

Putting it back, they then lay in wait to see who would come and pick it up. Two hours later, they were finally rewarded by the sight of a motorcyclist showing up on a Triumph 250cc bike. Wearing a crash helmet and leathers, he left the bike on its stand and cross the road to the sign post. There he looked all around quickly, as they took several photos of the bike and rider and several more of him handling the contents, as he shoved his hand in the hollow. He returned to his motorcycle, put the stand up, kick-started it and roared off in the direction of the Armagh Road, with the detectives following at a discreet distance.

'What's the betting he takes us to Father Behan?' Garrick asked, as he sat in the passenger seat next to Dougherty who was driving.

'A fiver says you're wrong,' Dougherty said, making sure he eased up on the speed and gave the motorcyclist enough leeway as they followed behind.

'I just hate to take your money,' Garrick said, smiling sardonically.

Dougherty did not like admitting it later on, as sure enough the motorcyclist pulled in to the driveway of Father Behan's residence. But what was better than that, and what amazed them both, was that as the man removed his crash helmet, the motorcyclist was revealed as none other than the Undertaker. Garrick eagerly took the photographs of the suspect climbing off the bike, removing his helmet and entering the garage with the bike. He looked pleased as punch as he looked at Dougherty and said, 'I told you so.'

Now the chief inspector and Dixon had confirmation of their suspicious connection between the three men. Garrick knew his superiors would be very pleased with his work and that of his colleague, which was a bonus!

Having taken the photographs, Garrick looked at Dougherty and said, 'Let's go home, constable.'

Both Dixon and the chief inspector were most impressed with the photographs, observation and recorded conversation of O'Flaherty. The diagram was most welcome too and the little notes on it were soon deciphered as referring to the number of men, personnel and departments attached to the Loughgall RUC station.

The handwriting on the circuit diagram was professionally compared to notes found in the waste bin in O'Flaherty's kitchen at the back of the shop. A handwriting expert confirmed the notes were made by the hand of Michael O'Flaherty and the same as that on the diagram. With this evidence, and once the photographs had been printed and developed and blown up, Captain Dixon and the chief inspector had no trouble acquiring the appropriate paperwork and authorisation for the arrests, and warrants to search the premises of the three suspects at the same time. All three men, O'Flaherty, the Undertaker and Father Behan, were arrested in synchronised dawn raids by three teams of police officers that swooped quickly and without warning.

It was not yet light when the unmarked car drew up outside Richhill Electrics. No one was around and all was deathly quiet as two uniformed officers disappeared down a side street and round the back of the shops, to prevent an escape out the back. Captain Dixon and a uniformed constable stood on the doorstep and gave the officers enough time to get in position. Looking at his watch Captain Dixon said, 'Time's up, let's go,' as the constable knocked loudly on the door.

There was no answer as the person inside either didn't hear it or chose to ignore it.

'Right,' Dixon said, to the young constable in the RUC, 'Break it down and let's get inside before our pigeon flies!'

The sledgehammer firmly in his grip, he swung several times and smashed both the glass and the door in with no trouble. The noise threatening to wake up the whole neighbourhood. Cracking and splintering, the door gave way and both men rushed inside and upstairs and collared Michael O'Flaherty before he could fully awake. Dragging him out of bed they apprehended him and brought him downstairs.

Sat at the table in the poky and cluttered kitchen, with dirty dishes in the sink, dazed and half awake, Michael O'Flaherty demanded to know, 'And jus' what is this all about?'

To Dixon he looked like a short, silly, sleepy dwarf in his striped pyjamas, sitting there trying to comprehend what was going on.

Looking him square in the eye, Dixon said sharply, 'I am arresting you on suspicion of passing information likely to cause a breach of the peace and a terrorist incident.' Then he continued, 'You have the right to remain silent but anything you do say may be written down and used in evidence in court. Should you require a lawyer one will be provided.'

Standing up, the dazed Michael O'Flaherty said, 'You must be jokin', an' I'll jus' be goin' back to bed, so I will.'

'There's no mistake,' Captain Dixon said with relish. 'We have evidence of your connection with known criminals and so,

Constable, cuff him and we'll take him with us.'

The constable took out his handcuffs and before Michael O'Flaherty could move much more, slapped them on his wrists. Before he turned to go, Dixon issued one last order to the two constables who had effected entry from the rear. 'You two stay behind and tear this place apart. I want you to look for anything further that may be incriminating.'

Picking up the sledgehammer by the door, Captain Dixon, the constable and the prisoner made their exit and got in the car.

The law courts in Belfast are to be found sandwiched between Oxford Street and Victoria Street, tucked away in the centre of the city and housing the Crown Court. It was there that the accused, Michael O'Flaherty, Father Behan and the Undertaker, were brought for trial in the Autumn of 1981. After he and his family had been in protective custody for years, the prosecution finally produced their main witness, 'Fat Billy', for corroboration of the three men's guilt and wrongdoing.

Through one thing and another, and the fact that the jury was most scrupulously chosen, and many jurors discounted, the trial began late on Monday 28 October. Cameramen and crowds pushed and shoved for the best view outside the swingdoors that allowed lawyers, the public and defendants easy access.

The court case, like so many others, was expected to drag on for weeks, but even so, outside the court onlookers waited anxiously for a brief glimpse of the four accused as they arrived in Black Marias with a heavily armed police escort. There was a thick police and army cordon both in and around the building, and the people jostling for position at the metal barriers changed their minds every day as to the final outcome of the trial.

The courtroom was high-domed and situated in the old part of the building. Though only a modest size, the room reeked of history and the curious mysteries of other famous trials. The judge, Mr Justice Avery, was fifty-five and had a great deal of experience with such important trials, and had presided over IRA cases before. He was a thick-set man and looked rather forbidding, with his long, sombre face, his scarlet robes and powdered wig. Flanked by his clerk, the judge looked down imperiously from his solid leather-backed chair over a small but fairly crowded well, from where the barristers and their clients faced the jury over a packed two rows of eager pressmen.

The public were sitting on steeply ranged benches high behind the lawyers, that afforded them the best view in the house of both witnesses and defendants. The dock was below the judge's bench and to the side of him under thick-paned glass windows that allowed much needed light to flood into the dark and sombre room.

Should you want to go in or out of the court, there were two ways only: through a glass door to the public section, or down a steep staircase to the gloomy cells below.

Queen's Counsel and the representative for the Crown Prosecution in the criminal case was Mr Hodgkinson, a tall, upright man of forty-three, with a cheery disposition and many years of experience at the bar. Defending Counsel was Mr Taylor, fifty-one, who was short and fat and whose black silk gown gave him the appearance of a barrage balloon. His gait was slow and his speech ponderous, but his brain was soon to be shown to be razor-sharp.

There was a great hush as the judge took his seat and the court usher offered him a stick of chewing gum, which the judge promptly took and popped into his mouth. He made himself comfortable and faced the court again. Then, said the judge, 'Let the proceedings begin, and proceed with your opening argument Mr Hodgkinson, if you would be so kind.'

Pacing the floor, Mr Hodgkinson directed his argument both at the packed room and the jury at the same time.

'This, dear people, is a case where over the duration of the trial the prosecution will endeavour to prove the case that these men here seated are justly accused of the crimes that they are hereby charged with.' He stopped before the accused and stared at them unflinchingly, nearly unnerving Michael O'Flaherty who felt most uncomfortable at this treatment.

'That these men are guilty of aiding and abetting in the most heinous crimes imaginable. Namely, shootings, bombings and murder. That these men were responsible for the passing of information likely to cause a breach of the peace, and were culpable in the taking of innocent lives. Whether in the police and army or security forces, or ordinary citizens. Men so lacking in moral fibre that they secretly met with and passed information to the notorious gang of criminals otherwise known as Tricolour-7. Who in their parlance are an ASU, or Active Service Unit, that for months ran amok in this province and caused murder and mayhem wherever they sprang up next; with controlled explosions and personal attacks and fierce assaults on both the individual person in the police and army and surprise assassinations on both the body politic and the establishment.'

Having got their attention, Mr Hodgkinson waited a moment for that unpleasant information to sink in and then continued, 'And if you don't believe me, here are the photographs to prove it.' He handed out large six-by-ten colour photos for the jury to pass around and look at. Photographs that showed the carnage and the destruction and the wanton taking of life.

'This one in particular,' Mr Hodgkinson remarked, 'to the naked eye looks like a mere wreck of something. Well, let me tell you that moments before, that was a Morris Minor 1000 that was taking a woman who was a midwife hurrying to a young mother in labour.' He paused for them to absorb the shock and horror of it.

'That is before the controlled explosion in the road blew the little car to smithereens and showered debris over a one hundred yard radius, and instantly killed the woman at the wheel.'

A gasp of shock and horror run through the courtroom as people shivered at the ghastly thought. 'Yes, it's a horrendous thought and almost beyond belief that one human being should countenance such grisly violence on another human being. But there it is My Lord, ladies and gentlemen. Some people and some men show a complete lack and disregard for other people's feelings and other people's lives, and three such men are sat here today. And so, I ask of you the jury a guilty verdict, and from the judge presiding over these proceedings nothing but the stiffest and most stringent of sentences for all three men.'

Pausing for effect and playing to the gallery, he raised his voice, 'For I believe the punishment should fit the crime, once the evidence has been heard. These men are accessories after the fact and therefore I believe strongly and adamantly, like the public at large, that the punishment should fit the crime and these men pay for their wickedness to humanity!'

Spontaneous applause broke out from the floor and the public gallery at that, and the judge had to acknowledge it and let it run its course before he could continue. 'Thank you, Milord,' Mr Hodgkinson said, and sat down on his bench and immediately conferred with his juniors.

'Thank you, Mr Hodgkinson,' said the judge. 'And now you Mr Taylor, would you like to put the argument for the defence.'

'Yes, Milord, I would,' Mr Taylor said, and rose to his feet. He was not the type to go roaming all over the courtroom, and so he stayed put and simply let his quiet but effective voice and his proud stature sway his audience. Not one for dramatic gestures or displays of emotion, Mr Taylor spoke to those in the courtroom simply and without frills, telling it as he saw it.

'I thank my learned friend for his engaging if not deliberate Shakespearian drama, rather than an explanation of the facts.'

He stopped and smiled thinly at Mr Hodgkinson, who nodded back as Mr Taylor turned to the jury and said, 'But as always with Mr Hodgkinson, there is more emotion and sentimentality than actual fact. I grant you these pictures are a horrible sight, and every right-thinking member of society will be appalled by them. However, the fact of the matter is that none of these men took part in the grisly deeds so alluded to, and indeed were never anywhere near the scenes of these terrible crimes. It is a fact, ladies and gentlemen of the jury, that neither the police nor the army, with their range of resources, up-to-date, high-tech computer system, their comprehensive records and files of known suspects and their accomplices, their superior intelligence and their round-the-clock surveillance, even with all this, they cannot put any of these men "in the frame" as the common vernacular goes. All the evidence the prosecution has doesn't amount to a hill of beans, being in the main hearsay and circumstantial. For, quite simply, they were not there, and I think that the security forces and Mr Hodgkinson in particular are cock-a-hoop to have brought these allegations, and think rather foolishly that they have an open and shut case. But they will find as the proceedings endure, that the reality of the situation is quite the reverse.'

'That was a bit brazen,' the judge said to Mr Taylor before he sat on the bench.

'Yes, Milord,' Mr Taylor replied, 'but I felt it had to be said all the same.'

'Very well,' the judge said. 'Call your first witness, Mr Hodgkinson.

'I call to the stand Captain Dixon,' Mr Hodgkinson said.

From the floor, Captain Dixon in a charcoal grey suit made his way to the dock and was stopped by the court usher, who made him lay his right hand on the copy of the Bible and take the oath, repeating 'I swear to tell the whole truth and nothing but the truth, so help me God.'

'Good, take the stand,' the usher said as Captain Dixon stepped into the dock.

Rising to his feet, Mr Hodgkinson approached the dock. 'Would you like to tell us your name and rank in the army?'

'My name is Frederick Dixon and I hold the rank of captain.'

'What branch of the army is that Captain?'

'I serve in the branch of the army known as the Special Investigation Branch.'

'Commonly referred to as SIB, yes?'

'Yes sir.'

'And would it be fair to say that it's more concerned with intelligence than the police side of things?'

'That is correct, sir.'

'Even though it is an umbrella branch of the Royal Military Police, is that correct?'

'That is correct, sir.'

'Now then, is it fair to say that while there is some rivalry between SIB and our own RUC over these matters, that generally you pull together?'

'Generally we do, yes sir.'

'Now then, Captain, tell us who are Tricolour-7 exactly?'

'Tricolour-7,' Captain Dixon explained, 'are the IRA ASU that—'

'Forgive me for stopping you there, but could you shed a little light on these abbreviations you have just mentioned.'

'Certainly sir,' Captain Dixon said, 'glad to be of help. For the uninitiated, IRA means Irish Republican Army of course, and an ASU is an Active Service Unit in their parlance.'

'Thank you for that,' Mr Hodgkinson said, 'please continue.'

'The ASU known as Tricolour-7 comprises Mairead and Liam O'Connell, Sean Maguire and Padraic Duffy. All are young members of the Provisional IRA and until recently were not very important or too active in the violent side of things.'

'Their ages and background if you will?' Mr Hodgkinson enquired.

'Mairead O'Connell was a school teacher at Crossmaglen school and is the oldest at twenty-seven. Her brother Liam is twenty-five and the unit commander, and posed as a caretaker at the same school. Sean Maguire and Padraic Duffy are twenty-four and twenty-three years of age respectively, and both unemployed and drawing benefit from social services.'

'And where are they now?' Mr Hodgkinson enquired.

'All our intelligence points to the fact that they are probably lying low and possibly scouting out targets on the British mainland, as some two years ago we had reports they had boarded a ferry for Liverpool and have not been seen since.'

'In fact, it is fair to say that they have vanished and there's not a trace of hide or hair of them, yes?'

'Yes, that is correct.'

'And where is Padraic Duffy these days, is he with them?'

'I shouldn't think so,' Captain Dixon said, surprised by the question.

'And why should you sound so surprised at that idea, Captain?' Mr Hodgkinson said, as he worked his magic and slowly built up a picture and a framework that the public and press could equally understand and imagine.

'Because he's dead, that's why.'

'How did he die?'

'He died at the hands of two frightened constables, who shot him in self-defence on the night of the attack by Tricolour-7 on their RUC station at Markethill.'

More gasps of horror and shivers of excitement ran through the courtroom and in particular the public gallery, as the trial promised to be one of the juiciest for a long time.

'On the night in question, how did the attack on the RUC station in Markethill begin?'

'The four members of the ASU drove up in a funeral hearse, and from witnesses that were later hospitalised we found out that they chatted in friendly fashion before they shot the two constables manning the lookout post and barrier. They then lobbed a grenade through a downstairs window.'

Mr Hodgkinson let that sink in as well with those in the courtroom and was just about to continue, when the judge interrupted.

'This is all very interesting,' he said, 'but I fear my stomach thinks that my throat has been cut. Let's adjourn for some lunch,' glancing up at the clock on the wall, 'and reconvene at half past two, if that's all right with you and Counsel.'

'That's all right with me, Milord.'

'Good.' The judge stood up and left the courtroom, and with the usher entered his private chambers at the back.

Everyone in the gallery streamed for the exit, only too glad to stand and be able to stretch their legs and leave the sombre room after two and a half hours of sitting on the polished but uncomfortable benches. The pressmen were making a beeline for the telephones, to call their editors and give them the latest update on the trial so far, while staff and court officials made their way out with a little more decorum and composure.

One of them was the tall, slim Mary Edwards, who was a pretty brunette, twenty-four years old and a court stenographer. She took down the official version of the trial in the weird symbols that were shorthand. She got to the exit and walked out and down the steps. In front of the metal barriers, she was hailed by the driver of a white Zephyr taxi, who called out loud above the clamour of the crowd, 'Mary Edwards, your taxi, Mary Edwards!'

'Here I am,' she shouted back to the driver hanging out the door, as she hastened towards the barrier where a polite policeman waited to let her through.

'Excuse me, please,' she said, as the policeman responded.

'Certainly miss,' he said, as she made her way over to the taxi.

She pulled her collar up above her ears as a cloud broke over their heads and the heavens opened up and it began to pour. 'My goodness,' she said, 'cats and dogs,' looking skyward.

'Never mind me darlin',' the driver said, 'you'll be safe and dry in there, so you will.' He shut the back door and then got behind the wheel and drove off.

'Take me to the Crown Saloon.'

'I can do that me darlin',' the driver said and drove off down Oxford Street.

After a while, the worried Mary Edwards said, 'Hang on a moment, this is not the way to—' She had hardly uttered the words when the driver braked hard and she was thrown forward; producing a pistol, the driver hit her on the back of the head.

Letting her slump unconscious on the back seat, Liam O'Connell remarked, 'And that'll be enough talk out of you today.'

Mary Edwards always relied on the court usher to order her a taxi a good fifteen minutes before the judge trying the case adjourned it. It always went as smooth as clockwork: the judge would tip the wink to the usher and he, out of the goodness of his heart, would order the taxi for her. Being a nice old boy, he did it for her so as to save time and give her a longer break. The only trouble with the arrangement was that Mary Edwards, after months of the routine, had taken it for granted that he would oblige without fail, every time. There was just one catch to it, and that was that the usher was a man of strong Republican sympathies. And furthermore, he was a fully paid-up member of the Sinn Fein political party.

When the hour was up and lunch was over Mary Edwards returned to the courthouse, smiled at the relief policeman at the barrier and flashed her identity badge and sauntered through. Though dressed the same, no one noticed that Miss Edwards had substituted her usual spiked heels for thick platform soled shoes. As so often in life people hardly take a second look at people they know, and so Mary Edwards entered the courthouse without a backward glance and without being challenged.

Like all judges and persons of good breeding, Mr Justice Avery tended to enjoy his lunch unhurriedly in the comfortable setting of his private chambers. He paid the hotel around the corner for the service and convenience of delivering his meal, which on that day was roast beef and Yorkshire pudding followed by apple pie and custard. He tucked in heartily and wallowed in the quiet time away from the hubbub of the courtroom, the time being the last thing on his mind. He knew full well that the courtroom would take a while to fill. And besides, there was the faithful usher, who would knock on his door and remind him, and so he carried on eating, blithely unaware of anything else.

This meant that the courtroom itself was empty for just a little while. Time that would give Mary Edwards the breathing space to do what she had rehearsed and had been planned. Sat on a chair on the periphery of the court, she reached down and took off her right shoe and retrieved a cassette from the hollow. Deftly she primed it, and palming it she walked across the floor and towards the judge's bench. She was nervous and her heart was in her mouth, but even so she was fiercely determined.

Suddenly, someone opened the door and said, 'What do you think you're doing?' It was the usher.

She turned, and giving him a disgusted look replied, 'It's for the Cause.'

'That's all right,' he said, and closed the door and walked away.

Mary Edwards approached the judge's bench and pretended to go through the notes he had scrawled in his large book. Bent over the full waste bin at the foot of his chair, she concealed the cassette under the rubbish and walked away. Then quickly she resumed her chair, and changed the platform heels for the spiked ones in the plastic bag she carried, before leaving the room. She had to push through the pressmen and the public who were just now beginning to crowd back into the courtroom.

The cassette bomb was one of a long line of ingenious devices thought up by the IRA in this period. They had no choice, as better security on the ground saw a squeeze on explosives, which meant it was virtually impossible to carry out the familiar car bombing. The cassette was ideal, easily concealed and weighing a mere four ounces but containing a highly flammable mix of everyday chemicals. A detonator, battery and timing device were all packed into the small but deadly casing.

Within minutes, Mary Edwards had left the building and gone through the barrier again. She got in the back seat of the white Zephyr taxi that waited to collect her. Quickly the driver whisked her through the traffic and across Belfast to the waiting car ferry at the terminal.

The driver, Liam O'Connell, turned to his sister in the back seat and asked, 'How long till it goes off?'

'About now,' Mairead said, checking her watch. 'And then, it's goodbye to them, an' goodbye to you especially,' she continued, as she flung the identification badge of the court stenographer with Mary Edwards' name on the floor.

The court was reconvened, and the judge was saying, 'I hope you all had a pleasant lunch, and now let's get on with this afternoon's proceedings,' when the bomb went off.

There was a loud bang and a flash as the bomb in the bin ignited and a searing fireball engulfed the judge and everyone within a nine foot radius of it, the resulting blaze quickly escalating out of control and into a roaring inferno.

Chapter Twelve

When the bomb went off the blast and the flames caught everyone by surprise, including Father Behan, Michael O'Flaherty and the Undertaker, the three IRA suspects. Mr Hodgkinson was on his feet and about to approach the bench and commence the proceedings when the bin exploded, catching the whole of the first two rows of juniors and important lawyers and barristers, along with the jury, who were wiped out to a man in the growling fireball that overcame them. To everyone's horror, and that of Dixon himself, it seemed to happen so quickly – in milliseconds almost. One moment everything was all right and the next, a fiery inferno, in which everyone was trapped disastrously.

Fortunately for him, Captain Dixon was slow to get to his feet from his seat at the back of the court and enter the dock to resume his position on the stand, where he had left off before the judge had adjourned the proceedings in favour of lunch.

Straight away the judge went up in the blaze, and screamed shrilly as tongues of flame licked him from head to foot, while others caught in the scorching heat and flames walked around as lighted human torches. Fear and panic filled the room, and all was confusion and terror as the press and public alike scrambled hysterically for the swing door exit through the choking, thick smoke and wall of flames. The bright red and orange fire set alight to everything combustible it touched. Paper, soft cushions, furniture, floor and ceiling all caught light as the flames spread rapidly and the heat became intense.

Two minutes after the bomb had gone off and people were scuffling with one another and fighting and trampling to get out of the crammed exit. The place was pandemonium, and those still trapped in the room and not overcome by the heat and choking smoke were wondering if this was it, if they had had their chips and were about to face death and meet their maker.

Coughing and spluttering like those around him, Captain Dixon got out his personal radio and made contact with the chief inspector outside. 'There's been a bomb attack. Alert the emergency services and get as many people out of here as you can.'

'How are you going to get out?' the chief inspector asked.

'By breaking open the fire door near me and hoping to God it gives. No matter what, get Fat Billy from the cells and escorted away from here. Make him your top priority and get him out!' Dixon emphasised: 'He has to survive, otherwise all our work's going to go up in smoke.'

Taking in all the information, the chief inspector thought to himself that his army counterpart had made a rather sick pun, though he knew it would have been in bad taste to have reminded him of it in the circumstances.

Instead, he did as he was told and giving orders set into motion the rudiments of a safety and rescue plan for those still in the courthouse and dying.

The bar of the fire door was stiff with lack of use, and so Dixon coerced two other men to help him. Shoulders to the door and several hefty kicks later, it gave, and those still trapped, including Captain Dixon, poured out of the room and collapsed in the hallway heaving from their exertions and coughing and blackened with smoke.

It was now over seven minutes since the blast and time was running out, as timbers crashed to the ground along with plaster and brickwork and other debris. People screamed in horror and dread as the fire threatened to trap them, many were already trapped under the falling masonry and debris.

It was now that the first of the emergency services arrived; the fire brigade in their thick protective clothing, plastic helmets and breathing apparatus and masks. In their hands were high pressure hoses that connected to the fire pump outside and supplied the enormous amount of foam they used to quench the fire. They hosed down every surface and every wall and every charred object before them as they fought the fire, their valiant effort bringing the conflagration to a successful conclusion a couple of hours later.

Meanwhile, Captain Dixon had recovered, and though a little shaken and still coughing he formulated a plan in his feverish brain. There was no time to lose, and he pushed and shoved his way through the ambulance men and those survivors milling about in the crowded corridors, still wandering aimlessly and muttering to themselves in shock.

Making his exit, the chief inspector said to Dixon, 'I got your message loud and clear. Now what do you want me to do?'

'Act on your initiative and take care of things here,' Dixon commented, already walking past him.

'But what do I tell my superiors?' the chief inspector said worriedly, as he saw a row looming over this.

In his mood Dixon said, 'I don't care, tell them anything. Only don't bother me, this is an army matter now.'

'So where are you going?'

'To the airport.'

'Why?' the chief inspector said out of sheer exasperation.

'To get out of this country.'

'Why?' the chief inspector queried again, not knowing what else to say, as he trotted after Dixon.

'I should think it was so obvious, a blind man could see it. Fat Billy is not safe here, and so I'm taking him where he will be.' With emphasis Dixon stated, 'I've put too much into this to lose him now.' And with that, he climbed into the passenger side of the Black Maria and ordered the driver, 'Let's get moving, and don't spare the horses.' He shut the door and they moved off.

The Black Maria escort included a patrol car with siren screaming and a motorcycle outrider at the front. The small cavalcade hastened to RAF Aldergrove, across Belfast and out of the teeming streets, pulling out all the stops and accelerating through red lights as they hurried with their precious cargo of Fat Billy to the key military airbase in Northern Ireland. Captain Dixon was sure in his purpose and determination to keep his agent Fat Billy, the key witness in the trial, alive to testify against Mairead O'Connell and the bloodthirsty gang of criminals that was Tricolour-7.

The sign stated categorically, 'MINISTRY OF DEFENCE LAND – KEEP OUT. ALL ENTRY PROHIBITED EXCEPT BY AUTHORIZED PERSONNEL.' The escort approached the airbase along the road that ran parallel to the six foot perimeter fence. Turning in to the base, the outrider and everyone else came to a complete halt at the barrier across the road that barred their path. A corporal in RAF uniform stepped forward, and rather officiously challenged them, especially Dixon as he climbed out ready to deal with the guard.

'Can I see your identification, please sir?'

Dixon played along and produced his wallet and his SIB warrant card.

The guard stared at it a good while and inspected it and then finally announced, 'What's this, then?'

'That, Corporal,' Dixon said politely, 'is my Army Special Investigation Branch card.'

Handing it back to Dixon the guard explained, 'It may be, sir. However, it won't cut any ice here, I'm afraid.'

'Pity that,' Dixon said, 'I was so hoping that it would.'

'Well it won't,' the officious little corporal stated. 'So you lot can just turn around and go back where you came from.'

'And is that your final word on the matter?' Dixon asked.

'It is, sir,' the guard said, rather pleased with himself. 'So you and your chums can just hop it!'

'Fair enough,' Dixon said, as he approached the motorcycle outrider who had his stand down and his feet on the ground with the bike parked.

'Give me your pistol please, Patrolman?' Dixon said, and the patrolman snapped his holster and handed him his sidearm, adhering to his orders to give the good captain every assistance.

'Thanks. Now then, where were we?' Dixon remarked, as he turned on the corporal and pointed the Walther PPK at him. 'Do you know what this is, Corporal?' Dixon asked, less politely.

'It's a gun, sir,' the corporal said, looking a little less officious now.

'Yes, it's a gun. A gun that's going to blow your head off, if you don't do as I ask.'

'I'm afraid I can't do that,' the corporal started to explain, while Dixon took off the safety and tightened his finger on the trigger.

'Now then, I'm going to count to three,' Dixon said, in a firm voice. But he need not have bothered, as after the count of one, the corporal jumped to it and lifted up the barrier hurriedly.

As he jumped back into the Black Maria and the patrolman kick-started his motorcycle Dixon warned, 'And no going to let the control tower or your CO know the minute my back is turned.'

As a reminder Dixon shot out the window, and with several shots he destroyed the gate telephone in the hut next door to the barrier. 'And remember, I'm coming back,' Dixon remarked as he shut the door.

The escort sped through the open barrier and on to the military airbase, past the large hangars and refuelling trucks, the radar moving around on a concrete bunker, and on to the concrete apron. They finally halted beneath the concrete and glass control tower that loomed large above them.

Out jumped Dixon and the four armed policemen from the patrol car, with Heckler and Koch automatic weapons in their hands. Stationing two there, Dixon took the two others into the building and climbed the stairs two at a time until he reached the inside of the control room at its summit.

Every control tower was similar to look at, though no two were exactly the same, but they all had the same job to do and that was controlling the planes. Airbase control had sole charge of all movement on the ground, on the taxiways and runways. It also directed the planes on their final approach to the runway and the first minutes of their take-off. Airbase control was to be found in the upper part of the tower, with windows all around allowing the controllers peripheral vision of the whole of the concrete apron.

Just below the control room was a darkened radar room, where Approach Control guided the planes in towards the airbase. Each operator was responsible for keeping track of several planes at once. The operators had to concentrate hard and usually only worked for two hours at a time before having a much needed half-hour break. However, a plane could not take off unless the pilot had called the control tower for permission to begin its flight.

First of all, Dixon and his men burst into the radar room of Approach Control, darkened so that the operators could clearly see the radar screens before them more easily. One of the operators sat at his screen was saying, 'You're clear for landing, Delta One Nine.'

'Roger and out base,' the pilot of the aircraft said. 'Am turning now and heading for home, approaching glide path.' The aircraft was some seven miles away.

One of the operators looked up at the strangers in the doorway and said, 'What do you want?'

'Never mind,' Captain Dixon said. 'One wrong move out of you gentlemen and this man will blow you and your screens away.'

He stationed one of the two patrolmen and then, with the other armed policeman, burst into the control room above. The controllers sat behind the green tinted glass, were startled.

'My name is Wing Commander Bostock-Smith,' said the man rising with the handlebar moustache and public school tones. 'What is the meaning of this outrage, man?'

Producing his pistol, the Walther PPK, Dixon said, 'This is a hijack. I want a plane fuelled and ready to take me and one other man out of here.' He handed the commander a piece of paper with the coordinates and final destination scrawled on it.

'Don't be ridiculous,' the fifty-year-old wing commander said. 'Are you off your head, man, or what?' as he glanced at the paper.

'I suspect I am,' Dixon stated smiling. 'But anyway, I want the plane double-quick, and you're coming with me, Wing Commander.'

'What as?' he queried in a stunned voice.

'My hostage and ticket out of here,' Dixon said. 'Now jump to it.'

The windows had been smashed, and glass and timber and debris from the roofless, torn building littered the inside of the courthouse on Oxford Street. It looked and smelt horribly like some sickening charnel house: outside on the grass verge a row of blue body bags was visible, and growing longer as the search and rescue teams probed inside the gutted building.

Ambulance men played an important role ferrying the patched-up burn victims and administering first aid in a procession of green and white ambulances parked in and around the grounds. The paramedics hurried to and fro with stretchers. And all the while, the hand-held, lightweight cameras of the news teams focused on the strained and serious expressions of the rescuers and the rescued. The firemen put their axes away in their scabbards, packed up the kit and rolled up the long, dripping hoses. The police and army were not standing by idly either, as they did their best to cordon the place off, direct traffic and hold back the eager press and ghoulish onlookers.

Uniformed constables and women police officers took statements from surviving eyewitnesses and saw to the injured, as they were given tea and sympathy while they sat outside in the drizzling rain. The pictures of the news team relayed the usual aftermath of a disaster or terrorist incident.

'Today, shortly after 2.30 p.m. there was a bomb explosion here at the law courts in Belfast. Dozens of people were caught in the blast, many were hurt and killed,' Dennis MacMourne began in sombre tones, as he stood before the smoking shell of the building.

'Has anybody been able to ascertain how the bomb was planted?' Andrew Simmons asked the correspondent.

'Yes, it seems that a court stenographer on her lunch break was abducted and then impersonated by a female bomber, who, wearing her clothes and personal ID, gained access to the court, thereby eluding the high security surrounding the immediate building and this high-profile criminal case that had only begun only a matter of hours previously.'

'I suppose it is a foregone conclusion that it was the IRA, in a bid to kill the key witness for the prosecution?'

'That's right, Andrew,' Dennis MacMourne said. 'A man that I am told had been a long-serving member of the IRA and an army agent for years, and who up to this trial had been in hiding for over two years.'

'Was it Tricolour-7 and the female bomber by any chance, Mairead O'Connell?'

'The police and security forces here on the spot, and intelligence services now investigating it, are almost certain that that is the likelihood.'

'How and where was the bomb planted?'

'From eyewitness accounts it would seem that the bomb exploded on ignition in a bin, just feet from the judge's bench.'

'What kind of a bomb was it, and how many were injured?'

'Eyewitness accounts say the bomb was only small, probably a cassette bomb that the IRA have recently developed and used on attacks on DIY and furniture shops and places of that nature. Highly volatile and easily concealed. The death toll is thirty-five and still rising.'

'What will they think of next,' Andrew Simmons said, most uncharacteristically, to himself. 'And who abducted the court stenographer, do we know?'

'From a description by the woman, although she was shook up and frightened by the incident, police have got a sketchy idea. But everything seems to point to Liam O'Connell.'

'The female bomber's brother, is that correct?'

'That's correct, Andrew.'

'Two members of the Tricolour-7 gang that had gone to ground?'

'That's right, but the pointers are that they did this and fled very quickly, and the police do not hold out much hope that they will apprehend the gang on this side of the Irish Sea.'

'There have been reports coming in, as yet unconfirmed, that some army officer, soon after the bomb explosion, got hold of the key witness and ferried him out of the building with an armed escort and took the man concerned to an airport. Is that true, and can you shed any light on this?'

'It is in fact true, Andrew. The officer was, I believe, Captain Dixon and in charge of the prosecution witness's security. And so he took it upon himself to get the witness out and, as you say, escort him to RAF Aldergrove.'

'What happened?'

'Well it seems from the accounts we've received that the captain went duly mad and threw his weight around and demanded a plane be fuelled for a secret destination. Then at gunpoint he took the wing commander as a hostage, and shortly after he and the prosecution witness took off in a VC10 for their secret destination.'

'Do we know where that is?'

'It could be anywhere, the authorities are not saying. Some have suggested Gibraltar, but no one really knows.'

'I see, well, thank you as always Dennis,' and Andrew Simmons in the London studio turned to the rest of the day's news.

Gibraltar is a UK territory on the southern tip of Spain. Most of it is a great rock that rises 1,400 feet above the blue waters of the Mediterranean Sea. The rock makes Gibraltar look as if it is a giant's castle, but in fact the colony was a fortress guarding the western entrance to the Mediterranean. Cut inside the rock there are ten miles of tunnels for storing the supplies of food, water and ammunition needed in days gone by; and there was also plenty of room for soldiers and a hospital.

Gibraltar has a harbour and dockyard, where ships sail to and from the eastern Mediterranean, and stop to refuel and take on fresh supplies. About 30,000 people live on Gibraltar, mostly of Italian and Spanish descent. The Rock is a tourist centre also, people flocking to see the naughty Barbary Apes, who clamber over the Rock and the old Moorish castle. Africa lies across the Strait of Gibraltar, which is only nine miles at its narrowest point, the ferry boats plying regularly between Gibraltar, Morocco and Tunisia.

Deep in the bowels of the Rock, two men sat in a poky little office with the door open, creating a well-needed draught. A single, bare wire hung from the nicotine yellowed ceiling, with a light bulb to illuminate it, while a dirty grey and dented filing cabinet held a buzzing fan that blew cool air to the stifling room. The two men sat there with glasses in their hands, filled from the Grant's whisky bottle on the desk before them, as they listened intently to the news report from Dennis MacMourne in Belfast.

When it had finished, Captain Dixon got up and switched the TV off and said, 'Well, they fell for that, hook, line and sinker.'

'Let's hope the IRA do too,' the wing commander pointed out, fingering his handlebar moustache.

'I'll drink to that,' Dixon said, and chinked his glass with the other man's. 'And I want to thank you for your part in this little ruse of ours.'

'Will it work?'

'God knows it better. These bastards have been giving us the run-around for too long.'

The assailant came at him with the knife and Strong was forced to defend himself. So he turned inwards on the attacker and grabbed the sleeve on his leading hand with the knife in it with his left, then grabbed the jacket collar as well, and with a good grip on that swivelled inside the man and attempted to throw him over his shoulder.

But to no avail, as it ended messily and not quite right. Out in the field it could have been dangerous and he could have lost his life. However, it was fortunate for Martin Strong that all this was taking place in the barracks gymnasium at Hereford, home of the SAS, where Strong was just one of four men in his unit that wore judo gear and tie belts. They were practising their moves and falls on the rubber mats on the polished floor.

'No no, no no!' the wiry instructor, who was a Northerner and seasoned campaigner in the regiment shouted. 'Don't chuffin' play with 'im, take out the bastard, instead.'

Panting and heaving, 'I'm trying,' Strong said annoyed. 'I'm bloody tryin'.'

The instructor gave him a cold-eyed look and commented, 'You don't need to tell me you're tryin'. I chuffin' well know that. Now do it again.'

There was a collective sigh, and, 'Oh Sarge, not again,' from the assembled lads.

'Only this time stop being bloody ballerinas and do it as if you mean it.'

So Strong and the assailant, East Acton, squared up to one another again. And East Acton lunged at him again with the knife, and Strong was about to grab his sleeve when the instructor intervened.

'No-no, no-no!' the instructor stated emphatically. 'You two are like a couple of chuffin' prima donnas for God's sake.' Not happy with the situation he said, 'You sit down on the bench over there,' to East Acton, as he took no more part and sat on the sidelines. 'And you, Strong, take the knife and come at me like you're going to stab me through the heart.'

Strong did, and to his amazement and his embarrassment, and the hilarity of his mates in the unit, ended up flat on his backside in no time at all.

'That's how you have to do it,' the instructor said, 'with a fluid movement like in the Castrol Oil ad on TV.'

Looking at Strong he said, 'Right, get up and sit on the bench.'

'Now you,' the instructor said, pointing to Man United. 'You come at me from behind and stick this gun in my back,' handing him the weapon.

'What me?' Man United said, not wanting to be shown up like Strong.

'Yes, you. You've been laughing as much as anyone. So let's see how you fare.'

The instructor turned his back and Man United duly stuck the gun in his back. Immediately the instructor reacted and back-heeled him in the shin, knocked the gun up and elbowed him in the face, then knocked him to the ground and bent his arm half way up his back.

'Agh, let me go, it hurts,' Man United squealed like a stuck pig in pain.

Unconcerned, the instructor carried on calmly telling the others, 'From here you can question the assailant should you wish to. Otherwise, chop him at the base of the neck and put him out of his misery.'

Suddenly, the colonel appeared in the room and approached them. 'Soon be finished here sah,' the instructor said, letting up the winded and pained Man United.

'Never mind about that,' the colonel commented. 'These lucky lads are off to the sunshine and Gib. Get packed now. You leave within the hour.'

The flight was a Britannia Airways one, and had flown all the way from Gatwick and grey, miserable England to arrive over blue skies and sunshine over the Mediterranean. The announcement over the intercom caused a ripple of expectancy to run through the passengers seated on board the aircraft.

'This is the captain speaking. Will all passengers please put the safety belts on as we are about to land at Gibraltar airport.'

With that, the red sign went on in the cabin and out again as those nearest the window saw the landing gear come down. Mairead O'Connell was one of them, as she looked out at clear skies and the wheel coming down under the wing. She felt herself suddenly excited at the prospect of what the coming week might bring, looking out at the blue sea and the great, magnificent rock looming before them as the plane made its gradual descent on to the runway. The runway was nothing more than a single landing strip beside the packed and picturesque small boat marina.

'Here we go,' Mairead said to Liam, her brother, beside her. He winked at her before turning around and looking at Maguire seated behind him.

'Ready?' he asked.

'Ready as I'll ever be,' Maguire shot back.

'Good,' he said and looked at his sister again.

'Good,' she said. 'Let the adventure begin.'

'Yes,' Liam said, 'let it begin and be over again just as quickly, so that we can all go home just as quickly.'

Picking up on the pessimistic tone, Mairead asked, 'Are you worried about this?'

Shrugging his shoulders, he replied, 'No, I'm not worried. What makes you think that? We are only going to an English speaking state with English speaking police and military and we're Irish for God's sake.'

'Stop worrying,' Mairead commented, 'lots of Irish people come here.'

'I know, that's what I'm afraid of,' Liam remarked.

Kissing him on the cheek, his sister said, 'Stop worrying, we have friends here and they will help us, so it won't be as if we're all alone.'

'No, sometimes I wish we were though.'

'It will probably be all right and you will have worried for nothing.'

'Maybe, but someone has to. You can't just enter into this blind.' And with that, the plane touched the ground and the wheels bumped on the tarmac as the plane taxied to a halt.

This was when the passengers craning their necks out the windows got a glimpse of the least attractive part of Gibraltar, that of the industrial area along the north front. Here names such as Lipton, Bland, Saccone, Speed and Gaggero reminded you of those seen in the main street shops. The warehouses and workshops were divided in two by the 2,000 yard runway, not long enough to take the largest of jet aircraft.

Both civil and military planes shared the airport, and it was at this time in the early 1980s that the Vulcan bomber, 'City of Gibraltar', was proudly put on regular display where the road crosses the runway. It was there now, but only hours before it had flown in a four-man SAS unit. The four-man IRA ASU – the usual three with the addition of Tommy Boyd, a new member – had no inkling of this however.

Not many people know it, but Gibraltar airport is unique in being the only one in the world that has an international highway crossing its runway. But some of those that did were Mairead O'Connell and Liam, and Sean Maguire, their friend; and also the four-man unit of the SAS headed by Martin Strong, Man United, East Acton and a new member, Dave Forrester.

The three Irish terrorists soon left the plane and headed through the small terminal and past the seven check-in desks, restaurant and duty-free shop. They carried their hand-held luggage of zippered holdalls with the GIB labels on them, and had their false passports checked and unbeknown to them, their photographs taken by an army intelligence man behind the scenes. During their exit they only made one momentary stop, and that was for Maguire to visit the toilets and Mairead to make a quick phone call. She looked at the piece of paper in her hand, memorised the number and screwed it up and threw it in a nearby waste bin, not knowing that soon after it would be picked up out of the bin when she had gone.

The phone ringing in her ear, she waited patiently for it to be picked up at the other end and said, 'The Emerald Isle is always green.'

The voice the other end responded, 'Always green and always raining.'

'So what do I do now?'

'Book in at your hotel and you will be contacted by tomorrow.'

'Very well,' she said, and put the phone down.

Walking away from the telephone, her luggage in hand, Liam caught her up and said, 'Well, what did he say?'

'We'll be contacted.'

'Right,' he said, and all four made their way outside to the taxi rank. They climbed in to the first empty one.

'Where to?' the taxi driver asked Liam, as they settled with the luggage in the back.

'The Gibraltar Beach Hotel, please driver,' Mairead said politely.

'It'll be my pleasure,' the taxi-driver said. It was Man United, in his casual dress of open-necked, colourful shirt and beige hipster pants.

Settling back in the seat, Maguire remarked, 'Mmm, I think I'm going to like it here.'

Part Four
The Rock

Chapter Thirteen

Day One on the Rock

Strong, Man United, East Acton and Dave Forrester were in the 'basha' sleeping quarters, and getting some shut-eye after the jetlag of the journey and a good few beers. They had also watched a really dreadful Wilfred Hyde-White old black and white movie in the TV room, part of the extensive barracks and accommodation for the troops within the miles of tunnels hewn out of the sheer rock.

When they woke up they started a pillow fight out of boredom, and in between the stupidity, East Acton stared at the new member, the flap-eared, pimply-faced Dave Forrester, and said, 'There's something wrong here. You ain't got a nick-name. Everyone in our unit has one of them.'

'That's right,' agreed Martin Strong, stopping a while from bashing East Acton with his feather-filled striped and stained pillow, coming apart at the seams.

East Acton chipped in too: 'We'll have to remedy that and quick. So what sport do you like?'

'Swimming,' Dave Forrester, the shy twenty-three year old, said.

'Then that's it,' Man United said with glee. 'We'll call you Fish, OK?'

Smiling and a bit embarrassed, 'OK,' he said. 'Fish it is,' glad that he was, for the moment at least, being accepted as one of them.

Then he turned to Martin Strong and asked, 'What's yours then, and why?'

Quick as a flash East Acton piped up, 'Clown, for being in love with an IRA tart, that's why.' At which, Strong resumed the pillow fight and even began using his fists, punching East Acton in the arm and leg.

Then a sergeant entered the 'basha' and called out, 'Strong, where are you?'

'Here, sergeant.'

'Well get along to the CO's office a bit smartish. He wants to see you.'

When Strong entered the room, there was the colonel of Stirling Lines, with his tough, craggy face, and one other person at the desk with him. He turned round as the colonel introduced him.

'I think you know Captain Dixon, don't you?'

'Captain Dixon,' Strong said, surprised to see him.

'I'm flattered you remember me. It must be all of three years since then. Your CO tells me you've served all over the world, and in Gibraltar in particular, with aptitude and leadership at all times.'

'Thank you, sir,' Strong remarked. 'How could I forget you after all that Mairead O'Connell business.'

'It's the Mairead O'Connell business that I've come about now,' he said, and pulled out a chair as the colonel excused himself and left. 'I wanted to have this private chat with you as I wanted to determine whether you are fit mentally as well as physically for the most important mission of your army career.'

'I think so,' Strong said, a little hastily.

'You're over the girl and can deal with this mission coolly and dispassionately when she is an integral part of it?'

'I think so,' Strong said, a little too eagerly, his mind refusing to listen to the complex arguments for ducking out of it.

'Good, then send in the others,' said Dixon as Strong opened the door and the rest, dressed in green t-shirts and shorts like Strong, entered. 'Now then, listen up and listen good,' Captain Dixon said, as they lounged around the room. 'This is the most important missions of your lives and no one had better fuck up! Or it'll be curtains for the trooper concerned and any successful outcome.'

'What is the nature of the mission?' Strong asked.

'To finish off the IRA ASU known as Tricolour-7. To finish all business with them here on the Rock, where we have the advantage, the manpower and the resources.'

Tentatively, Dave Forrester asked, 'When you say finish you mean…'

'I mean exactly what I say,' Captain Dixon said, with a hard edge. 'No one in that ASU leaves the Rock, unless it's in a body-bag. Is that clear?'

'It's clear,' they all chorused.

'Are you sure?' Dixon asked, peering into the face of Martin Strong.

'Crystal clear.'

'What about the police?' East Acton asked. 'Won't they have something to say about that.'

'The police are not to know and will not be notified of our presence and intent. So as always the Special Air Service will go at it alone.'

'Should they try to intervene, what do we do?' Man United wanted to know.

'Take care of them, but for Christ's sake don't harm them or injure them. Or you'll face criminal proceedings afterwards. Any more questions?' Dixon asked.

'Then report back here in two hours' time for full briefing after weapons training on the indoor firing range.'

They tramped down the corridor and soon entered the firing range, where they picked up their own Browning 9mm high-powered handguns and started to familiarise themselves with their weapons. On the table were the Heckler and Koch MP5 machine guns first used in the Iranian siege in London the previous year.

They put on their safety glasses and ear-muffs to protect their eyes and ears against the noise and loss of hearing. It was not long before they were loaded up and shooting the hell out of the metal targets with a man silhouetted on them.

★

Day Two on the Rock

The Gibraltar Beach Hotel was known as the Both Worlds Aparthotel, that is, until it was taken over by Best Western

International in November 1986. It was the longest building on the Rock, stretching from one end of Sandy Bay to the other. It had 123 rooms, of which only a dozen were in the conventional hotel while the others were self-catering apartments. It was these the four Irish terrorists had plumped for, not expecting their stay to be long.

There were others on the beach with their sun umbrellas up and their deckchairs and mats out, but there was one girl that knocked the spots off all the others. She looked gorgeous, her slim and curvaceous body on show and her long limber legs splayed out in front of her as she lay on her back in the shade. Her large breasts rose with the motion of her breathing and the skimpy black bikini hardly held her ample charms.

The woman was on the beach soaking up the sunshine in the small hours of the afternoon. For even though it was November, it was dry and the temperature was fast approaching the mid-70s mark, as the sun reached its zenith in a cloudless sky. Running his eye over every gorgeous square inch of her, Strong felt the sap rise in him as he looked at her through the magnification of the German-made Zeiss binoculars. He was leaning on the rail of the balcony from another of the apartments overlooking the beach.

Suddenly his reverie was disturbed by a knock at the door. Strong put down the binoculars and walked across the apartment. He opened the door, and there stood a small boy. '*Senor*, the lady on the beach she says will you join her?'

'How much did she give you to tell me?'

'One pound, *senor*.'

'Then here's another,' Strong said, as he handed it to the boy. Grabbing the note quickly, the boy soon ran off with it leaving Strong with his thoughts as he found himself locking up behind him and entering the elevator to take him down to the beach.

It was not long before he was making his way across the soft sand and towards the blue Mediterranean lapping at its edge. She heard his footsteps, and looked up. 'I wondered when you would get here.'

'Getting a nice tan?' Strong replied conversationally.

'You know I am,' she said, smiling. 'You've been watching me for about the last hour.'

'How did you know it was me?'

'I felt your eyes boring into my hot flesh,' she said teasingly.

'How do you know I wasn't birdwatching?' he said, as he sat down on her towel and she sat up next to him.

'Oh, you were,' she laughed. 'Only it was the Mairead O'Connell late nesting variety.'

'And which are you today,' Strong asked with a hint of sarcasm, 'blonde, brunette or redhead?'

'As you can plainly see, I am a brunette.'

'A brunette today, yes, but what were you when you planted that bomb and killed all those innocents in that Belfast court?'

'There are no innocents in war,' she said, 'only combatants and non-combatants. And besides, I was trying to kill a traitor to the Cause. A treacherous man, betraying our trust. You would not have been any different.'

'That's debatable,' he said, 'I don't go around planting bombs.'

'I should hope not too,' Mairead said. 'That would not be fitting for one of Her Majesty's soldiers.'

'Are you mocking me?' he said. 'You damn bitch!'

'No I'm not, I really am proud of you and your beliefs. You're like me, really, we believe in the same things. But we're on different sides and no matter how we preach to the other we will never change. So please, let us not waste this precious time in argument.'

'Is this the redhead or the brunette speaking?'

'Neither, it's me and it's from the heart. So don't be dreary and talk shop all your life. You know a girl has to change her appearance every once in a while to keep the man in her life interested in her.'

Not believing a word of it, and trying to be hard and not let her get to him and his emotions he said, 'And who is that?'

'You,' she said, startled at the very question. 'It's always been you, ever since I popped up out of that coffin and surprised you for the first time.'

Now the accusations came thick and fast.

'If you loved me like you say you do, would you have kept running off like that?'

'I had to; the Cause is my lifeblood and the fight for a united

Ireland my ambition. Maybe it won't be in my lifetime, but at least in some small measure I would have made it possible in generations to come.'

'It still doesn't explain why you kept running off.'

'I had to, I could not risk capture and confinement. I am a free and independent spirit and would rather die than have to face all that.'

'How about leaving me tied up every time?'

'I confess the first time it was a bit of a joke, little old Mairead O'Connell tying up the tough soldier type of thing. But later, it was the only way to stop you following me and to stop you alerting the authorities before I could get away.'

'Why should I believe all this simple dogma and communist claptrap?'

'Look my love,' she said and kissed him briefly. 'I know you hate all I stand for and I don't blame you for that. But at least I thought you understood I was a freedom fighter. And that I was doing it out of the best of motives, just like the Israelis after the Second World War and later, the Palestinians.'

'Killing and shooting is no motive, what do you hope to achieve?'

'To stir up the powers that be, the Margaret Thatchers and the Ronald Reagans and the Irish Assembly, so that there can be a new peace initiative, and free elections and an Irish Assembly represented by those elected by the people, and not governed by Stormont or the civil servants in Whitehall or the politicians in London.'

'But that still doesn't justify the killing and bombing, does it? I say it, as I care for you.'

'You sit here and say you care for me, and hit me with these questions with scorn in your voice and yet, if you were given the order, you as a soldier would kill me without the slightest hesitation.'

'That's different, you're part of the IRA and a known terrorist.'

'Granted, but I'm also a person with rights and loved ones, and what have I done to you to justify such an act and to deserve that?'

'But you're a killer…'

'But what have I done to you personally? Nothing, is the answer. We do it for our beliefs and to carry out our orders, and for the fact we are opposite sides of the coin, don't we?'

'Yes,' he said reluctantly, finally worn down by her penetrating arguments.

'Now don't think for one moment I expect you to go all soft on me or love me because of it. But if you could manage to love me in spite of it, it would be a help.'

'I'll do that,' he said, and kissed her long and full on the lips, a kiss sweeter than wine, and one that promised much as he felt the passion in her kiss and she turned him on with her warmth and response.

Breathless they broke from the embrace, and happy she demanded, 'Again'.

They kissed again, and Strong fairly ate her up with his passion and years of emotions finally released.

'Now my three year wait is over, and you, Mr Soldier, are going to take me to bed and we're going to make love all afternoon,' she said. They picked up all the things and strode up the beach towards the apartments.

The best meal in town was, quite simply, to be found at the best restaurant and that was at the Casino by the Rock Hotel. Here you could try your hand at blackjack, American and French roulette, punto banco and poker. But the two lovers wanted nothing more than to eat, after their hectic activity all afternoon.

They sat hand in hand at the best table in an alcove, with a quite splendid view of the South Mole and the moored shipping and luxury yachts in Gibraltar Bay as dusk fell.

'I want to thank you for today,' Mairead said contentedly. 'It's been really lovely.'

'I know,' Martin Strong said, as he gazed at the most beautiful woman he had ever known, dressed in a figure-hugging black dress with splits up the sides to show off her gorgeous long legs. 'But it's still not over yet, we still have to order.'

'Oh, that's easy,' Mairead commented, 'I trust you and I'll just have the same as you.'

She too was pleased, and proud of his smart appearance in a white tuxedo, shirt and black tie. He looked suave and young and dishy, and every inch the good-looking Englishman she took him for when dressed up.

'You're sure now?' he said, not wanting to make a faux pas.

'I'm sure,' she said and smelt the fresh cut roses in the vase on the candle-lit table was complete with shiny silverware and a bowl of fruit in the middle of the white linen cloth. Giving him a peck on the cheek she said, 'I'm also sure I've never been happier in my life.'

'That's good, I am glad,' he said. 'So shall I order?'

The busy little dark-skinned waiter came over, intuitively, and said, 'Are you ready to order now?'

'Yes, we'll have something Spanish on the menu. What do you recommend?'

'There is paella, the national dish of Spain, *senor*. You cannot do much better than that.'

'What's in that?' Mairead asked out of curiosity.

'Oh, *senora*, you will adore it,' he said going into raptures. 'There are fresh shrimps, and spicy sausage, and chicken in garlic and green peppers, and rice, and you will adore it.'

'Oh, good,' she said, amused by his quick, sharp gestures and Spanish accent. 'And for starters?'

'Gazpacho from Andalusia, an ice-cold soup to cool you down on such a warm evening, *senor*.'

'And to drink?' Mairead asked.

'The beautiful fresh sangria, as red as the roses on your table and as lovely as your wife.'

'She's not my wife,' Strong added hastily, 'but you're right, she is beautiful and so, we will have that, thank you,' putting down the menu. They both laughed at the funny little waiter, and everything was dreamlike and just perfect for the couple; they never wanted the evening to end.

Soon the waiter brought the bottle of sangria and poured a little in a glass for Strong to taste. Then, when Strong nodded his approval, the little waiter hurried into the kitchen and minutes later, returned with the gazpacho for both of them. When that course was over he brought the paella, cooked in a shallow, two-handled black skillet brought from the stove to the table, and dished it out for them. Looking out the window as she sipped her sangria and ate her paella, Mairead asked, 'What's that view over there?'

'That is Africa,' the passing waiter explained.

For hours in the afternoon the mist had lain over the Strait of Gibraltar and now it had cleared, revealing a most enchanting view.

'Oh—' she said, and somewhere the tune was heard, 'The Carnival Is Over', by The Seekers with Judith Durham's plaintive voice.

'Say goodbye my own true lover, As we sing a lover's song, it breaks my heart to leave you…'

Suddenly there were tears in her eyes, and Strong said anxiously, 'What is it,' as he handed her a handkerchief.

Taking it, she could not tell him but said instead, 'Oh nothing, don't mind me,' as she dabbed at the tears. The emotions were coming thick and fast as she was reminded of a promise she had made earlier not to take part in any illegal activities on the Rock for the sake of her lover, Martin Strong.

Pressing his hand she said, 'Don't worry, I won't be there tomorrow. I'll stay at home like a good girl.'

'Good,' he said. 'You know it makes sense.'

'Would you stay the night with me, please? I don't want to be alone.'

'Sure I will,' he said confidently. 'Now eat up, your dinner is getting cold.'

★

Day Three on the Rock

During the night Mairead was restless and could not sleep in the small hours of the morning. So she left the sleeping Strong beside her and got up to take a glass of water for her parched throat. But as she padded quietly to the bathroom, she saw something pushed under the hotel door. When she picked it up it was a note that simply said, '97 Irish Town, ten o'clock.' Memorising it she ripped the note up into small pieces and flushed it down the toilet, and went back to bed.

When Mairead woke at 8 a.m. Strong was gone, and had not even left a thank you note. 'Men,' she mused, 'they are all bastards, even the nice ones,' and smiled to herself. Never mind, she was in love and knew she could forgive him anything for one kiss, one smile and one caress from him. She met the others in the breakfast room and began with cornflakes as a starter, joining the others in chit-chat and an unhurried English breakfast. They had a tasty meal with the full works, and umpteen cups of tea and rounds of toast.

Then she sat in the lounge in an armchair and wrote out several postcards, leaning on the low table before her. The others did the same, all except Liam, who read the *Sun* newspaper and lingered long over a picture of Sam Fox thrusting her big breasts at the camera. To all appearances it was as it should be, with all four of them doing and acting no different from all the other tourists on holiday.

Tommy Boyd, like all the other men, was dressed in casual trousers and summery shirt. He was the replacement for the killed Padraic Duffy. He had a hard face and a broken nose, with a mass of curly black hair on his head. Tall and wiry, he was twenty-two years of age. More showy than the others, he proudly displayed an array of gold rings adorning his fingers like ornamental knuckle-dusters. Of a similar age and background as the others, he too came from the same predominantly Republican Newry council housing estate.

At 9.30 a.m. the taxi they had ordered with reception arrived, and the ASU left the Rock Hotel and made themselves comfortable for the short ride.

'Where to, folks?' Man United asked. He was still posing as a taxi driver in the intense surveillance operation being instituted by the SAS unit and being conducted back at headquarters deep in the Rock by the colonel and Captain Dixon.

Sharp as a razor, Mairead commented, 'You're the driver we had from the airport.'

'That's right,' Man United said, not knowing whether to laugh or cry. He hoped to God that his play-acting was not so bad that they had rumbled him. 'So where do you want to go?'

'Can you drop us at the post office? We can make our own way from there, so we can,' Liam said, in a conversational voice.

They did not know it, but the fact he was so close to known terrorists and the sound of a thick Irish brogue so far from Ireland had made the hairs of Man United's neck stand up. He was decidedly uncomfortable, but he hid it well, with his easy and friendly manner.

'That's OK,' he said to Liam in the passenger seat beside him. 'But while you're here you really must take a ride on the cable car and see the Rock from up there. I promise you, it really is quite spectacular.'

'Yeah, that would be great,' Boyd said in the back.

'Wouldn't it just,' Maguire agreed, as Man United turned round and clocked all three in the back with one glance. Despite the snide remarks they all had made about Mairead O'Connell and Strong, Man United had to admit she was some looker.

Leaving the Rock Hotel, Man United took them up the Europa Road, through Southport Gates and hung a left into Kings Yard Lane and up Main Street, a narrow thoroughfare with an architectural style of its own.

'Well, we're here,' Man United said some time later, and the rest got out, while Liam paid the taxi driver and then Man United drove off.

As he did so, he pushed a button on the radio before him and spoke into it. 'This is Oscar 34 to base. Have made contact with bandits and dropped them at the post office in Main Street.'

'Well done 34, keep driving then park in Casement Square until further instructions are issued.'

'Will do base, this is Oscar 34, over and out.'

As soon as the taxi drove off, the ASU headed for the post office to buy stamps and post their cards at the box outside. A few people were in the queue, but Mairead was a tourist on holiday, and so she did not mind waiting to take her turn at the stamp vending machine outside. There was also a list of thirty-five businesses in town licensed to sell postage stamps.

While they waited, Liam read from the tourist guide he had bought in the hotel's reception.

'The colony's post office was built in 1858 and an inscription on the outer wall reads, Lieutenant General Sir James Ferguson KCB Governor.'

'So it does,' Maguire said, pointing to the very spot.

'It does, doesn't it,' Mairead said quite interested too.

Continuing, Liam read, 'It opened for business on 1 September of that year and was also the Mediterranean headquarters of the British GPO at the time. Not until New Year's Day 1886 did Gibraltar take control of its own postal affairs at short notice, as for eleven months the colony had no choice but to be content with Bermuda stamps with "Gibraltar" overprinted on them. That was when Gibraltar was using Spanish currency with twenty-five pesetas twenty-three centimes to the pound sterling, and as the post office was losing a half centime on every penny stamp, the July 1889 issue was priced in pesetas instead of pence. Rare stamps that are now worth thousand of pounds.'

'I wouldn't mind gettin' me hands on a few of them, by jove,' Boyd said, in a cheerful manner.

'No, we could all use a few thousand quid,' Maguire agreed.

'Will you lot shut up an' let me read,' Liam said, put out, as the others shot each other a look of, 'What's up with him?'

'In 1898 the Rock changed to British currency when the peseta lost its value due to the Spanish American War. The first pictorial stamps were issued on 1 July 1931. They showed a view of the Rock from Spain and carried the colony's coat of arms, bequeathed by Queen Isabella in 1502.'

From the post office, the ASU walked into Irish Town. It was a little past ten thirty in the morning. About this time a bobby on the beat approached from the direction of the police station. He was Martin Strong in disguise, and more worried about being spotted by a genuine policeman and the sentence imposed for impersonating one, than the fact that known terrorists were just across the street from him.

North from the Piazza, almost to Casement Square, ran a narrower street parallel to Main Street, this was Irish Town. It had a few public houses and commercial offices, but peculiarly, no one could remember the origin of the name; while the north end recalled Cooperage Lane and the barrel-making industry there in the days of the Duke of Medina Sidonia, between 1465 and 1502. This was where the note said to go to, 97 Irish Town and the Free House, a rough and ready drinking establishment.

All four walked in, and were immediately accosted by a man at the bar. He was a colourful character in pure white trousers and bright red t-shirt, with an emblem of the Rock emblazoned on the front and a mass of yellow hair in the popular afro hairstyle. About forty-six years of age, he was their contact and a person with connections to the Spanish Basque separatist organisation, ETA.

Smiling cheerfully, he greeted Liam with a warm handshake and said effusively, 'I am so very glad to meet you. Your exploits are legendary and well known to us and it will be a great pleasure to do business with you and your comrades-in-arms.'

'Thank you,' Liam said, but before he could say much more, Mairead interjected.

'Isn't there something you are forgettin' first,' she said, looking him in the face.

'Uh oh, the recognition code, *si senors* and *senorita*,' he being so pleased to see them that he had forgotten all about it.

'The Emerald Isle is always green,' she started and he finished.

'Always green and always raining.'

'Thank God, that's out of the way,' Boyd remarked.

'Yeah, you could've been anyone,' Maguire said, echoing their feelings.

'Me *senors*, anyone – with this hair?' he said, touching it as he laughed and showed a row of gold-capped teeth. 'Not anyone, *senor*. But Emmanuel Santa, at your service.'

'And we're at yours,' Liam said succinctly. 'Now let's do business. Have you the hardware, the information and the transport to do the job?'

Santa beckoned the sullen barman over, who brought a suitcase that Santa opened and revealed the hardware, Polish Skorpion 4.263 sub-machine guns.

Picking one up, Maguire said, 'Hmm, nice and light and easy.'

'Easy but deadly,' Santa added, with his customary cheer.

'But of course,' Liam said, admiring the automatic weapons and Tokarev pistols.

'They'd be no use to us otherwise,' Mairead pointed out, picking one up and checking it out and the firing mechanism. 'Seems OK,' she said.

'The car?' Liam urged Santa. 'Where's that?'

'Oh *si*, that is out the back.'

'Let me see it,' Liam remarked. They all followed Santa out into the bright sunshine of the courtyard.

'There, isn't she a beauty?' Santa asked with pride. They stared at the car, with its peeling paint and flat tyres, and wondered what was so marvellous about it.

'Is that all you could get, a stinking Fiat 124?' Mairead said with disgust, as she looked down her nose at the little car.

'It has a fine engine—'

'It better have,' Boyd pointed out.

'And I can give it a new coat of paint,' Santa said, like a used car salesman.

'Yeah, yucky yellow,' Maguire said, utterly unimpressed. 'Just the colour to be seen miles away at night.'

'Ah, but I left the best for last,' Santa said, as he approached the vehicle. 'There are only ten thousand miles on da clock.'

'Probably been rewound that's why,' Maguire said, unimpressed by a single feature yet.

'Oh *senors* an' de *senorita*, never. I never do that to my friends.'

Suddenly Boyd caught a glimpse of something, and froze. 'What do you know,' he said. 'We've been here five minutes and already there's a policeman wrapped around our getaway vehicle.'

'Get rid of him,' Liam instructed Boyd and he crept up on the cop and pulled a knife on him.

The uniform of the Gibraltar constabulary was not much different from those in the British Isles; the same uniform, but a different cap band and badge design. Just as the cop turned away from looking in the rear view window, Boyd lunged at him with the knife. That was a mistake, for then the policeman was forced to defend himself. Grabbing Boyd by the arm and the collar of his t-shirt, the cop got him in a judo hold and threw him to the ground so quickly he had no time to catch his breath. Then he stamped on his hand, disarming Boyd of the knife.

'Next time I won't be so polite,' the cop said to Boyd, pinned to the ground by a foot on his stomach and knife in hand.

'Neither will I,' Liam said. 'Now let him up before I kill you.'

The policeman he did as he was told, and Boyd took his knife back as Liam stood there with the automatic weapon.

'You can't kill him,' Mairead burst out. 'Not before the job is done, or we'll have the cops and goodness knows what else down on us like a ton of bricks.'

'I guess that's common sense,' Liam said. 'But you can get rid of your soldier boy.'

'How did you know?'

'You were never very good at concealing the heart on your sleeve, even as a little girl.'

'Then let me speak to him.'

'I don't care, just get rid of him, that's all. We have important business to conduct an' he mustn't affect that.'

Approaching Strong, she turned him around and walked away with him. 'You shouldn't be here,' Mairead said, 'I just stopped them from killin' you.'

'Maybe so, but neither should you. What about your promise?'

'I remember that,' she said, and kissed him long on the mouth. It was a kiss of passion and desperation. 'Now go: and remember I will always be true to you, my love.'

He hurried away, and did not see the tears on her cheeks as she blew him a kiss. 'Farewell my love, till we meet again.'

As soon as he could, Strong ducked down a darkened alleyway out of the sunlight and, making sure he was not followed, got out his personal radio and contacted base headquarters.

'Bravo 123 to base, over. Have made contact with bandits and eyeballed getaway car complete with registration, make and colour. Also eyeballed automatic weapons and been made by hostiles. Retreated before any provocation. Have description of one new target male, yellow hair afro style, age forty—'

'Base to Bravo 123, that will be Emmanuel Santa, known underworld associate and resident of Irish Town. Where you are, confirmed?'

'Bravo 123 to base, confirmed and location is the back of the premises of the Free House pub. Have backed off for own safety and awaiting instructions.'

'Base to Bravo 123, have your location and instruct you to proceed back to base. Over and out.'

'Bravo 123 to base, understood and over and out.'

When Mairead returned they all went back in the rough and

ready shaded drinking establishment out of the warm sun. As soon as they sat at the table, near the open door casting shadows inside, Santa, being the ever hospitable host called to the barman, 'Guinness all round for my friends, *si*,?' looking at Liam for confirmation.

'*Si*,' Liam confirmed and then businesslike, 'Now where's that treacherous bastard, Fat Billy?'

'He's been holed up in a suite on the fifth floor of the Rock Hotel ever since he arrived some days ago. They put him there for his safety, and he's not moved in all that time.'

'Not for anything?' Boyd asked.

'*Si senor*, not for anything.'

'What about the guards?'

'There are four and they are on four hour shifts. Four hours on and then change.'

'I think we've got that,' Maguire said patronisingly. 'Where do they guard?'

'One in the suite, one in the corridor outside, one in reception by the elevator and another patrols de car park.'

'Do they have radios?'

'*Si senor*, all are in contact with one another.'

'There goes the element of surprise,' Liam said flatly. 'What do you think?' he said, turning to his sister.

All she could think of was that Strong had changed in the three years she had been away. She could not put her finger on it, but he was different somehow. She wondered how much.

'Uh oh,' Mairead said, bringing herself back to the subject at hand. 'Seems to me,' she continued, 'you need a brave girl to do a man's job.'

'Catch yourself on,' Boyd said intrigued. 'And jus' how are you going to do that?'

'Listen very carefully an' I'll tell you,' Mairead said, as intriguing as ever. 'But first, get rid of that car and get another.'

★

The Last Night on the Rock

It was 2 a.m. in the morning and all was dark and quiet as the grave. Nothing stirred except the tropical date palms and bougainvillea grown in the town's tiny gardens, blown by a light southerly breeze. A royal blue Fiat 124 turned out of Cooperage Lane on to Line Wall Road and picked up two hitchhikers with holdalls slung over their shoulders. They soon got in the back seat of the vehicle, and it drove off down Line Wall Road.

The hitchhikers had come from a set of steps that linked Fish Market Road with Line Wall Road, a road that ran a good way along the top of the original Line Wall which were sea defences built by the Moors and continually improved over the centuries. It was in 1776 when General Elliot took over as governor from Colonel William Green that most of the Rock's three hundred cannon and mortars were sited along the Line Wall.

Not that any of that interested Captain Dixon, who was watching the stirrings of the IRA ASU known as Tricolour-7. All the other tourists had gone to bed long since and there were just those good people out for a night ride. Captain Dixon adjusted the night glasses and got a good close look at them through the green lenses as they got in the back of the car. He did that easily, from his vantage point high on the roof of the House Assembly building, a position in Main Street that overlooked the surrounding area for miles. The House of Assembly was a smart, white building that stood back from the pavement, allowing space for ice cream vendors and postcard sellers to have kiosks beneath the two tall trees.

Switching on his personal radio and putting down his night glasses, Captain Dixon spoke softly, 'All units this is 510. They are coming. I repeat, bandits are on their way. So get ready.' Picking up his night glasses again he continued, 'They are in a small Fiat registration M for mother, 1881, F for Freddie and W for whisky. Now heading in a southerly direction down Main Street and past the piazza.'

The piazza was customarily known as John Mackintosh Square, after a local benefactor. Set into the pavement there were mosaics showing the crests of the famous regiments that helped capture the Rock in 1704, or had been garrisoned there since. Some of the more recognisable ones were the Royal Scots, King's Own, the East Lancashire, East Surrey, Royal Welsh Fusiliers, King's Own Scottish Borderers and the Suffolk, Essex, Dorset and Northamptonshire regiments. Without mentioning of course the special relationship of the Royal Air Force and the Gibraltar coat-of-arms displayed.

'All units ready,' Captain Dixon said, 'then stand by for immediate action. This is 510 over and out as bandits continue down Main Street.'

The Fiat kept on along Main Street, passed the Holiday Inn and King's Chapel on the right, and the Methodist church on their left as they continued along by John Mackintosh Hall and the Garrison Theatre. They turned by the Queen's Hotel into the Europa Road that led eventually to the Rock Hotel, a journey of some twenty minutes' duration driven casually and unhurriedly through the night.

Undoubtedly, the Rock was the only five-star hotel in Gibraltar, with a reputation second to none ever since the building began in 1930 and opened early in 1932 with a mere eighty rooms. The owners made themselves personally responsible for the best-in-house, with the Marquis of Bute, whose family had long lived in Tangiers, bringing dining room furniture from Seville and that of the bedrooms from Granada. Not to mention the linen from Ireland, bedcovers from Turkey and an exceptional orchestra from Hungary, the original decor enthusing two Prime Ministers and the Queen's son, Prince Charles when he was younger and in his seagoing days.

Cautiously, the driver of the Fiat circled the block and went several times around the car park. Each time Liam said, 'I don't like it at all, it's too quiet for me likin', so help me.'

'What did you expect,' Mairead said. 'A big brass band and a parade?'

'Not exactly—'

'Not exactly, but at least there would have been a bit of life,' Boyd said. 'Liam's right – it's damn right creepy.'

'Creepy and unnerving,' Maguire agreed, 'I don't like it either.'

'You big girl's blouse,' Mairead said in a confrontational mood. 'It's on for tonight an' we have to do it, so help me God. So let's get on with it.'

All four donned their black balaclavas and helped themselves to the weapons in their holdalls on the floor of the car. Liam remarked, 'Well, I guess this is it?'

'I guess it is,' Maguire said tentatively.

'I guess it is and let's go to it before we change our minds,' Boyd urged.

'This *is* it, unless you want to be the one to call the Army Council and tell them that it's all off,' Mairead pointed out.

'No,' Liam said, his mind made up.

Liam stayed in the car as the other three got out and, weapons beneath their zipper jackets, entered the Rock Hotel. The place was deserted with no one at the desk in reception, as the three of them rushed through the foyer, Mairead as oblivious as the others to the sheer luxury and elegance of the place. All she could think of was the hate and contempt she had for the treacherous Fat Billy, her brain racing as to how she was going to kill him after missing him on two previous occasions. But there was no one in the foyer or surrounding corridors, and increasingly the situation was looking somewhat dubious.

Boyd voiced their fears. 'I don't like it. If I didn't know better I'd say we've been set up.'

'Set up or not, this goes ahead,' Mairead warned Boyd and Maguire. 'We may never get another chance. And I for one intend to get him this time if it's the last thing I do.'

'At this rate it probably will be,' Maguire said, as they all piled in the elevator and Boyd pressed for the doors to close. Maguire pushed for the fifth floor.

Soon they arrived, and the doors opened. The three walked down the thick carpeted corridor and passed the large conference room and on to the suite they wanted. With all three stopped outside, and after looking up and down the corridor for anyone approaching them. Mairead tried the lock of the door. She turned the knob but it did not give to the touch, so knocking the safety off the Polish Skorpion automatic weapon she put it on rapid fire and fired a short burst that chewed up the lock. Stepping back, she and Boyd kicked in the door and entered the suite. They stormed in firing short bursts and ruining the décor, exploding valuable vases and shattering the glass drinks cabinet in the main room as the two of them went on a mad rampage throughout the suite as they searched for Fat Billy in vain. Turning over the bed and throwing the clothes all around the room, they left with curses of contemptuous frustration towards Fat Billy, who was nowhere in sight.

Mairead and Maguire tore out of the room on the run and, along with Boyd, made for the elevator. Just then the door opened in the next suite along, and an army intelligence man in plain clothes with gun in hand warned, 'Stop right there and lay down your weapons.'

With no hesitation all three spun round and began firing with their automatic weapons, slung on harnesses around their necks.

While the intelligence man took out Boyd with three quick shots, Mairead and Maguire riddled him with a fierce volley of bullets that tore into him from knee to neck and left him bloody and dying as he hit the floor. The only consolation for him was that Boyd was done for too; Mairead and Maguire left him where he lay and dived in the elevator. They pressed anxiously for the ground level and ran out of the Rock Hotel, straight into a hail of bullets from behind a parked vehicle to the left of the front entrance.

Firing from waist level, Mairead and Maguire desperately ran across the car park looking for Liam, who met them with a squeal of brakes and tyres and they threw themselves inside the Fiat. As bullets punctured the paint and bodywork, Liam kept a cool head and asked Maguire next to him as Mairead ducked in the back, 'What happened to Boyd?'

Before he could answer, Mairead remarked, 'Don't ask.'

'And Fat Billy?'

'The same.'

'Then I won't,' Liam replied, as he put the car in gear and shot out of the car park like a bat out of hell, on to the Europa Road and towards Main Street. Behind them, the army were in pursuit in a black Renault.

The speedometer was creeping up towards the seventy-five miles per hour mark as Liam drove at breakneck speed through the narrow, dimly lit streets. The black Renault was still on their tail and doing its best to force them to stop as bullets pinged and whined all around them. Flashing through the night, fighting the steering and zig-zagging to make things harder for those in pursuit, Liam asked Mairead in the back seat, 'What's happening now?'

'They are still there,' Mairead said in answer. 'Where else would they be?'

'Then do something to slow them down.'

'It'll mean knocking the window out.'

'Just do it,' Maguire said, as impatient with her as Liam.

She knocked out the window, and began firing in retaliation. Her first short burst took out the windscreen, her second shredded the right tyre and the third caught the driver, right across the eyes. He wrenched the steering wheel sharply and slumped over. The car turned over and skidded across the road, and burst through the glass paned window of a paint shop and promptly exploded, blowing out the storefront. All four men inside were fried in the heat and flames and died instantaneously.

Mairead and the others whooped for joy at the sight of the loss of the pursuit car. But their joy was short-lived as the Fiat started to slow down. 'What's wrong, now?' Mairead asked.

'I think one of their bullets must have hit the petrol tank, and now we're running out,' Liam said in explanation.

'Never mind,' Maguire said, 'I'm sure I remember a petrol station just up here, somewhere.'

'But it will be shut,' Mairead said, being practical.

Liam replied, 'Then, we'll just have to open it, that's all.'

The little Fiat slowed down to almost walking pace as it approached the petrol station on Bernard Montgomery Avenue. A Mobil filling station by the sundial at Waterport, where a four-man SAS unit were in hiding. They were in radio contact with base headquarters and the colonel. The officer commanding on the spot was Captain Dixon, on the roof of the House Assembly building.

Shortly before the IRA turned up in their little Fiat, the leader of the unit Oscar 123 received a terse message. It said, 'Bandits heading your way. ETA approximately two minutes.'

'Thank you 510, received. Over and out,' Strong said, and turned his radio off just as the Fiat 124 slowed to a crawl on the bend in South-Dorrien Avenue that led into Bernard

Montgomery Avenue. For the last hundred yards the three had to get out of the car and push it into the filling station. Not a very glorious way to arrive, but then, needs must when the devil drives.

A tall sign advertised Mobil and the forecourt and pumps were painted in the same colours, with a glassed in office and sliding window for serving customers. A Thames van was parked beside the office with its doors shut.

Maguire was chosen to scout the site, and approached the glass office. After a brief look round he blasted the door and shattered it. Stepping inside, it was not long before there was more gunfire and Maguire stumbled out again holding his leaking insides where he had been shot in the stomach. He clutched himself finally once more and then crumpled to the ground, dead.

When Man United emerged triumphantly, Browning pistol in hand, looking down at him Liam and Mairead lost their cool and gunned him down in a vitriolic rage. As they opened fire the back doors of the Thames van burst open and three SAS tumbled out, firing as they did so their Heckler and Koch automatic weapons.

The adrenalin pumping, they fired fierce bursts at the Fiat. Liam was hit in the eye by flying glass as the windscreen was shot out and, blinded, he got out of the vehicle and was promptly mown down by three SAS kneeling and squatting across the forecourt. Liam fell in a heap as Mairead ducked out of sight in the backseat and moaned and groaned to sucker the ambushers as they got to their feet, and gradually approached the rear of the car.

Dave Forrester stuck his head inside, and that was the last thing he ever did, as Mairead jumped up and blew out his brains with a rapid fire blast of the Skorpion weapon, chunks of him were sent flying through the air as he was decapitated and East Acton froze in horror at the sight. This was just what Mairead needed, as she stuck her head out and stitched him in the arm and leg. He fell away wounded as she jumped out of the side door and Strong gave chase.

'Come back you bastard,' he shouted, 'I'm not finished with you yet by a long chalk.'

Running away from the forecourt out of fear of capture, Mairead turned round and fired a short burst that made Strong duck behind the petrol pumps. Mairead was not having that and fired some more, holing the tanks and making them leak. One more burst had the desired effect, and they exploded into great gusts of flame. As she stood there, out of bullets, he gunned her down before she could draw her Tokarev pistol.

The terrorist crumpled to the ground and Strong was pleased, as he waited some seconds before finally approaching. Kicking away the weapons he bent over his adversary and ripped off the balaclava with the words, 'Let's see your face. I want to see who you are.'

As soon as he did, he wished he had not, for to his shock and horror, the dying terrorist was none other than his love, Mairead O'Connell. Cradling her in his arms as she coughed up blood where he had shot her, he said in agonised tones, 'But you promised. You know you promised to stay away.'

'I know, but I just couldn't,' she said, nearly choking. 'Much as I loved you I still had to be true to myself and the Cause.' Perplexed by her words, Strong was speechless. 'Kiss me one last time,' she said; he did so, and at the end of it she was dead.

Minutes later, Dixon and the other pursuit vehicles turned up. But it did not matter to Strong. He was beside himself with grief, as the one person who had shown him what real love was lay lifeless in his arms. He did not care about Fat Billy, who had long since been moved to a concrete bunker at the airport for his own safety. All that mattered was that his love was dead as the sobs racked his body and were torn from his very soul.

'She promised!' he cried. 'She damn well promised!' he kept crying out, as friends and comrades came and prised him apart from his fierce grip round her, and their separation was complete.

Printed in Great Britain
by Amazon